Evelyn

Evelyn James has always been fascinated by history and the work of writers such as Agatha Christie. She began writing the Clara Fitzgerald series one hot summer, when a friend challenged her to write her own historical murder mystery. Clara Fitzgerald has gone on to feature in over thirteen novels, with many more in the pipeline. Evelyn enjoys conjuring up new plots, dastardly villains and horrible crimes to keep her readers entertained and plans on doing so for as long as possible.

Other Books in The Clara Fitzgerald Series

Memories of the Dead

Flight of Fancy

Murder in Mink

Carnival of Criminals

Mistletoe and Murder

The Poison Pen

Grave Suspicions of Murder

The Woman Died Thrice

Murder and Mascara

The Green Jade Dragon

The Monster at the Window

Murder Aboard Mary Jane

The Missing Wife

The Woman Died Thrice
by
Evelyn James

A Clara Fitzgerald Mystery
Book 8

Red Raven Publications
2018

© Evelyn James 2018

First published as ebook 2016
Paperback edition 2018
Red Raven Publications

The right of Evelyn James to be identified as the Author of this work has been asserted in accordance with the Copyrights, Designs and Patents Act 1988.

All rights reserved. No part of this book may be reprinted or reproduced or utilised in any form or by any electronic, mechanical or other means, now known or hereafter invented, including photocopying and recording, or in any information storage or retrieval system without the permission in writing from the author

Chapter One

Clara concluded that a charabanc was the only way to travel. She had boarded the elegantly painted brown and cream vehicle in Brighton to begin a tour of the Lake District. Two hours later she was already convinced this was a very fine way to view the world. She was sat on a comfy leather seat, like the sort you found on smart omnibuses, with her legs stretched out and her damaged foot snugly installed on a cushion. She was very cosy in fact and, with the charabanc driver sticking to a decent 20mph, she was finding it a very settling experience. Unlike her last ride in a car which was at very high speeds and hugely disturbing. Clara could get quite used to this sort of travelling.

Clara had been gifted this little holiday through the gratitude of Mr Hatton, the owner of the Brighton Charabanc Touring Company. His little buses went all across the country, taking people to see the best sights and to visit the most interesting places England, Scotland and Wales could offer. Mr Hatton had been the victim of a nasty blackmailer and Clara, Brighton's first female private detective, had saved him from scandal. As a thank you, Mr Hatton had offered her a free charabanc holiday, for herself, her brother Tommy and their maid and friend,

Annie.

Clara had not at first been enamoured with this idea. Charabancs looked big and daunting, and she suspected they went rather fast round corners. But Annie found the whole idea exciting and Tommy was determined to go. In the end, Clara really had no choice.

As it happened, once aboard the charabanc, Clara had discovered it was neither overly large nor daunting. And the driver and conductor were both very professional and friendly, there seemed no reason to fear that this would be anything but a truly enjoyable jaunt around the countryside. Admittedly, at 20mph, it was going to take a long time to reach the Lake District, but the driver had promised his passengers that there would be ample stops for comfort breaks and a hotel for an overnight stop halfway.

Mr Hatton had an eye to the future; his charabanc was not the open-topped nightmare that mills and factories hired for day trips for their workers. For a start his had a properly built roof and glass windows to protect his passengers (the usual charabancs had a canvas roof that was kept collapsed until needed, like the soft roof of a sports car). While he could do little about the rather hard suspension, he compensated by providing well-cushioned seats that acted very nicely to smooth out the shocks caused by the bumps and lumps of the road. Mr Hatton predicted that luxury coach travel would prove a booming industry soon and had plunged a lot of his own money into having specially designed coaches built for his company. So far his investment had proved wise. Many of his customers enjoyed travelling around the country in his charabancs and appreciated the extra comforts he had gone to great lengths to provide.

Mr Hatton had once been told that, technically, what he actually had was a fleet of 'motor coaches' not charabancs. But he found this a rather confusing idea, after all, coaches were pulled by horses. In any case, his customers were not familiar with 'motor coaches' but they did understand the concept of a charabanc and it sounded much nicer in his company name. The term 'motor coach' had a rather cumbersome ring to it, so Mr Hatton remained head of the Brighton Charabanc Touring Company and had nothing to do with this 'coaches' nonsense.

Clara was sitting one row from the front of the charabanc, to her right sat Tommy with his dog Bramble on his lap. The small black poodle seemed almost as intent on watching the world flash by as Clara. Ahead of them both sat Annie, on a seat all to herself. This had caused her some mortification when she first sat down, not only was she sat on a seat alone, but she was right at the front of the vehicle where everyone could see her. Fortunately, she had her picnic hamper beside her – Annie had insisted on bringing a selection of sandwiches and cake, as she was convinced that once they strayed past Brighton's outskirts they would be subjected to unusual and unfamiliar foods – and this took up a good place on the seat beside her and provided Annie with a barrier between herself and the world. If anyone looked in her direction, she could console herself with the thought they were looking at the hamper and speculating on its contents, rather than looking at her.

Outside the windows of the charabanc the landscape had merged into a vista of never-ending fields. Clara found herself impressed by how rural some parts of England could be, though, she also had to admit, the endless ranks of green were rather boring after a while. She switched her attention from the view outside to her fellow travellers.

The charabanc could hold twenty-four people, excluding the driver and conductor. It seemed virtually full to Clara's eyes. The passengers were largely female and mostly in their later years. Clara was certain she and Annie were nearly the youngest women aboard. There were also a few men, usually accompanying wives and apparently retired from the strains of a working existence. Tommy had said earlier he felt a little out-of-place. He had just about managed to stagger aboard the charabanc using a walking stick. Though he was regaining some use of his legs – Tommy had been left crippled by a bullet in the Great War – he was a long way from being able to walk around on his own and relied on a wheelchair. The chair had been stowed behind the driver's seat, which was rather a tight squeeze. Tommy, therefore, had a valid reason to be jaunting off on a holiday in the middle of the working week, but he couldn't help but feel that everyone would wonder about him.

Then there was Clara with her bandaged foot. She was also hobbling about on a stick. She had had her foot run over on her last case and was still suffering the consequences. Clara found it amusing as she and Tommy stumbled around on their sticks. Tommy just found it embarrassing.

"I could murder a cup of tea," Annie pondered from the seat in front. She glanced at her hamper, knowing that inside she had a full tea set, but, alas, no means of heating water to place in the teapot she had carefully packed. One could never be sure what sort of facilities would be available on a trip such as this, it was better to be prepared.

Almost as if he heard her, the conductor rose from his small seat beside the driver and wobbled into the aisle of the charabanc, hanging onto the edge of a chair as the vehicle hauled itself around a corner.

"We have our first stop coming up in a few minutes," he declared. "Mrs Woodcock has a dear little house and has turned the front room into a small tea shop. Refreshments will be awaiting us at no added expense. There are also facilities should anyone require a comfort break."

Everyone seemed pleased with this announcement.

"You may be interested to know that Mrs Woodcock's house dates back to the days of Charles I and there are some particularly fine beams in the front room, one of which is said to bear the initials of a Cavalier soldier who was secretly housed there during the Civil War. The fireplace incorporates stones from a former priory that used to exist just along the river, but which fell out of use during the Reformation. The stone was reclaimed for local properties. Mrs Woodcock informs me that the house is said to be haunted by the ghost of a serving maid, but that she has never had her night's rest disturbed. Ah, here we are now," the conductor held on to the back of the driver's seat with one hand as the charabanc rolled to a halt. There was a gentle groan as the brakes took hold and the passengers were lightly jerked forward and back.

Mrs Woodcock, a dapper country lass with broad arms and a rosy face, waved at them and brandished a brown teapot.

"I believe we are quite welcome," Clara smiled. "That makes a change. Usually when I visit people they don't want to know me."

The passengers were ushered off the charabanc onto a little grass verge. There were several wooden chairs and tables outside Mrs Woodcock's property, and plenty more inside. Her guests could choose between sitting outside in the sunshine or going indoors where they could sit beneath her famous roof beams. The 'facilities' were at the back of the house and consisted of two lavatories in a brick outhouse. These proved initially more attractive to the passengers than the pots of tea Mrs Woodcock was rapidly brewing. An orderly queue soon formed.

Clara and Tommy found themselves at the back of it, being, as it were, the least mobile of the passengers. Tommy preferred to leave the charabanc after everyone else so he would not hold up anybody and Clara stuck with him. By the time they had visited the facilities and made their way back to the front of the house all the tables, both outside and in, were taken. It looked for a moment as if there would be no space for either of them, then Clara spotted Annie waving her hand. The little maid had nabbed three seats for them at a table on the verge.

Clara helped Tommy to the table and they sat down with a nod and words of greeting to the ladies already present. These proved to be a very upright woman, with a sharp nose and black hat, an older lady who had brought her knitting with her and was busily clattering out a cardigan sleeve, and a plump woman who sat back in her chair and contentedly rested her forearms on her sizable belly.

"Clara and Thomas Fitzgerald," Clara introduced herself and her brother to the ladies.

"Mrs Siskin," the plump lady said. "And this is my friend Mrs Palmer. Are you first time charabanc tourers?"

"Indeed," Clara answered. "It is much nicer than I imagined."

"Mr Hatton's charabancs are very nice," Mrs Siskin nodded, folding her hands on her stomach. "Not like those dreadful things we used to see before the war. Not that I ever travelled on those."

"I did a few times," Mrs Palmer spoke up, her needles clacking away at speed. "Back when I worked in the elastic webbing factory. They would organise day trips for us and we would travel by charabanc. I stopped after that dreadful accident where several girls were killed."

"Accident?" Clara asked anxiously.

"Yes. It rolled over, you see, and being open topped and all, everyone tumbled out."

"Don't let Lizzy scare you," Mrs Siskin interceded, noticing Clara's face. "Mr Hatton's charabancs are perfectly safe, else I would not get on one."

They all paused as Mrs Woodcock appeared with plates of cake and a large pot of tea. For a while everyone was intent on eating and drinking and talk was stifled. Then Mrs Palmer gave Tommy a long look up and down.

"May I ask, were you in the war?" she said at last.

Tommy almost choked on a crumb of cake. It was not

that he was unused to the question, but it still amazed him how perfect strangers could find it acceptable to quiz him on his past. Tommy preferred not to think of the war, but the rest of the world would not let him be.

"I was," he admitted reluctantly.

"I take it that is how you acquired your limp?" Mrs Palmer pressed on, oblivious to the discomfort she was causing. "My grandson was also in the war."

Mrs Siskin had suddenly become very absorbed in her cake as her friend spoke. Clara was observing them both with interest, she sensed this was a topic of conversation Mrs Palmer referred to often and not with the approval of Mrs Siskin.

"He never returned, you know," Mrs Palmer continued. "But I am certain he is out there still somewhere. They never declared him dead, only missing. I keep knitting things for him, because when he comes home he is bound to need new clothes."

Mrs Palmer's needles clacked, for a moment no one was sure what to say, then the stern looking woman sat beside Annie carefully put down her slice of cake.

"You do realise being declared missing by the army is as good as dead?" her tone was icy and her words cut through the silence like a razor.

It was a cruel thing to say, and the woman knew it. Mrs Palmer's needles came to a halt.

"Missing. Only missing," Mrs Palmer repeated. "I saw the telegram myself."

"Missing only means they don't know where his body is," the stern woman said as if talking to a very dull child.

"Here now, don't say things like that!" Mrs Siskin jumped to her friend's assistance. "You don't know that, you are only saying it to be spiteful. Lizzy, of course your grandson is out there somewhere. You keep on knitting."

For a moment Mrs Palmer didn't move, then the clack of the needles began again and she slipped into the rhythm of knitting. It seemed to soothe her. The stern woman observed her for a while longer, then finished her tea and excused herself.

"Right cow," Mrs Siskin informed the others once she was gone. "You can tell by her face she has nothing but nastiness inside her. Right cow."

Clara did not reply, merely finished her cake and tea. The conductor appeared among them again and announced they should be on their way. Mrs Woodcock was complimented on her hospitality and waved off her guests as if they were old and much-loved family members. Tommy struggled up the charabanc steps, followed by his sister. They returned to their seats and settled for the next leg of the journey. Clara tried to relax as she had done before, but the atmosphere had changed aboard the charabanc. There was a tension hanging in the air now, as if everyone was on edge, yet only Mrs Palmer, Mrs Siskin and the stern woman had anything to be upset about. Mrs Palmer was sat with her friend in the opposite row, knitting automatically. If the incident had upset her badly it did not show. Mrs Siskin looked a little uncomfortable, the unpleasant conversation had tainted her day perhaps more than it had her friend's. The stern woman was too far back on the charabanc for Clara to see. She wondered who she was and why she had felt the need to be so sharp with Mrs Palmer. Perhaps she was merely one of those people who speak without thinking. Clara decided it was not worth dwelling over, she was here to enjoy herself, not ponder on other peoples' affairs. Even so, the countryside proved less distracting than before and her mind kept turning over the strange conversation. What a cruel woman, she mused, what a cruel, cruel woman.

Chapter Two

After the initial excitement of charabanc travel had worn off, Clara found herself feeling a little bored. The problem was the monotony of it all; the rolling countryside interspersed with quaint, but very briefly seen villages, the constant thrum of the engine and rumble of the wheels, the sitting still in one place for far too long. Clara was beginning to find it all very tiresome. She had never travelled in a vehicle for this long before, even a train ride to London was only a couple of hours. She had been on a steamer once for several hours, but that was different, you didn't sit still on a steamer.

The only way Clara could distract herself was by observing her fellow passengers and even that grew monotonous, for most either stared out the window or dozed. Clearly they were more experienced at this sort of travel than her. Mrs Palmer busied herself with knitting, it seemed to be an unconscious habit, she could knit while looking out the window. Clara wondered how many jumpers she had made for her lost grandson and where she kept them all. Beside her Mrs Siskin was sound asleep, her head slumped back and her mouth emitting the sort of snores more suited to an elephant or hippopotamus. The gentleman trapped sitting behind her looked most aggrieved by the disturbance.

Further back on the bus Clara could just spy the unpleasant woman who had caused such a problem back at their first tea stop. She was sitting looking straight ahead, as if the countryside rolling by her window held no appeal for her. Another woman was sitting beside her and reading a magazine. They didn't talk and didn't appear to know each other. Clara could not look any further back in the charabanc without appearing obvious, so she concentrated on the first few rows of seats and, when that grew tiresome, she switched her attention to the conductor.

He was sitting next to the driver, smoking a cigarette and making occasional comments on the passing landscape. He was young, though not so young that he would be deemed unsuitable for his role. He was probably around twenty-eight and handsome enough, if a little gawky. Clara found her interest wane, she wished she had brought a book, though, more than anything, she wished she could get up and stretch her legs. Next to her Tommy had his eyes shut and may, or may not, be dozing. Clara looked down at the black poodle sitting in his lap. The dog returned her gaze.

"I don't know why I agreed to this," Clara told the dog. His response was to yawn at her.

It was almost one o'clock when they paused at their next stop. This time they found themselves outside a hotel. Mr Hatton had arranged with the hotel owners that a table be set aside for his passengers in their private restaurant (reserved normally only for hotel guests) and that a cold luncheon be served. Naturally the first priority, as before, was for the travellers to avail themselves of the hotel facilities. They were then ushered into a smart restaurant that had a hint of fresh paint about it, and shown to one long table that had been set aside for them.

Due to being in a wheelchair, Tommy was sat at the head of the table and Clara and Annie sat either side of him, facing each other. Next to Clara was sat a gentleman and his wife; he was a portly fellow with one of those continuous moustaches that sweep from the nose around to the ears, where they merged with the gentleman's sideburns. His wife was tall and lean, with rather a hooked nose and a slight over-bite. They were the epitome of a 'chalk and cheese' couple. Next to Annie sat a quiet woman in her forties, who dipped her head and tried not to make eye contact. Reminding Clara of a little mouse caught out of its hole. Clara gave her a smile and the woman's head dropped even further.

Luncheon consisted of a cold chicken salad served with freshly cooked bread and either a cup of tea or lemonade. Clara opted for tea, it was not yet warm enough to tempt her to switch to cold drinks. The portly man next to her seemed to have the same idea. He was elated when he saw the salad placed before him, he was clearly a man who lived for his stomach.

"I say, they are feeding us well!" he jabbed his fork into a slice of chicken. "Last charabanc trip I was on it was bring your own sandwiches or starve."

"Henry, that was many years ago, before you were a professional," his wife interjected rather sharply. She didn't want people overhearing they had been on a cheap charabanc tour.

"Quite right, my dear. That was before I became general manager," the portly man winked at Clara. "Back then I was just a humble supervisor in a shoe factory."

"Henry!" his wife scolded once again.

"And you were just one of the girls who sewed up the inner soles," Henry continued unabashed, grinning from ear-to-ear as he picked up a fat spring onion from his plate.

"You are not eating that!" his wife declared, looking half prepared to swipe the onion from his hand. "You know they give you appalling wind."

On this Henry had to concede defeat. He did know the limits of his digestive capacity. He looked at the spring onion forlornly and then offered it to Clara.

"Would you care for my spring onions?"

Clara, who was rather a glutton when it came to such things, agreed at once. The portly Henry forked his three spring onions onto her plate and smiled with satisfaction.

"Henry Wignell," he introduced himself, deeming it appropriate since he had just shared his lunch.

"Clara Fitzgerald," Clara answered.

"Is this your first charabanc excursion?"

"Yes."

"Honeymoon, perhaps?" Henry Wignell had his eye on Tommy.

"Oh no!" Clara laughed. "This is my brother, Thomas, and our friend Annie."

"My apologies," Henry blushed a little at the error. "Nice to meet you all."

"I take it you have been on a charabanc before," Clara said to change the subject.

"Well, yes, though not as nice as this one. In fact, my previous experience had rather put me off the whole concept," Henry attacked a large tomato on his plate. "However, we have several friends who said Mr Hatton's tours were most delightful and worth the expense. So far I quite agree with them."

"And you get to meet new people."

This comment had come from the unremarkable woman next to Annie who had been trying to avoid them as much as possible. "At least, that is what mother says. She thought it would be good for me to travel on my own. I'm not very good at speaking to people."

"Nice to meet you," Clara said to her gently, noting how much effort it had taken this shy creature to speak to them. "What is your name?"

"Eleanora Smythe," the woman said. "I must emphasise it is Smythe, not Smith. Mother is quite particular about that. She won't even have a letter in the house that is addressed with the incorrect name."

Eleanora suddenly decided this was quite enough

talking for the time being and became acutely absorbed in her salad, ignoring all further questions or attempts to speak to her.

Henry Wignell rolled his eyes at Clara, signalling his puzzlement at this behaviour.

"Have you met the other members of our travelling party?" he enquired.

"Only a handful," Clara admitted. "Mrs Siskin and Mrs Palmer introduced themselves at our last stop."

"Mrs Palmer is the prodigious knitter?"

"That she is. We also sat with a woman who failed to introduce herself. She is down at the far end of the table," Clara gave a slight tilt of her head to indicate where she meant. "Second up from the bottom, opposite to our side of the table."

Henry Wignell was not opposed to staring down a table at a stranger. Fortunately, the unpleasant woman did not notice.

"I believe her name is Mildred Hunt," he said after he had blatantly observed the woman for several moments. "I do recall hearing her give it to the conductor when we were boarding. Isn't that right, dear?"

It was a while since Mrs Wignell had been drawn into the conversation and she looked a tad startled by the sudden question.

"Pardon?"

"That woman down there, isn't her name Mildred Hunt?"

Mrs Wignell glanced down the table, a little perplexed.

"Oh, yes, I do believe so."

"There you are," Henry turned his attention back to Clara. "Now you know her name."

"That's about all I know of her," Clara noted. "She seems to be here alone."

Henry Wignell merely shrugged, as if that was really unimportant.

Lunch concluded, they returned to the charabanc and

resumed their seats. It was going to be another three hours before they stopped again and Clara settled herself for the tedium. Tommy seemed to noticed.

"Charabanc travel not for you?"

"Lengthy travel in general, I fear, is not for me," Clara answered. "I suppose you get used to it."

"You have to learn to use the time productively," Tommy observed. "That's what we did during the war when we were stuck on troop transports for hours. Best thing was to get some sleep, since you never knew what was going to be awaiting you at the other end."

"In this case I rather hope that will not be necessary," Clara said with a wry smile. "I rather imagine Mr Hatton is not sending us off to spend a week in trenches."

"No, probably not," Tommy smiled with amusement. "Though it would save on costs."

"It crosses my mind, that it is bad enough travelling this far in the first place, but at some point we will have to travel back just as far to get home," Clara returned to her earlier train of thought. "There is a part of me that would rather turn back now than face that long trip later on."

"Once we arrive this will all be worth it," Tommy assured her. "I hear the Lakes are lovely."

"Well, I hope you are right."

There was a pause, then Tommy said;

"What do you make of this Mildred Hunt woman?"

"Unkind," Clara answered. "Bitter. A bitter soul makes people lash out at others."

"Doesn't strike you as the sort to take a charabanc tour, does she?" Tommy mused.

"Perhaps she just likes the chance to aggravate people," Clara shrugged. "She was just awful to Mrs Palmer. It was so cruel."

"I know it was cruel, I would never say something like that. But, Mrs Palmer is deluded. Her grandson is dead, we both know that."

"And probably she knows it too, but to spare herself that crippling realisation she has created this false pillar of hope. I don't see that any of us are in a position to deny her that."

"Probably not," Tommy said after a moment. "Though, I am not convinced it is healthy."

Clara shrugged again.

"Who is to say?"

The charabanc continued on its winding route. There was to be one final stop before they reached the hotel where they would spend the night. Not all could wait that long. The copious amounts of tea drunk at Mrs Woodcock's and then at the hotel, had weakened the resolve of a few and the charabanc had to make an impromptu stop by a remote hedge to allow some of the passengers a chance to relieve themselves. Mr Hatton had envisioned just such an emergency when arranging his long road trips. He had provided his charabanc with a folding screen that could be positioned against a convenient hedge to provide privacy to his passengers who were unfortunately caught-short. It was rather amusing, Clara found, to watch the small queue of passengers availing themselves of this rudimentary lavatory arrangement. Though she was most glad she did not have to be one of them.

The journey continued and, in the late afternoon, they arrived at yet another teashop, this one a professional establishment run for the benefit of tourists and visitors to the little village where it was set. A husband and wife ran the shop, buying in a vast array of tasty delights for their customers, rather than baking themselves. Mrs Woodcock might have been disheartened to learn that her customers were now comparing her home-run affair to this deluxe establishment with its factory made scones and twelve types of cake. She would have been consoled to know that despite all the glitz and glamour of the place, the business owners had overlooked one vital point – they had not emptied their facilities that day.

When Mr Hatton's charabanc unloaded its usual cargo of passengers and they all descended on the relevant conveniences at the back of the shop, it caused a serious overflow issue and there was quite the commotion as the toilet had to be hastily emptied before anyone else could avail themselves of it. Clara had, fortunately, been at the head of the queue for the conveniences, so she could watch the drama unfold from the comfort of the outside seating before the teashop. There was quite a queue lined up on both sides of the gate that led to the back of the shop and the outside lavatories. Somewhere among them were Annie and Tommy. Clara decided it would be best to order tea and cake while she waited for them.

She found herself a spot on an empty table, but was soon joined by Mrs Siskin, who had clearly taken a shine to her company.

"Rather unprofessional," Mrs Siskin nodded to the grumbling queue. "I always have thought this place was rather slapdash."

"You have been here before?"

"Yes, on a previous excursion," Mrs Siskin flagged down a waitress in a pinny and ordered tea. "I thought then this was all shine and no substance. Factory made scones, after all!"

"Not quite Mrs Woodcock's style," Clara smiled.

"Definitely not!"

"Where is your friend?"

"Lizzy? Oh, she is just across in the Post Office buying a postcard," Mrs Siskin pointed across the road to a dear little shop that had 'Post Office' over the door and a small stand of postcards and souvenir booklets set on the broad sill of its picture window. "She will send one home every day to her daughter. It's very sad, you know, she is a widow and so is her daughter, and her only grandson is lost as well. Three generations of the same family all stung by war."

Clara was about to say something more when there was a cry from behind her. Both she and Mrs Siskin turned in time to see Mrs Hunt yelling at an unfortunate waitress, who had just upended a full teapot on the woman. Luckily most of the scalding contents had hit the ground, but enough had found their way onto Mrs Hunt to make her most indignant and, indeed, rather wet.

"I apologise, madam, I swear a rat ran over my foot!" the maid said, trying to assuage the damage.

"A rat?" someone cried out.

There was a panicked commotion among the teashop patrons as they began looking under their tables (and, in one case, under their plate) in search of the mystery rat. Rather than improve matters and excuse her behaviour, the girl had made things worse and now incurred the wrath of her employers.

"You foolish girl!" snapped the woman who ran the teashop with her husband. "Of course there are no rats here! Everything is completely clean and hygienic."

The last statement was said loudly enough for the benefit of her customers.

"What about the toilets?" someone pointed out rather brusquely. Clara was uncertain if it was the same person who had picked up on the word 'rat' earlier.

"This is a professional establishment," their host insisted in a clipped tone. "No rats, no mice, no vermin of any description."

"Then what caused her to drop that tray?" Mrs Siskin kindly pointed out, indicating the maid who was now stood looking morbidly unhappy at the predicament she was in.

"She is a foolish girl who does not know how to carry a tea tray," their host said crisply. "And, as of this moment, she is no longer in our employ."

The maid, who was probably only around sixteen, burst into tears and ran from the garden of the teashop.

"Don't forget to bring your uniform back tomorrow clean!" her employer yelled after her.

"What about my skirt?" Mrs Hunt demanded. "I am soaked through!"

With profuse apologies Mrs Hunt was led inside by both owners of the teashop. It was at that moment Clara's scone and tea appeared. She eyed the scone with a look of uncertainty. Had there been a rat? After the debacle over the outside lavatory she was beginning to imagine it a possibility.

Mrs Siskin had no such concerns and bit into her scone without hesitation.

"That will be something to tell Mrs Woodcock!" she grinned.

Clara turned her head again to look where Mrs Hunt had been sitting. To her surprise she saw Eleanora Smythe bend down by the table and seem to pick something up, before she calmly walked off. How curious?

"Eat your scone, dear, and don't worry about rats," Mrs Siskin said. "I peeked in the kitchens while I was waiting to use the loo, and they looked extremely clean."

Mrs Palmer appeared just then.

"What happened to Mrs Hunt?"

"A tea drama," Mrs Siskin laughed. "At least she won't be bothering us this time!"

Mrs Palmer pulled a face.

"Wish I had had the courage to pour hot tea over her!"

Clara had nothing to say to that.

Chapter Three

The charabanc rolled up to their hotel for the night at eight o'clock and the passengers were all very relieved to have finally reached their destination for the day. Clara was amazed at how exhausting sitting still and doing nothing could be.

The hotel had laid on a three course dinner for them, and there was a bit of a rush to get to their rooms, change for dinner and reach the dining room. Clara flopped down on her bed as she changed her stockings and wondered if she could be bothered to sit for the next couple of hours eating and talking. She did not really feel hungry and all she wanted was a good night's sleep. It still pained her to think that they had another whole day of travel tomorrow. How unbearable! Why had she ever thought this was a good idea?

She did go down to dinner, however. Partly because she did not want to appear ungenerous to the hotel's hospitality – the owner of the hotel was Italian and very prone to fawning over his guests as if they might abandon him at any moment – and partly because she was curious about her fellow passengers and wanted to learn a little more about them. Seeing as tomorrow was going to be spent sitting with little to do, it seemed rather a good idea to learn what she could about everyone else and give herself something to mull over on the journey. It was better than counting cows, which she had been reduced to on this last leg until it got too dark.

Clara found Annie and Tommy in the hotel lobby. Tommy was looking smart in his dinner jacket and bowtie. Annie was busy talking to the hotel owner who she had struck up an instant and very cordial friendship with. It was rather like she had found a kindred soul; they both knew what it was like to have to deal with the whims of other people. Not that Clara or Tommy were particularly prone to whims, but Clara could be a nightmare for getting home for dinner on time. In any case, Annie had taken to the little Italian who was close to three times her age and a fount of wisdom on the subject of serving others. They were currently comparing notes on the best way of making an egg custard.

Suddenly, seemingly from nowhere, Mrs Hunt swept in. She took one look at Tommy and Clara and declared;

"Are you being ignored?"

"Why, no," Clara smiled at her. "We were about to go into the dining room."

Mrs Hunt gave a hostile look to the hotel manager, as if she did not quite believe Clara and thought she was just being polite.

"These foreigners don't know how to treat English guests correctly," she said sharply. "I'll join you, if you don't mind? Shall I push?"

With that she had the handles of Tommy's wheelchair and he was being propelled towards the dining room. He glanced up at Clara, who had to hasten to follow, with a look of utter outrage on his face. He hated people making assumptions about him when he was in his wheelchair and insisting on taking him places without his consent, as if he was mentally deficient too. He started to open his mouth, but Clara interceded.

"Please, let me," she stepped in and almost wrestled the handles of the wheelchair from Mrs Hunt. "We are still waiting for one of our party."

"Very well," Mrs Hunt looked mildly offended. "I shall save us some seats. Presumably you will need to be at the head of the table?"

Despite referring to Tommy, she never took her gaze off Clara.

"Well, yes…"

The woman bustled off before Clara could say anymore.

"That woman!" Tommy spat out the words in an utter temper. "The impudence of it all! Treated me as if I didn't exist!"

"I know," Clara groaned. "And now we look doomed to sit with her."

"I think not!" Tommy declared stoutly. "There are two ends to a table, we shall just happen to go to the one opposite her!"

That plan might have worked except, by the time they had collected Annie and made their way to the table, someone had already acquired the seat at the bottom of the table, and it would look extremely odd to oust them when it was apparent a space had been set aside for Tommy at the top end. Defeated, the party joined Mrs Hunt. She was sitting like some mythical griffin on guard duty, stiffly glaring down her beak-like nose at the other dinner guests and resting her talon-like hands on the table.

"I saved the seats," she informed Clara as they arrived. "There are three of you, yes?"

"Yes," Clara admitted.

Tommy was wheeled into his place in the top spot, with Mrs Hunt directly on his right. She had saved two chairs opposite herself for Clara and Annie. None of the other guests near them had yet been introduced to Clara, so there seemed no sparing them from an evening talking with Mrs Hunt.

They had barely sat down when the first course arrived; a cream of mushroom soup.

"Look at the ghastly stuff," Mrs Hunt lifted up a spoonful of soup and tipped it off back into the bowl with a plop.

Clara, who thought the soup rather tasty, merely smiled as she consumed hers.

"At least there are no rats," Tommy said testily. He had been informed of the incident at the teashop. He was still cross with Mrs Hunt's abrupt manner towards him, and couldn't resist the jibe.

"There was no rat," Mrs Hunt said, eating her soup despite her criticism of it. "The girl was stupid and clumsy."

Clara said nothing. The strange behaviour of Eleanora still had her puzzled. What had she seen under the table? Had something been dropped?

"I shall still complain to Mr Hatton, naturally," Mrs Hunt continued.

"Naturally," Clara mumbled, trying to avoid conversation and knowing it was not going to work.

"Well? Are you going to introduce yourselves, or do you intend to sit there like lemons?" the sudden change in Mrs Hunt's tone, the sharpness of her pronouncement, made them all look up.

For an instant they were all too stunned to say anything, then Clara regained her composure.

"Clara Fitzgerald. This is my brother Thomas Fitzgerald and our friend Annie Green."

"Mildred Hunt," the woman opposite them said. "I've heard of you, Miss Fitzgerald. I believe I saw your name in the papers."

Clara uncomfortably waited for her to elaborate on that statement, Mrs Hunt was the sort of person who you were never sure about what they might say next.

"You are a detective," Mrs Hunt informed her.

"Yes. I am," Clara agreed. "Though, for the moment, I am on holiday."

"I was not about to employ you," Mrs Hunt snapped. "I was merely observing the matter. I must say, I do like to see a woman taking charge of her own life. And what do you do Miss Green?"

A look of sheer panic crossed Annie's face. She was terrified of admitting to this woman that she was actually the Fitzgeralds' maid.

"Annie is my assistant," Clara interceded swiftly. "She helps with my cases."

"Indeed? She is rather a quiet thing for a detective."

"I find saying less is often the way of finding out more," Annie found her tongue with some relief. Her panic gone she met Mrs Hunt's eye. "And what do you do?"

"I used to teach," Mrs Hunt declared. "Until I retired on a small inheritance that is."

Mrs Hunt's hand holding the spoon began to tremble. It was subtle, but her spoon splashed into the soup and suddenly she dropped it. Mrs Hunt masked the unexpected loss of control swiftly, raising her napkin to her mouth and mumbling about how she had had enough soup. She placed her hands in her lap, but not before Clara noticed that her right hand, the one that had dropped the spoon, was still trembling.

The main course that evening was duck with a redcurrant gravy and boiled potatoes. Annie was taking notes on everything served, as if she was studying for an exam on dinner party menus. She was intrigued by the redcurrant gravy, which was new to her. Her gravies were made from the juices of the roasting joints, mixed with a bit of cornflour and gravy salt. The blacker it came out, the better. But she had to admit that the redcurrant gravy, despite being pale and thin, was not altogether unpleasant. It distracted her, at least, from Mrs Hunt, whose attention was once more on Clara.

"Do you live with your parents?" she asked.

"They are deceased," Clara replied, feeling annoyed by the bluntness of the query.

"So you live alone?"

"I live with my brother."

Mrs Hunt's eyes travelled to Tommy at last.

"And he is not married?"

"I am not," Tommy answered the question, annoyed that Mrs Hunt refused to address herself to him.

"Difficult, I suppose, being a cripple."

Mrs Hunt was close to getting an earful from Tommy, Clara was not far off herself. The woman was obnoxious and nosy, no worse combination was there.

"I take it you are married?" Clara interjected, deciding attack was the best form of defence.

"Once, many years ago. Do you…"

Before Mrs Hunt could unleash her next question Clara jumped in again.

"Are you widowed, then?"

Mrs Hunt actually had to pause.

"Not precisely," she said at last.

"How can you be not precisely widowed?" Clara asked, being more pointed with her questions than normal because the woman had rattled her temper.

"I do not know where my husband is," Mrs Hunt said at last, her voice less certain now. "He vanished thirty years ago."

Tommy gave a huff under his breath. They all heard it.

"I occasionally deal with missing husbands," Clara said, deflecting attention once more.

"I don't particularly want him back," Mrs Hunt toyed with her duck, her hand was still trembling though she had it mostly under control. "I have managed quite well these last three decades without him."

Clara's interrogation of Mrs Hunt had, for the moment at least, deflated the woman's curiosity, and she turned her attention to her meal. For a happy fifteen minutes Clara, Tommy and Annie were left in peace to enjoy their duck. Then dessert arrived; a chocolate torte from an Italian recipe. Mrs Hunt looked aghast as she was handed hers.

"Chocolate cake? For dessert?"

Clara said nothing.

"I am appalled by this place," Mrs Hunt told them all. "I have never known such an awful meal."

She prodded at her torte.

"I cannot eat this!" Mrs Hunt stared down the table, looking for someone who would support her in this culinary outrage. Unfortunately, the other dinner guests were quite content with their dessert. "Do you consider this adequate service?"

Clara glanced up at the question. She had been attempting to ignore Mrs Hunt.

"I have found the meal most enjoyable," she said, quite honestly, though with a frisson of pleasure at seeing Mrs Hunt so put out.

The woman puffed out her cheeks and clearly could not fathom why no one else was as outraged as her by their evening's meal. Abruptly, and rather violently, she drove her fork into her torte so that it stood upright.

"I am going to my room," she told no one in particular, before rising sharply and leaving the table.

"Good riddance," Tommy whispered as soon as she was out the doors of the dining room. "What an utterly appalling woman!"

Clara was watching the fork that Mrs Hunt had stabbed into her torte, it was still vibrating from the force of the movement.

"I rather hope we don't have to eat with her again," Annie added. "I don't think I could face it."

"Did anyone not think…" Clara stopped herself.

"What were you going to say?" Tommy asked her.

Clara shook her head.

"No, nothing," she said, but she was still watching the fork tremble and thinking of Mrs Hunt's hand.

Chapter Four

Clara discovered that the perils of charabanc travel included the misfortune of indigestion caused by eating too much and doing too little when she sat in her hotel room a little after dinner. She felt rather queasy – too much cake, too many meals in one day, just too much. She patted her bloated stomach and sighed. How was she ever to sleep? She was exhausted, but felt too ill to relax into slumber. She was really beginning to regret this holiday.

She had just decided to mix up a glass of bicarbonate of soda and water (the bicarb had been packed by Annie in the luggage as a precaution against foreign foods – ie. anything cooked outside of Brighton) when there was a quiet knock on the door. It was so quiet, in fact, that Clara was at first uncertain she had heard it at all. She paused halfway across the room. For a moment she waited, but there was no other sound and she was just moving to her suitcase again when the knock was repeated, this time rather more firmly.

"Who is there?" Clara asked.

"Excusa me, madam," the heavily accented English of their Italian host was at once recognisable to Clara. "Might I, aska you to assist me?"

Clara was curious. She went to her room door and

opened it. The hotel owner was stood just outside looking very worried.

"What has happened?" Clara asked.

"I do not know," the Italian gave a very dramatic shrug. "But your girl Annie, she say you are a detective?"

"Yes?" Clara said cautiously, wondering what she was about to be embroiled in.

"Then, maybe, you coulda come and help? I don't wanna have to call the polizia," the unfortunate man wrung his hands together. Clearly something serious had occurred.

"You best let me see what has you so upset," Clara said, deciding that at least this late night drama would keep her mind off her indigestion. Fortunately, she had yet to change out of her day clothes, having felt too unwell to be bothered about them when she flopped on her bed. "And you best explain this all to me, as well."

The hotel owner motioned for her to follow him down the hallway.

"You saw, I hope, that all the rooms are a fitted with call buttons?" he asked as he walked.

"I had," Clara said.

"They linka to my office downstairs. A few minutes ago the call button for room twenty-one rang. I come up. I knock on door twenty-one. No one answer," again he shrugged dramatically, causing his neck to appear to disappear into his suit. "I go back down, the call button is still ringing. I getta out my master key and I go back to room twenty-one…"

They were at the door of the room as he spoke. The hotel owner pushed the now unlocked door open wide enough for Clara to see in.

"…this isa what I find."

Clara peered in the door and saw Mrs Hunt lying slumped across her bed. The call button, fixed for convenience at the side of the bed, had been knocked on by Mrs Hunt's arm, which lay against it. Clara crept into the room softly. The woman did not move.

"She is dead," the hotel owner stated in hollow tones. "She don't breathe!"

Clara walked to the bed and carefully lifted Mrs Hunt's hand. She felt for a pulse in her wrist. After a couple of minutes she had to admit she could not find one. Mrs Hunt had fallen face first across her bed, she could have been struck down by a heart attack or an apoplectic fit, whatever the case, they would need to call an ambulance.

Because it was part of Clara's nature to be suspicious about unexpected deaths (it came with the day job) she took a good look about the room for any signs that something more serious had occurred. Mrs Hunt's luggage was standing on the floor, apparently yet to be unpacked, though probably most would not bother to empty their suitcases when they were only staying one night. Her handbag was on the nightstand, unopened. When Clara undid the clasp she saw that it was intact, Mrs Hunt's purse and other belongings were still inside. There was no evidence of anything untoward. Clara decided it was time they summoned that ambulance. She turned to the hotel owner.

"You better call…"

Before she could finish they both heard the sound of someone taking a long, awkward breath, and the hotel owner's face turned into a mask of horror. Clara spun round in time to see Mrs Hunt pushing herself upright on the bed. She was breathing in ragged croaks and her face was flushed. Clara would have sworn the woman was dead – at least by all the signs that she had been trained to recognise – but now here she was sitting upright. The hotel owner looked like he had seen a ghost. Clara was less astounded and more curious.

"Mrs Hunt, are you quite all right?" she asked the woman.

Mrs Hunt looked up at her. Her eyes were a little bloodshot and she was having to breathe through her mouth.

"I'm perfectly..." she coughed, "all right. Why is that man in my room?"

She was eyeing up the hotel owner, her expression disapproving.

"You pressed the call button," Clara explained.

Mrs Hunt glanced accusingly at the button on the wall.

"I certainly did not!"

Clara was not about to argue with her. She doubted she would win.

"Would you like us to summon a doctor for you?" she asked instead.

"Certainly not!" Mrs Hunt near yelled at them. "Why would I need a doctor?"

"You had stopped breathing," Clara persisted calmly, wondering why she was bothering. The woman was obnoxious and belligerent, and clearly not impressed by their help.

"I am perfectly fine," Mrs Hunt wheezed.

Clara was not going to contradict her.

"You can leave," Mrs Hunt continued.

The hotel owner, looking very relieved, headed out the door. Clara went to follow him.

"Not you Miss Fitzgerald," Mrs Hunt called out suddenly. "I would like you to stay a moment."

"Is that necessary?" Clara asked. If the woman was just going to be argumentative and volatile Clara really didn't have the energy for it. Her stomach ached and she wanted to rest.

"Please Miss Fitzgerald," Mrs Hunt's tone abruptly softened, taking Clara by surprise. The woman was almost beseeching her. "Stay just a moment longer."

Clara wanted to walk away, but the pathetic plea made her turn back.

"Close the door," Mrs Hunt went back to her commanding voice as soon as she saw that Clara was obeying her.

Clara grumbled to herself as she shut the room door.

She really had no call to be ordered around by this woman, she should go back to her room and be done with it.

"I will stay just a moment," Clara said firmly. "Do you want anything from your suitcase? A nightdress perhaps?"

Like herself, Mrs Hunt was still in her day clothes.

"No, don't bother with that. Come stand beside me, please," Mrs Hunt emphasised her words with a beckoning hand. "I want to talk to you."

Clara joined her by the bed.

"You are a detective?" Mrs Hunt asked.

"Yes," Clara admitted. "What is this about, Mrs Hunt? I really am too tired to talk."

"Then just listen," Mrs Hunt snapped out the words. She was anxious, her breathing still erratic and her voice raspy. "I don't talk to strangers about private matters lightly."

Mrs Hunt undid the top button of her blouse and this seemed to help her breathing.

"I just need you to listen. I don't want the police summoned and I don't want any fuss, but I need to tell someone," Mrs Hunt rubbed at her throat. "I think someone tried to poison me."

Clara was caught by surprise. This revelation came unexpectedly, when Clara was feeling the full weight of her weariness dragging down on her.

"That is a very serious allegation," Clara pointed out.

"I know, but what happened to me was very serious!" Mrs Hunt was angry again and she started to cough.

Clara patted her on the back and she began to breathe normally once more.

"I don't say such things lightly," Mrs Hunt said. "But, I came into my room tonight and there was a parcel waiting for me on the dresser. It was addressed to me and had a tag stating it was a gift from the hotel to welcome me. I had no reason to doubt the statement. It was a very pretty and expensive box, though not very big. When I opened it, I found it contained four marzipan fruits, the sort one buys people at Christmas as an extra special treat. I am partial to marzipan and, after the disappointment at dinner, I decided to eat the fruits. I had consumed all of them bar one. I came to this last fruit, shaped like a strawberry and very detailed in its design. It had even been carefully painted to mimic the fruit. I bit into it and, almost at once, I knew something was wrong. I tasted something metallic! I spat out the marzipan at once, but I must have consumed some for, within a few minutes, I began to feel quite unwell. I don't recall what occurred after that. Not until I roused and found you and that suspect little Italian in my room."

Poisoned food, as Clara was well aware, was a popular means of despatching people from a distance. But she still found it hard to believe that a stranger on a charabanc tour had taken such a dislike to Mrs Hunt in the last few hours that they had attempted to kill her.

"What became of the marzipan?" Clara asked.

"I spat it out the window and, in my haste and disgust, threw out the piece that remained in my hand too."

"And the box?"

Mrs Hunt pointed to the floor down beside the dresser. From the angle Clara stood she could not see behind the dresser but, when she walked towards it, she spotted a small box lying on the floor. It was made of tin and very prettily enamelled with pink flowers on a green background. It was, indeed, the sort of tin people sent Christmas gifts in and it was only just large enough to contain four marzipan fruits. Clara opened the tin and smelt inside; she caught the scent of almonds, unsurprisingly since that is what marzipan is made of, she could also smell the metallic odour of the tin. But nothing else struck her. She turned over the little box and looked to see if it had a maker's name underneath. There was a small label, the sort used to discreetly price goods in quality shops. Clara read the name and realised this tin had been bought in the last village they passed through.

The one with the Post Office that sold souvenirs. She had spotted a sweet shop two doors down from the Post Office, but had paid little heed at the time. Now it appeared someone had bought sweets there and handed them to Mrs Hunt. But was it really an attempt to poison her? Or had some other illness overcome Mrs Hunt and she had wrongly associated it with the marzipan? In any case, Clara thought it prudent to keep the tin.

"Mrs Hunt," Clara returned to the bedside. "Why would anyone on this trip wish you harm? Surely they are all strangers to you?"

"Strangers or not, someone left that box for me. Can you deny it?"

Clara could not deny the tin, though she was uncertain about its contents.

"I really am quite tired now," Mrs Hunt rubbed a hand wearily over her forehead. "I just wanted to let someone know."

"I should call a doctor if you suspect you have been poisoned," Clara repeated.

"No! I don't want the fuss!" Mrs Hunt glowered at her. It was an aggressive, even a threatening look. Clara decided she had no more time for this woman.

"Then I shall return to my bed," Clara replied, heading to the door and mightily glad to be going.

"Miss Fitzgerald!" Mrs Hunt called out one last time. "If anything should occur to me... Well, I have given you due warning."

Clara did not understand what she meant. Was she warning her that if someone harmed Mrs Hunt Clara would be seen to have failed? Or merely wishing to warn her that something might happen and Clara would need to investigate it? Whichever it was, Clara was too tired to care anymore.

"Goodnight Mrs Hunt."

Clara left the room and headed down to her own. She spotted the hotel owner hovering by her door, clearly waiting to hear what had gone on after he had left.

"Is the lady all right?" he asked, looking flustered.

"She seems so," Clara answered, thinking it would take more than poisoned marzipan to see off such a creature as Mrs Hunt. "I don't suppose you leave little gifts for your guests in tins like this?"

She showed the hotel owner the tin. He shook his head.

"Gifts? We don't leave our guests gifts. How odd a thing?"

Clara had expected such an answer, after all, there had been no tin in her room to welcome her. If it was hotel policy, why had she been missed out?

She thanked the hotel owner and went to her room, locking the door behind her and deciding that if someone knocked for her in the night again she would not answer. She went back to mixing a glass of bicarbonate of soda with water and dropped the marzipan tin unceremoniously in her luggage. What a load of nonsense! Mrs Hunt had been taken bad, perhaps with a coughing fit or something like that. Clara had already noted the tremble in her hands. She was not a well woman. Probably this was yet another symptom of her condition which she wrongly attributed to poison. Still, it was rather strange that someone, presumably from the charabanc crowd, had left Mrs Hunt a gift. But people do strange things without there being any evil intent behind them. Clara decided it was not something to be dwelled on. She supped her drink, which almost made her gag, and hoped to get some sleep before morning arrived and they made the next leg of their journey.

Chapter Five

There was no indication of the dramas of the night before when everybody boarded the charabanc the next day. The driver and his conductor seemed bright and breezy, ready for another day of endless travel. Clearly it suited them. Most of the guests were equally alert and eager to be off, having indulged in a hearty breakfast their Italian host had laid out for them. Clara had found it impossible to contemplate kedgeree and herring after her night of indigestion and declined food. Annie couldn't even tempt her with porridge, which she insisted was a good lining for an upset stomach. Clara just wanted to avoid food altogether for a while.

Clara had wondered if Mrs Hunt would continue her journey with them, but she should have realised that the woman was made of sterner stuff and a bout of poisoning was not about to deter her from her holiday. She appeared in the dining room looking as stern and neatly turned out as ever. There was no sign of her indisposition from the night before, though she did seem to rather glower at her fellow charabanc travellers as if she suspected them all of a conspiracy against her.

Clara had spent most of a restless night pondering the question of whether or not Mrs Hunt had been the victim of poison. It was certainly intriguing that she had received a gift, which had clearly been made to appear to be from the hotel. That was odd. Clara had left the dining room early with the excuse that she wanted to stretch her legs and get some fresh air before they continued on their journey. She had hobbled on her walking stick around the side of the hotel and to the window that served Mrs Hunt's room. Beneath it were some thorny rose bushes, not quite in bloom as yet. From the angle of the window Clara thought it most likely that the discarded marzipan fruit would have fallen into the bushes. She poked around with her walking stick at the base of the roses. She didn't spot the lost sweet, but she did find a dead rat.

It was a curious set of circumstances and Clara was just wondering whether the rat should be retrieved as evidence when she heard a yap behind her.

"There she is!"

She turned and spotted Tommy and Annie walking Bramble. Tommy was limping along with his own walking stick, having been sternly told by his doctor that if he wanted to recover the use of his legs he must take a short walk every morning. Clara thought they must look a right pair hobbling along together on their respective sticks. Annie had accompanied Tommy as much to keep an eye on him as to check up on Clara. She knew something was afoot. Clara didn't turn her nose up at breakfast lightly.

Clara stepped back from the rose bush and gestured to the window above her with her stick, almost unbalancing herself in the process.

"Mrs Hunt was taken ill last night. She claims she was poisoned by a box of marzipan fruits left in her room," Clara turned her stick to the rose bush. "She threw the last sweet out the window and I suspect it landed in this bush, where we find our one and only witness to the crime."

Clara used her stick to lift up the bottom branch of the rose bush and reveal the rat. Annie pulled a face at the sight, while Bramble tried to grab the rat and was hastily restrained.

"You think the rat ate the sweet and died?" Tommy asked.

"Well, it's possible. Of course, it could have been there a while, or died of some other ratty illness."

"It wouldn't surprise me if someone tried to kill that woman," Annie interjected suddenly. "She has a way about her that makes enemies rather than friends."

"But in such a short space of time?" Clara said. "We have only been on the charabanc a day!"

"Perhaps that is all the time it took?" Annie remarked, pulling Bramble back from the bush sharply. "So it wasn't just indigestion that kept you awake all night?"

"No," Clara admitted with a blush. "I just can't seem to get away from being a detective."

"Yes, well Mrs Hunt is alive, so you have no need to do any more investigating. You are supposed to be on holiday," Annie wagged her finger at Clara. "Just stop trying to find crimes for the sake of something to do."

Her tone was firm, but there was amusement in her eyes. Clara couldn't help but smile. She shrugged and left the dead rat for nature to deal with.

Their second day aboard the charabanc followed the pattern of the first. They stopped for morning tea at ten and Clara found herself sitting at a table with two fellow passengers who she had not spoken with before. One was a young man, with a serious face and an inclination to peer down his nose at people. The other was a woman in her twenties, dressed smartly if not expensively who had the feel of a schoolmistress about her. While they were waiting for tea and cake Clara made the introductions.

"Clara Fitzgerald, this is my brother Tommy and our friend Annie Green."

"Edwin Hope," the young man introduced himself. Hope was still young enough to be infused with the arrogance of adolescence. He didn't look like the sort of man who took charabanc tours.

"Madeleine Reeve," the woman followed suit. She looked rather anxious and certainly not like someone on a holiday. She kept glancing around as if someone might suddenly ask her something or accuse of her being in the wrong place.

"This is my first charabanc trip," Clara told them to draw out some conversation. "Have you been to the Lakes before?"

"Never," Madeleine answered at once. "This is my first time away from home."

So she was not a schoolmistress, or at least not one that worked away from home at a boarding school. She could be a teacher at a local school.

"Are you enjoying it so far?" Clara asked. Her tea had arrived along with a large slice of Victoria sponge and she was feeling rather queasy again.

"I don't know," Madeleine gave a self-deprecating smile. "It's all rather different."

"What made you decide to book the excursion?" Clara continued, wondering where a woman of Madeleine's standing found the money for such an expensive thing as a charabanc tour.

"Oh, well I didn't, that is…" the woman gave a little cough. "It was a present from a friend."

"How nice," Clara smiled politely. "And you Mr Hope? How do you come to be here?"

"Curious, aren't you?" Hope said sharply. "Typical woman, needs to know everything."

"Watch your tongue, old man," Tommy grumbled like a dog that has seen a cat. "It was only a polite question."

Hope glanced at Tommy, contemplating arguing the issue. But, while Tommy's infirmities might make him look like someone who would be a push-over, his confident demeanour quickly altered that perception. Tommy was a fighter through and through, he had survived a war because of his gut determination and he wasn't someone to be taken lightly. Hope shut his mouth and concentrated on his cake.

Clara was beginning to feel she was travelling with a coach-load of rogues. No one, except perhaps Mr Wignell and his wife, seemed typical holiday-makers. They were all rather surly and keen to be left alone – which was altogether odd when travelling with a crowd of people on a charabanc. Clara wondered if this was the usual sort of folk Mr Hatton attracted to his trips?

"I saw you had the misfortune last night to dine with Mrs Hunt," Madeleine spoke up, trying to ease the tension which had fallen over everyone.

"You know her?" Clara asked.

"Everyone knows her by now!" Madeleine laughed, though it seemed a little forced. "Mrs Siskin was not particularly discreet about how Mrs Hunt upset her friend."

"It was an unfortunate comment," Clara agreed, her eyes twitching to Hope to give him the hint. "We all say them from time to time."

"Then she had tea dropped over her, and that poor girl got the sack," Madeleine added.

"The girl deserved it for being so clumsy," Hope said, the words seeming to roll down his arrogantly long nose.

"Yesterday I dined with the Wignells," Madeleine pressed on, not acknowledging Hope's interruption. "They had sat in front of Mrs Hunt that afternoon and she had complained the whole journey about this and that. Not to them, but to her unlucky neighbour on the next seat. She also said some cruel things about her fellow travellers, according to Mr Wignell."

"Gossip!" Hope scowled at Madeleine. "Is that all women are capable of?"

Madeleine was cowed into silence, much to Clara's annoyance. She decided to turn her attention on Hope.

"You don't feel the need to take an interest in your fellow passengers then?" she asked him bluntly.

Hope tilted his head before saying.

"I keep my thoughts to myself. If more of us did that then we would not be having this discussion, Mrs Hunt being a prime example of a person who clearly cannot keep her own thoughts silent."

"Or maybe she doesn't care to?" Clara suggested. "Some people like to say things that hurt."

She held Hope's gaze for longer than necessary and was certain he received her message. A moment later he excused himself and left his cake and tea unfinished on the table. Madeleine pressed crumbs together on her plate with her cake fork.

"I met Edwin yesterday, he's a student and a little full of himself," she confided. "He doesn't seem right for a charabanc tour, does he?"

The similarity of this insight to Clara's own, made her almost smile.

"No, Mr Hope does not seem the sort."

"He is one of those people who seem to think the world owes them something," Madeleine said. "You know the sort?"

"I do," Clara nodded. "I also know such types of people tend to end up with a lot less than they could have achieved because of the chip on their shoulder."

Madeleine considered this thoughtfully.

"You know, I rather imagine that sums up Mrs Hunt."

It was Clara's turn to consider this idea.

"You know, I think you may be right."

~~~*~~~

They carried on until noon. Clara found it possible to doze in her chair if she lowered herself slightly and rested her head against the window. She woke with a stiff neck and feeling like someone had knocked her over the head for her efforts. Dinner was served as a picnic, prepared at the last stop. Unfortunately, the weather had turned to drizzle and, as beautiful as the countryside was, no one felt eager to disembark and endure English rain for the sake of it. So the picnic was served onboard and discreet toilet arrangements were prepared for those who could not wait until their next convenience break.

Clara accepted her portion of the picnic from the conductor. It was in a cardboard box tied with string and when she opened it she found ham sandwiches, a boiled egg still in its shell, a slice of pork pie and an apple. This was sufficiently plain and rustic to restore her appetite. Annie engaged with her boiled egg with the eye of an expert; she would know at once how fresh the eggs used were and whether they had been given sufficient time in the boiling water. Tommy shovelled pork pie into his mouth with a look of satisfaction, the water pastry almost melting on his tongue. For once the entire charabanc party seemed content.

Sadly, Mrs Hunt had to spoil it.

"As we are all gathered so agreeably, perhaps someone would like to admit to leaving me a gift in my room last night?" she asked the passengers, sounding all too much like an accusing headmistress. "Well? Will no one admit to their act of generosity? A shy gift giver are they?"

Aside from Clara and the person who sent Mrs Hunt the marzipan fruits (presuming they were one of the travellers) no one knew that the sweets had been poisoned. So everyone was more curious than disturbed by this question.

"Why would someone leave you a gift?" Mrs Siskin remarked, perhaps wondering why she had not been treated to such generosity.

"If I knew who had sent them I would be better set to answer that," Mrs Hunt responded in a condescending tone. "All I can say is they were most delightful."

Mrs Siskin obviously could not understand why anyone would want to give Mrs Hunt a gift. She screwed up her round, fat face.

"Perhaps it was a friend from home?"

"They would not know where I was staying," Mrs Hunt corrected her. "I did not know the address of the hotel until we arrived."

"Perhaps they gave it to the conductor?"

Everyone turned to the conductor and the driver, who both quickly denied any knowledge of a gift.

"Isn't it curious?" Mrs Hunt said in a jovial voice. "Well, if they will not declare themselves I can hardly thank them, can I?"

Mrs Hunt finally turned to her lunch, taking a very small bite from her sandwich.

"My word! This ham is salty!" she declared loudly and in a disparaging voice.

Everyone ignored her, especially as no one else had noticed anything particularly salty about the ham. The atmosphere aboard the charabanc had taken a cold air, which was all the more curious considering that the real nature of Mrs Hunt's 'gift' had not been revealed, and the question she had asked would have seemed innocent enough to anyone who did not know about the marzipan fruits.

Clara found her eyes straying about the charabanc, looking to see if anyone seemed uneasy or guilty. No one did, but, then again, no one looked particularly happy either. Mrs Hunt had cast a cloud over them and it seemed the only one to be taking delight in this was the culprit herself. Mrs Hunt seemed to almost smile as she ate her salty ham. Clara suspected the woman was pleased with herself and perhaps believed she had rattled her would-be murderer (if there was one aboard). Clara saw things differently; she feared Mrs Hunt was making things worse. But what could Clara say? Nothing at all. She concentrated on peeling her hard-boiled egg and wondered why some people are so fond of unpleasantness.

Chapter Six

When they finally arrived at the hotel where they would be spending the next five nights Clara was most relieved. The first thing she did was retreat to her room and lock herself in, enjoying the reprieve from all the strange characters on the charabanc.

After their picnic the atmosphere aboard the vehicle had deteriorated. Mrs Hunt's words seemed to loom in the air for no real reason, after all, only one other person was aware that Mrs Hunt had nearly died the night before, so why should the entire charabanc party descend into melancholy? It was something in the way Mrs Hunt had burst out with her question. It had felt like an accusation, and no one could mistake that.

Clara thought the woman was foolish. If someone was trying to kill her why goad them? If they were on the charabanc, that is. Clara sighed and set to her unpacking, she would be glad to have some time to herself. She was emptying her suitcase when she came upon the pretty tin which Mrs Hunt had received her poisoned sweets in. The tin sat in her hand neatly, looking innocuous enough. Who had had the time to go to the sweet shop and buy it?

Well, nearly all of them, Clara supposed. As it happened, the seat she had occupied outside the teashop would have granted her a prime position to see who came and went from the sweet shop. Unfortunately, Clara had not been paying much attention, at the time she had had no reason to.

Clara was just arranging herself for dinner when there was a frantic knock on her room door. When she opened it Annie was on the threshold.

"You better come quickly!" Annie declared, before rushing away and assuming Clara would follow.

Clara grabbed her cardigan, for the evening had taken on a chill, and went after her. Annie led the way down the corridor and up the back stairs, the ones usually used by the servants. Clara started to ask a question, but Annie put a finger to her lips. They carried on in silence reaching the third floor and hurrying along. Finally Annie stopped outside the room ominously numbered as 13C (the C indicating the floor they were on). Annie pushed open the room door and ushered Clara inside before shutting it behind them.

Mrs Hunt was sitting in a low chair while a man who appeared to be a doctor took her blood pressure. The charabanc driver was also in the room and glanced up at Clara with an expression of relief and panic.

"Thank you for coming, Miss Fitzgerald. She was asking for you," the driver came over, wringing his cap in his hands.

"You'll wreck the rim," Clara told him gently. "Put that cap down and tell me what is going on."

They discreetly moved to a corner of the room to talk.

"I was taking Mrs Hunt's luggage up from the charabanc. She was the last to have her suitcase taken out, due to her being unhappy with her first room and insisting on changing it. She said we should not carry up her luggage until she had found a room to her liking."

That sounded exactly like Mrs Hunt, Clara thought.

"She finally settled on this room and I was just

bringing up her suitcases, we were on the second flight of stairs to be precise, when the most horrendous thing happened. A chamber pot, the old-fashioned porcelain sort, came flying down from above and hit Mrs Hunt on the head!" the driver grimaced at the memory. "I looked up almost at once, but I saw no one at all. It just came out of nowhere!"

Both of them glanced at Mrs Hunt who was delicately touching the back of her head.

"What happened next?" Clara asked.

"Well, I bent down and gave Mrs Hunt a little shake. She was lying on the stairs, you see, and I could not think what else to do. She didn't move, so I said her name, just quietly like," the driver was becoming agitated again and wanted to do something with his hands, but Clara had made him put down his cap, so he had to console himself with clutching his hands together. "I shook her again, it never occurred to me she was dead."

"Dead?" Clara said quietly, out of the corner of her eye glancing at the very alive Mrs Hunt.

"She wasn't breathing. I didn't realise that until that fellow over there came down the stairs and spotted us," the driver nodded at the doctor attending Mrs Hunt. "He said he was a medical man and at once realised we were in a pickle. He checked her pulse and her heart and her breathing. Mrs Hunt was dead! He said so!"

The word 'dead' had been loud enough for Mrs Hunt to hear and she cast an accusing glare across the room at the driver.

"I was temporarily indisposed," she told Clara stoutly. "Dead is rather exaggerating the fact."

"The doctor said she was dead," the driver whispered to Clara. "We carried her up here between us, she didn't rouse at all. I thought to myself, I didn't become a charabanc driver to spend my days carrying corpses about!" the driver pulled another face. "Can you imagine what it will be like explaining this all to Mr Hatton?"

"But it appears Mrs Hunt was not dead?" Clara said.

"She was, I swear it!" the driver hissed. "Only, when we had laid her on the bed, she suddenly starts to breathe again. Just as we were planning on calling for the police or something. She started groaning and said she needed to speak with you at once. The doctor thought I ought to fetch you, but in my panic I couldn't remember your room number. As it happens I stumbled upon your friend and she said she would fetch you."

The driver paused, his hands twitching to be wringing his cap rim again.

"Might I go now, Miss? I feel a bit queer and could do with a rest meself."

Clara agreed that he could go and the driver disappeared hastily. Clara now turned to the doctor who was finishing up with Mrs Hunt.

"Well? What verdict do we have?" Clara asked him.

The doctor was in his thirties, well-dressed, nice looking except for the residual scar from a hare lip. Clara thought he had a serious face, perhaps one that was even inclined to be depressive or stern. She couldn't immediately say if she liked or disliked him, only that he seemed a person not inclined to open himself to other people.

"Mrs Hunt sustained a bad blow to the back of the head. I expect her to have sustained a concussion," the doctor spoke with a very slight lisp, which perhaps explained some of his apparent sullenness for conversation.

"I do not like the sound of 'concussion'," Mrs Hunt said bluntly. "Therefore I refuse to have it."

The doctor gave her a rather cross look, but then Mrs Hunt had that effect on people.

"Is it true Mrs Hunt was technically dead?" Clara asked.

"There you go, using that word again!" Mrs Hunt snapped.

"Mrs Hunt had no life signs when I first saw her," the doctor said carefully, ignoring the outburst from his patient. "She was not breathing, nor did she appear to have a pulse or heartbeat. To most intents and purposes she was dead."

"But I am alive now, that is what matters," Mrs Hunt muttered impatiently.

"How can a person be dead then alive?" Clara pressed on.

"The easiest thing to suggest is that her heart had temporarily stopped, and then, for some reason, began to beat again. It has been known to happen. In fact, it is for this reason life-saving techniques focus on getting the heart to beat again," the doctor explained.

"But you had not tried any of those techniques?"

"Not at the time, no. I would suggest Mrs Hunt's heart restarted quite spontaneously. A miracle, if you will," the doctor did not seem much impressed by this miraculous resurrection. He reached down for his surgical bag. "Now, if you don't mind, I would like to change for dinner."

The doctor excused himself and left. Mrs Hunt scowled at the door as it closed behind him.

"Miserable sort," she complained. "Probably not a real doctor at all. Probably a dentist with ambitions."

She touched the back of her head and pulled a face.

"It was a nasty blow," Clara observed.

Mrs Hunt placed her hands, one on top of the other, in her lap and looked Clara squarely in the face.

"The second attempt on my life, Miss Fitzgerald. I do hope you will take me seriously now."

"I took you seriously before."

"No, you did not. I saw it in your face when you left me. You thought I was a silly old bat who had been taken unwell and had become fanciful."

Clara could not immediately say she had not thought that.

"I went to look for the marzipan in the morning, all I found was a dead rat."

"And so it seems I was right?" Mrs Hunt nodded

gingerly, trying to avoid hurting her head further. "I have a ringing headache, that doctor gave me something for it. Might you assist me to lie down on the bed?"

Clara helped Mrs Hunt to her feet. The woman suddenly seemed a lot frailer than she had the night before. She felt light as a feather, as if there was nothing to her. Annie pulled back the sheets on the bed and together they hoisted Mrs Hunt onto the mattress and settled her in an upright position.

"Shall I ask someone to send you up some dinner?" Clara asked.

"I should hope so!" Mrs Hunt pressed at her head again.

Clara shared a look with Annie, they were both thinking the same, that Mrs Hunt was truly insufferable.

"Did you see anyone on the stairs before your accident?" Clara changed the subject.

"No. Except that useless driver."

"Who knew you were changing rooms?"

"It was hardly a secret!" Mrs Hunt puttered. "I changed rooms on purpose, you know, to put a spoke in the murderer's wheel. I thought they might have arranged another little gift for me like last night."

"But who would be interested in killing you?" Clara found the whole situation baffling. "You are sure you knew no one on the charabanc?"

There was a long pause. Mrs Hunt stared thoughtfully at the bed linen, finally she spoke and in a very precise voice said;

"I know no one aboard that charabanc."

Clara sighed.

"Have you any enemies?"

"Probably," Mrs Hunt replied unhelpfully. "I am a woman who speaks her mind. I won't suffer mumblers or those who refuse to say what they think or feel. This world is half ruined because of those sort. If we had spoken our minds sooner the war may never have happened."

"I think that unlikely Mrs Hunt," Clara said calmly. "Have you spoken your mind to anyone recently?"

"Probably," Mrs Hunt admitted. "I don't keep track."

That didn't surprise Clara.

"Do you have family Mrs Hunt? Or anyone you might like me to send a message to on your behalf?"

"No," Mrs Hunt's voice for the first time became uncertain. "No, I am alone in this world."

"Not even a friend I could write to…"

"No!" Mrs Hunt glowered at Clara. "Enough, young lady! I am quite sick of you, of you all! Go! Leave me alone! Find who did this if you are any sort of detective and prevent them from succeeding the next time!"

Clara was quite ready to take her leave. She politely stated that she hoped Mrs Hunt would recover swiftly then left the room with Annie. They headed back downstairs almost without a word, then Annie piped up.

"I could think of several people aboard that charabanc who would be glad to see the back of her. Myself included."

"But you don't intend to kill her," Clara pointed out.

"No. Do you really think this was intentional and not some silly accident? A chamber maid perhaps not taking enough care?"

"Had there not already been the previous incident I might have considered that possibility, but someone appears to have made two attempts on Mrs Hunt in a short space of time. Whatever our feelings on the woman, we can't allow a murderer to succeed."

"I suppose not," Annie replied. "At least we don't have to worry about her sitting with us at dinner."

Clara was reluctant to admit that she was relieved by that thought too. They were just about to depart to their separate rooms when a man came rushing up to them. He was in a fine suit and Clara recognised him as the hotel owner. He was a tad out of breath as he stopped before her.

"Is it true?" he asked Clara. "Has someone tried to kill

a guest?"

"I can't say for certain," Clara told him gently. "It may have been an accident. Tell me, do you provide chamber pots for your guests?"

"Chamber pots?" the hotel owner looked aghast. "In a modern establishment like this? Each floor has two bathrooms, one at each end, I must point out madam. Chamber pots are so old-fashioned!"

"So there are no chamber pots at all in the establishment?"

The hotel owner began to speak, then hesitated.

"Actually, we did retain some for emergencies and, occasionally, guests request them," the hotel owner gave a polite look of disbelief at the ways of his older guests. "Some guests simply can't get out of the habit of using them."

"Have any guests requested chamber pots today?" Clara asked.

The hotel owner started to shake his head, then he paused as a thought struck him.

"Mrs Crimp did," he said at last. "Yes, she came to the front desk for one. Does Mrs Hunt require anything?"

"She would like dinner in her room," Clara informed him.

"Naturally, naturally! I will arrange that at once," the hotel owner began to bustled off, then turned back. "Be assured I run a safe and respectable establishment!"

He vanished with his new purpose in mind. Clara turned to Annie.

"Is there a Mrs Crimp on the charabanc?"

Annie thought about this.

"I believe so. But it's odd."

"What is?"

"Well, if she is the lady I am thinking of she is only in her forties. Not precisely what I imagined when the hotel manager spoke of older guests."

"Everyone has their quirks," Clara went to her room door and paused with her hand over the handle. "I wonder if Mrs Crimp is missing a chamber pot? Perhaps we ought to arrange to sit near her at dinner?"

Annie rolled her eyes at her.

"I just can't stop you being a detective, can I?"

Chapter Seven

Mrs Crimp proved to be a well-padded lady in her early forties, with a round happy face and a dimple on her chin. She had decided to try out the new fashion for shorter hair, which had not worked terribly well on her robust form. She rather looked like an egg someone had dropped an under-sized wig onto. Nor did the rather straight-waisted dress she had opted to wear to dinner do her figure any favours. It was in a rather unappealing puce colour, with a hummingbird design sequined onto the top. Perhaps on some emaciated model it would have looked becoming. On Mrs Crimp it gave the appearance of a badly stuffed sofa.

Her fashion issues aside, Mrs Crimp was a pleasant enough woman. She was the wife of a bank manager who liked to fund her little excursions to keep her amused. Mr Crimp did not travel, he was rather too busy with work and was one of those type of people who imagine themselves indispensable. But he was also a man who found his wife rather overwhelming at times, so he sent her off on these little jaunts to give himself a much needed break. Considering Mrs Crimp's rather larger-than-life persona, Clara could understand Mr Crimp's need for the occasional separation.

Apparently Mrs Crimp's life revolved around these short breaks. She confessed she did not have much in the way of hobbies. She couldn't knit or crochet. The garden annoyed her because things took so long to grow. She had never been much use at cooking. And she was rather a careless housekeeper, flicking a duster around when it suited her, usually just before some guest was due to arrive. Aside from reading (Mrs Crimp was a voracious reader) there was little else in the lady's life apart from her holidays. She spent a great deal of time planning for them and organising her wardrobe, as she explained to Clara;

"I always buy a new dress for a trip away. It is an indulgence, I admit, but I can't resist it. I saw this dress in the window of Kendril's Department Store and had to have it. Perfect, I said to myself, for our special evening meals."

In Clara's head she had a sudden vision of Mrs Hunt's disapproving face and imagined her muttering something derogatory about Mrs Crimp's fashion sense.

"I try to keep abreast of the latest trends," Mrs Crimp continued, fluffing up the side of her awful haircut. "One might not be so very young anymore, but one can still try. I tell my husband that all the time."

"Today's fashions seem to change so fast," Clara pulled a face as she toyed with the tomato soup they had been offered for that evening's starter. She rather had the feeling it had come out of a can. "Each month there seems to be a new trend for hemlines or seams, or a dozen other things."

"That is why I always buy something just before I am due to go away. So I can keep up-to-date. Mind you, that dress you are wearing is very pretty and most becoming," Mrs Crimp revealed that outside of the air-headed fashion follower she was in fact a very nice person. "I do like the little roses on it. They are just the right shade for your skin tone."

"Thank you," Clara said, touched by the complement.

Only later remembering how awful Mrs Crimp's idea of suitable colours was. "I am rather new to this whole charabanc lark and was beside myself as to what to pack."

"Practical clothes for the day-time," Mrs Crimp explained helpfully. "Walking shoes are a must on these things as they will drop you off at some footpath and expect you to walk the whole thing and be picked up at the other end. I always bring a thick jumper and a good coat. But in the evenings it is rather nice to dress up."

"And is this the usual sort of accommodation you would expect on one of these excursions?" Clara motioned with her soup spoon to the hotel at large.

"Yes, we generally stay in a hotel. Though once we had to spend the night in a private house due to the charabanc breaking down!"

"How awful!"

"Oh, the house owners were very accommodating. It was rather fun actually. We slept on chairs or rugs and rather 'roughed' it for the night," Mrs Crimp smiled. "It was quite entertaining."

"I'm rather glad we made it to the hotel!" Clara laughed. "The accommodation here seems rather good, though the bathrooms do seem rather a long way from the rooms."

Mrs Crimp gave a giggle.

"Don't mention to anyone, but I thought the same as you in regards of the distance to the bathrooms and so I asked for a chamber pot! You can still get them in hotels, you know, and they are much more convenient for the middle of the night," Mrs Crimp's eyes danced with amusement. "I grew up in a rather old-fashioned household and we swore by our chamber pots, really we did. It's hard to break the habit!"

"What a novel idea!" Clara said, playing along. "Isn't it odd that you are the second person to mention chamber pots to me, the first was another guest who was telling me how Mrs Hunt had had a misfortune with one of the things!"

"Mrs Hunt?" Mrs Crimp looked perplexed. "Oh, is she the opinionated woman who sits at the back of the charabanc and makes comments about people? I have been avoiding her. But, yes, you are right, she has not come down for dinner."

"That's because, just a few hours ago, she was mysteriously struck by a falling chamber pot."

Mrs Crimp's eyes went wide.

"Truly?"

"That is what I am told. It fell from nowhere and landed right on her head."

"Is she all right?" Mrs Crimp asked.

"As far as I am aware she is," Clara assured her. "She has opted to stay in her room for tonight, however. She has a nasty bump."

"I can well imagine. I wonder how it happened?"

"I couldn't say. Perhaps a careless maid? Your chamber pot is presumably intact? Wouldn't want to discover it was cracked in the night, would you!"

Mrs Crimp roared with laughter. It was a sudden and loud sound that took Clara by surprise. In fact, it took quite a few people around the table by surprise and caused a brief pause in the consumption of dinner.

"Oh my," Mrs Crimp dabbed her eye with a handkerchief she retrieved from her handbag. "Excuse me, but your suggestion brought such an image to my mind… well…"

Clara was not inclined to ask what that image was.

"As it happens, I personally collected the chamber pot from a cupboard where such things are kept. I wouldn't normally, but when I had asked about it the maid mentioned they were kept in a cupboard we had to pass to reach my room. It was therefore no bother to retrieve one as we went past."

"There is a cupboard of them?" Clara asking, feigning astonishment.

"Only about a half dozen of the things," Mrs Crimp shrugged her shoulders. "In an old armoire along the landing from my room on the third floor."

"Makes you wonder why anyone would be throwing the things around," Tommy interjected, of course, he was in on the notion that someone was out to kill Mrs Hunt, but before Mrs Crimp he wanted to give the impression of complete innocence of this idea. "They are hotel property, after all. People shouldn't be so careless."

"It was probably an accident," Clara said, joining in with the pretence. "Just very unfortunate for Mrs Hunt."

"Children causing mischief, perhaps?" Mrs Crimp added. "Though I haven't noticed any children in the hotel. I don't suppose anyone saw who did it?"

"Apparently not."

The conversation paused as the main course was served. Chicken in a white wine gravy, with seasonal vegetables. It looked a meal far easier on the stomach than that Clara had eaten the day before.

"I suppose it was an accident?" Mrs Crimp suddenly said as she carved into her chicken breast. "I mean, the relevant people are certain of that?"

"What else could it be?" Clara played dumb.

"Oh, you know, a prank gone wrong, perhaps?" Mrs Crimp waved her hand in the air. "I'm not making a great deal of sense, but, you see, I had noticed she was inclined for upsetting people. The sort of person who finds fault wherever she looks and likes to say so."

Mrs Crimp paused in the middle of eating and stared down the length of the table, though not looking at anything in particular.

"It occurred to me that someone who was of a foolish persuasion and did not realise the consequences, might have thrown the chamber pot at her," Mrs Crimp toyed with this idea a moment. "Yes, as soon as you said what had occurred it made me wonder. I mean, chamber pots do not simply fly off by themselves! And, I really find it hard to imagine how it might have accidentally been cast at her. How was the person not seen, for a start?"

"It was on the stairs," Clara explained. "The chamber

pot fell down from a higher floor."

"The third floor?" Mrs Crimp asked.

"I don't know. No one saw it coming."

"And no one confessed to the matter," Mrs Crimp nodded. "I see, yes, it all sounds a little too odd."

Clara had to admit it wasn't your usual sort of accident, not one to be easily explained away. As Mrs Crimp said, chamber pots did not magically take flight.

"I find it hard to imagine Mrs Hunt upsetting someone so dreadfully in the short time we have been on this trip for them to contemplate harming her," Clara eventually said. It was the truth, after all.

"People do spur of the moment things," Mrs Crimp countered. "Oh, but don't imagine I was retrieving the chamber pot for just such a thing! I honestly would not and mine is still in my room."

"I believe you," Clara reassured her. "Anyway, why would you want to harm her?"

"True, I have managed to avoid her so far. She is one of those people I dread getting into conversation with. I really wonder why she came on this trip at all, seeing as how she seems to detest everybody and want to make them all unhappy," Mrs Crimp gave a 'tsk' under her breath. "Why do those sort of people exist, I ask myself. What misfortunes of life have turned them so bitter? Mrs Hunt, and I don't say this lightly, but Mrs Hunt is one of life's nasty souls who take pleasure from making others miserable."

"Do you think so?"

"I do. I have heard her speaking to a few people aboard the charabanc and none have come away from their chats, shall I say, unscathed?"

That was a telling remark, but it did not surprise Clara. Her own encounter with Mrs Hunt had been less than pleasurable. Still, it was one thing to dislike a person and another to want to kill them. A brief conversation in a charabanc with a stranger seemed flimsy motive for murder, didn't it?

"I see I have you thinking?" Mrs Crimp winked at her. "It is certainly a strange thing. Mrs Hunt probably ought to speak to the police, but I doubt she will."

They finished dinner on a pudding of stewed fruit and clotted cream, and Clara found herself aching for her bed. She had not slept the night before and it had been a long day. She walked towards her room with Tommy and Annie. They were all housed on the ground floor as neither Clara or Tommy were up to much stair climbing, though Clara could if it was really necessary as she had demonstrated earlier. Their rooms were next to each other, with Clara's the furthest along. She said goodnight to her travelling companions and was headed to her room when a door even further up the corridor opened and the doctor who had attended Mrs Hunt emerged.

Clara noted the man looked a little dishevelled. His tie was draped loose about his neck and his hair was roughed up as if from sleeping. He glanced up as he closed the door to the room and saw Clara. For a moment he looked a little surprised, then he regained his composure.

"Oh, so you are on this floor too."

"Yes. I'm afraid I never asked your name," Clara said, the doctor seemed inclined to hurry down the corridor, so she deliberately stepped away from her door to prevent it. "Are you on holiday or business, Dr...?"

"Business," the doctor answered brusquely, his exit denied. "I have been called up to visit an old patient who has taken ill on holiday."

"Oh, how awful," Clara sympathised with the patient. "As you are here on business, might I ask you to look at my foot?"

The doctor looked down at Clara's feet. Her right one was visibly bandaged and only just able to squeeze into her shoe.

"I had an accident a few weeks ago," Clara told him. "My own doctor stated I was well enough for this trip, but I am in a lot of pain tonight and wonder if I have damaged the foot again. Might you look at it?"

This was all bunkum for the doctor's sake. Clara's foot felt fine. But she was curious about this man and his strange behaviour. The only way to nab him for a little longer was to give him a medical problem to deal with. The doctor sighed.

"Let me look at it then."

They went into Clara's room and she removed her shoes. The doctor carefully felt her foot and it was not hard for Clara to grimace and wince at certain points, for her foot was still sore and bruised.

"I don't think there is any great harm done," the doctor concluded. "Just rest it."

"Thank you. Now, how much would you like for the consultation? I shall write you a cheque," Clara reached for her handbag.

"No bother, really," the doctor stood up and hastened for the door. "I don't expect payment."

"Well, at least let me thank you properly. I still don't know your name!"

The doctor hesitated for a long moment. Why he was so reluctant to reveal his identity Clara could not say, but finally he spoke.

"Dr Masters," he said, clearly expecting a reaction from Clara. When he received nothing but a smile he added. "Dr John Masters."

"Thank you for your assistance Dr Masters," Clara said happily. "If I have a problem with my foot again, might I ask for you once more?"

Dr Masters was clearly still expecting some other response from her and seemed bamboozled by her lack of a reaction.

"Yes," he said, still baffled. "Goodnight."

He let himself out of her room. What an odd man, Clara thought to herself. He had clearly been expecting her to recognise, or at least to react to his name, but it rang no bells with her. She wondered just what trouble the good doctor had found himself in, for he certainly acted like a man with something on his conscience.

Another little mystery to solve, Clara mused. She lay back on her bed, forgetting to undress in her weariness, and very soon was asleep.

Chapter Eight

The first true day of the Fitzgerald holiday dawned. According to the brochure kindly supplied by the charabanc company, their first day in the Lake District was to commence with an excursion to Windermere, the largest natural lake in England. The brochure went on to explain that Windermere had been a popular holiday destination since a railway branch line had been extended there in 1847.

Clara thought a peaceful day by the waters of Windermere sounded just what the charabanc party needed to refresh and revive them. Therefore she was eagerly down for breakfast, freshly changed into her walking attire. She was intrigued to see that Mrs Hunt had joined them, clearly the woman was feeling better after her unpleasant encounter with a chamber pot. Clara was intent on avoiding her, however, she didn't need her relaxing day ruined by the woman's vitriol.

The party was due to depart just after ten. Clara found herself in the hotel lobby examining a selection of postcards the establishment offered for sale. She thought that perhaps she ought to send one back to Oliver Bankes in Brighton, her photographer friend and occasional accomplice. It seemed to be the thing to do. She was distracted from a pretty hand-tinted card that showed the picturesque road leading to the hotel by the arrival of Eleanora Smythe. The woman seemed to be greatly distressed, wringing a handkerchief between her fingers and giving occasional sniffs as if just about or just finished crying.

Clara paused her browsing to turn to the woman.

"Are you all right Miss Smythe?"

"Please don't talk to me," Miss Smythe hurried past in the direction of the dining room, the handkerchief surreptitiously dabbing at one eye.

How curious, thought Clara, what reason could Miss Smythe have to be in such a state? She found herself unconsciously glancing around for Mrs Hunt, as if that woman was responsible for every calamity befalling the charabanc party. She was almost disappointed not to see her.

The charabanc departed at ten on the dot. Clara wedged herself next to Tommy yet again, while Annie had opted to sit behind. She had been dubious about the rather continental style breakfast served at the hotel, and was still semi-convinced they had all been poisoned by the lack of boiled eggs and black pudding. She wouldn't admit it to anyone, but she was homesick and didn't really want to make conversation. So she sat behind the Fitzgeralds and told herself it was only for a few more days longer that she must endure this ordeal.

Windermere proved as pretty as the brochure had suggested. A thin mist was hovering over the surface of the lake, but their driver informed his party with certainty that this would soon burn off in the sunshine. The party disembarked and was shown to a pleasant rambling path around the lake's edge by the conductor. Everyone was free to roam as they pleased for the next few hours, as long as they returned to the charabanc by two o'clock when the driver had instructions to take them into the nearby village for high tea.

Full of a good breakfast, (Clara had not been fazed by

its 'continental' style) the Fitzgeralds and Annie set out at a gentle pace, keen to test their respective stamina. Tommy insisted on walking, though his wheelchair had been brought as back-up and the girls took it in turns to push it.

"Look, is that a heron?" Tommy raised his arm skyward as across the centre of the lake flew a greyish, long bird.

Clara could not say precisely what sort of feathered beast it was. She was just content to nod and assure Tommy that it must be. They paused by the water and watched it ripple about the lake edge.

"Beautiful day," Henry Wignell came up behind them, wife in tow. "Once the mist burns off it will be glorious."

Clara turned and smiled. Wignell, as always, seemed jovial and delighted to simply be there. His wife looked a tad sour-faced, but that might just have been her natural expression.

"It is beautiful," Clara agreed.

"You know, the name 'Windermere' is thought to translate from an old Germanic name, either 'Winand' or 'Vinand'. It has old Norse roots, or so my little guidebook says. So, at some point many centuries ago a chap called Winand walked this way and had a lake named after him," Wignell commented, a man who loved facts, especially when they related to a place he was visiting. "Another interesting point, the lake is more than 11 miles in length, but less than a mile in width. Oh, and it contains 18 islands!"

"I suspect they know quite enough about Windermere now," Mrs Wignell interrupted. "Why don't we go look for that island you mentioned that can only be seen when the water is a certain depth?"

"Bee Holme? Oh yes, I want to see that, the mist permitting. Good day, friends, have a very pleasant time," Henry Wignell tipped his hat to them and sauntered off with his wife.

"Chatty fellow," Tommy smirked when he was gone.

"Enthusiastic," Clara said. "And that is much nicer than the gruff attitude we would receive from Mrs Hunt, who, I am relieved to say, appears to have wandered in her own direction."

"She was on the charabanc," Annie observed.

"Well, let's not talk her up. I am enjoying the view and really don't need her obnoxiousness ruining it," Clara said firmly and they all made the determined effort to push Mrs Hunt from their minds.

The day became brighter. The mist on the lake, as the driver had said, burned off and it began to get quite hot for walking. The trio took their time wandering along the lakeside and by noon had agreed to rest beneath the shade of a large tree and share the bottle of ginger ale Annie had stashed in the wheelchair. Clara was beginning to feel quite relaxed, even her foot seemed to hurt less. The weather was just right to induce her to doze and she drifted off beneath the tree leaves with no one complaining.

When she woke a good hour later her companions were debating whether they ought to start sauntering back along their route, considering the time their out-journey had taken it seemed wise. They set off for the charabanc, the lake glistening at their side and some distant birds calling out a gentle harmony in the trees.

The charabanc driver had spent the day reading a newspaper and sleeping. He was not much of a fellow for walking, he much preferred the power of an engine to get him from A to B, and had been content to relax in his usual seat. The conductor had wandered around the near edge of the lake, casting stones into the water and mulling over the contents of a letter he needed to write to his girl back in Brighton. Neither were in any rush to leave, which was just as well as the passengers returned in dribs and drabs. By quarter past three it seemed everybody was aboard, but the conductor was duty bound to check the passengers off a list he had prepared when everyone first boarded. It was only then that it was noted

Mrs Hunt was missing.

"Give her five more minutes," the driver suggested, stretching back in his seat and clearly in no hurry.

Five minutes came and went without any sign of Mrs Hunt. A ripple of uncertainty went through the air. It was Mrs Siskin who finally said what everyone was thinking;

"She had that bump on her head yesterday, what if she has felt queer and fainted beside the lake?"

The conductor gave an anxious glance to the driver, who scratched his head beneath his cap.

"I suppose we better go look for her."

Almost everyone descended from the charabanc again and offered to assist the search. It was in their best interest, if they wanted high tea, to find the elusive Mrs Hunt. The passengers were split into parties of three, with Clara and Annie joining forces with the now decidedly worried driver. Tommy had been persuaded to stay aboard the charabanc as he was already exhausted from his walk.

The various search parties fanned out around the lake and began to walk the perimeter. Everyone had their eyes open for a person lying under a tree, or stretched on the ground, and they stopped other walkers who they passed asking if they knew anything.

The driver was now very concerned.

"Why did she go walking off on her own?" he asked Clara as they paced the lake's bank.

Clara had her eyes on the rippling water, expecting any moment to see a hand or a foot just beneath the surface.

"There was no call for it," the driver persisted. "What with that bump on her head she took yesterday."

The driver was in real danger of wrenching off his cap and wringing it merciless through his hands again.

"I asked her how she felt, I truly did. She said she was fine. I can't go around telling my passengers what they can or can't do, especially if they say they are feeling fine. I couldn't stop her going off alone."

"I don't think anyone would expect you to," Clara informed him gently. "She has probably just lost track of time."

The drive gave her a sharp look.

"You really think Mrs Hunt is the sort of woman who loses track of time?"

Clara had no answer to that.

They walked along the bank for at least an hour, this time going much more briskly than on Clara's previous saunter. They passed the place they had stopped at noon fairly rapidly, but there was still no sign of Mrs Hunt.

"How far could she have walked," the driver scratched his head again. "How far did you walk?"

"We passed the spot a long while back," Clara told him.

The driver nodded.

"That's what I thought. If we don't find her, I'm going to have to go to the police!"

Annie had wandered a little ahead of them. She thought she had seen something in the water that was causing strange ripples. She walked a little faster, then suddenly stopped.

"Hurry! This way!"

The driver ran ahead, Clara hurried as best she could on her sore foot. She was already in a lot of pain from all this over exertion. She caught up with Annie and the driver in time to see the latter almost breakdown with shock. She gently nudged him away from the lake edge and peered through the rocks and reeds that masked off this small portion of the water. Just beyond them was Mrs Hunt, lying face down in the water, her arms spread-eagled, her hat floating a little distance away. Her feet were still just on land. She appeared to have fainted forward into the water.

"Help me Annie," Clara took one of Mrs Hunt's ankles and Annie grabbed the other. Together they hauled her closer to them, until she was near enough that Annie could fix her arms around the woman's waist and drag her onto the bank.

Annie gasped with the exertion. Mrs Hunt had been heavier than she looked. Clara rolled the woman onto her back and felt for a pulse. There was none and the woman looked an ominous grey colour, but Mrs Hunt had defied death twice, could she defy it a third time?

"I was trained in a little first aid," the driver had recovered his composure a fraction and came forward to help. "Maybe if we clear the water from her lungs…"

He put Mrs Hunt on her side and slapped her back firmly. There was no reaction. He laid her on her back again and compressed her chest with his hands several times, something like a pumping action, there was still no response.

"I think she may actually be dead this time," Clara told him.

There was a sound of footsteps behind them as several of the passengers arrived on the scene to see what was happening.

"Annie, don't let them get too close," Clara said quickly, then she turned to the driver. "As much as this looks like a tragic accident, considering yesterday's drama, I think it prudent to summon the police."

The driver blinked at her rapidly. He was still trying to comprehend that one of his passenger's was dead.

"I thought…"

"Mrs Hunt intimated to me that she feared for her life," Clara interrupted him before he could protest. "I think, under the circumstances, we ought to take that fear seriously. I suggest you guide everyone back to the charabanc and drive into Windermere to alert the authorities. I shall remain here to make sure the body is not disturbed any further."

"Yes, oh…" the driver took off his cap and mangled it in his hands. "What will Mr Hatton say?"

"If you manage this situation correctly he will have no cause for complaint. Now go, or the police will never get here before dark."

The driver finally got to his feet and took charge. He ushered away the other curious passengers, reminding them that high tea awaited them in Windermere. Annie remained behind with Clara. She sat down beside her friend.

"Well, this was unexpected," she observed.

"Perhaps," Clara sighed. "Or perhaps Mrs Hunt was well aware that someone wished her harm. Two attempts on her life failed, and now we have this."

"It could still be an accident," Annie pointed out.

"It could. This might all be some strange coincidence. I don't think it is, but once the police are here that is no longer my concern."

Annie gave her an amused look.

"You really believe once the police take over you will just let this case be?"

"What else can I do?"

Annie smirked.

"What you always do," she said. "Investigate."

Chapter Nine

Clara and Annie waited a long time near the lake for the police to arrive. First on the scene was the police doctor who had wandered along the bank for a while wondering where this body he had been told about was before stumbling across the pair of women. By now the evening was setting in and the midges were out in force and hovering over the edge of the water and biting any person they could reach. The coroner swiped a hand in the air, sending several to their doom and wafting the rest away from his face.

"Is this the corpse?" he asked, scowling at the deceased Mrs Hunt who lay on the ground unmolested by the midges, who were not interested in the dead.

Clara thought that a wholly stupid question and was very uninclined to answer. The coroner glanced up at her.

"Well?"

"I'm sorry, I thought that was a rhetorical question," Clara answered coolly. "And yes, this is Mrs Hunt."

The coroner gave her a surly look and dropped his medical bag on the ground. He knelt by the late Mrs Hunt and felt for a pulse. When this proved absent he removed a pair of stethoscopes from his bag and listened for a heartbeat. Then he went through a series of examinations, everything from moving her head left to right, to pounding on her chest and lifting her arms up and down. Finally he seemed satisfied that she was truly dead.

"Drowned, by the looks," he observed to no one in particular.

He lifted up Mrs Hunt's eyelids and revealed bloodshot eyes.

"There's a nasty bump on the back of her head."

"She had an accident last night," Clara interceded. "A heavy object fell on her head."

"Hmm," the coroner examined the injury for a moment more. "Yes, definitely not a fresh wound. So it looks like our victim here had an unfortunate accident. Came over dizzy on the shore of the lake and fell in, resulting in her being drowned."

"I can't understand, if that were the case, why she would not call for help or even pull herself out," Clara objected, feeling frustrated by the man. He was being of no use at all. "Unless she was unconscious, she would surely have cried out?"

"I don't do speculation, I merely state the facts. The woman drowned. That is unfortunate, but not uncommon, especially in an area full of large bodies of water. I see a lot of drownings and they all look like this," the coroner stood and brushed grass off his trousers. "Now, where is the police inspector?"

Since Clara did not know herself she also ignored this question. The coroner clearly decided that this time he would leave it as a rhetorical query. It was another half hour (Clara was keeping an eye on her watch) before the local police inspector arrived. By which time they had all been severely bitten by midges.

The police inspector ambled along the lakeside, clearly in no hurry. He was in his late thirties, tall, lean and a dedicated smoker. He was smoking as he walked, puffing away as though cigarettes might suddenly become scarce. He had a broken nose and rather bad teeth, one at the front was missing, while the others were badly stained by nicotine. He looked more like a criminal than he did a policeman. Just before he reached the crime scene, he tossed the stub of his cigarette into the lake water. The coroner was glaring at him.

"What time do you call this?" he huffed. "I've stood here half an hour being eaten to death by these damn midges!"

"I was dealing with another case," the police inspector answered blithely, untouched by the coroner's ire. "Two fellows got into a fight outside the local, one drew a knife and now we have one fella dead and the other tried to scarper. We caught him though. Now that was a true murder. Wasn't going to rush it to get here for a suspected suicide."

"Is that what you were told?" Clara interjected.

The inspector saw her for the first time, he had not been paying a great deal of attention to his surroundings in the evening light and had only noted the two women out of the corner of his eye.

"Who are you?" he asked, a slight surliness to his tone.

"Clara Fitzgerald, and this is my friend Annie Green. We found the body of Mrs Hunt who is a fellow passenger of ours on a charabanc tour of the Lake District."

"Aha," the inspector said, drawing out another cigarette from a packet in his pocket. "And you don't like the idea of suicide, then?"

"Mrs Hunt did not seem the type. This might be an accident, or…" Clara felt she was being ignored, the inspector was busy lighting his cigarette rather than listening to her. "Inspector, I think this could be a case of murder."

The inspector gave a laugh, and slapped a hand on the coroner's arm, (who responded by looking annoyed).

"A murder! Women get such fanciful thoughts into their heads!"

"Mrs Hunt was concerned for her life," Clara persisted,

though she was now very annoyed. "The night before last a tin of sweets had been left in her room, when she consumed them she became ill, in fact, almost died. That was when she first made me aware that she thought someone might wish her harm. Yesterday, a chamber pot was thrown down a stairwell at her and she received a bad bump to her head. Again she was concerned and confided as much in me. Now here we are today standing by her corpse, apparently she is the victim of yet another 'accident'."

The inspector grinned at the coroner.

"Sounds like we have one of those armchair detectives on our hands here," he jested. "Any signs of a struggle or that she was held in the water, Jock?"

"No," the coroner said crossly, not pleased at the nickname the inspector had used. He had a Scottish lineage as long as his right arm, that the inspector seemed to take great pleasure in tormenting him over whenever he had the chance. "Can I remove the body now?"

The inspector nudged Mrs Hunt with his foot. Clara was about fit to erupt at him for his disrespect and lack of professionalism.

"Yes, why not? Nothing more I can tell here," the inspector glanced at Annie and Clara. "Just got to get your statements ladies, so you found the body?"

"Specifically I did," Annie put up her hand, as if she was in school. She always tended to get a little cowed before authority. "We were concerned that Mrs Hunt had not returned to the charabanc. We walked along the bank to look for her and I thought I saw something in the water, then I came around this little spurt of rock and there was Mrs Hunt lying face down."

"You dragged her out?"

"Yes, with Clara's help. We didn't realise she was dead, you see," Annie glanced at Clara. They both knew that was somewhat of a lie. When they had come across Mrs Hunt she had looked very dead.

"Did Mrs Hunt appear ill before this afternoon?" the

inspector persisted.

"She had not mentioned anything," Clara answered. "But I had noticed a tremble in her hands, it seemed to cause her distress and was uncontrollable at times."

"That's another thing for you to investigate, Jock," the inspector called out to the coroner, who was being helped by the two constables who had arrived with the inspector to bag up and remove Mrs Hunt's corpse.

The coroner scowled at him, but said nothing. The inspector turned back to Clara.

"So we have a sick woman strolling by herself near the water's edge, she perhaps takes queer and falls in, or she decides she has had enough of this life and her ailments and tosses herself in the lake. Seems straightforward to me."

"And if there had not been any prior incidents I would have agreed," Clara told him. "But there was the poisoned sweets and the chamber pot."

"Did you keep the sweets?"

"No. Mrs Hunt threw the last out of the window and I could not find it," Clara admitted. "But she was very unwell that night."

"But you told me already that she was a sick woman," the inspector pointed out, enjoying refuting her idea. "It could have had nothing to do with the sweets."

Clara pursed her lips. The words she wanted to say were not polite, nor would they help the situation.

"And what about this flying chamber pot? Another accident if ever I heard of one. I mean, who would use a chamber pot to kill someone?" the inspector laughed. It was rather a sneering sound that seemed to stem from his nose. "That would be a new one on me, death by chamber pot!"

"Sneer, inspector, but Mrs Hunt was concerned for her life."

"Women, especially old women, are prone to hysterics," the inspector shrugged. "Who is to say these 'murder attempts' were not all fits of fancy on the part of this woman?"

"Mrs Hunt was the last person to have a fit of fancy," Clara said stolidly, though she knew she was not winning, nor could she win against this obnoxious fellow. "Please do not dismiss her concerns so lightly."

"Don't try and tell me how to do my job," the inspector's laugh turned to a snarl. "I've been at this game five years and made plenty of arrests, young lady, which is more than can be said for you."

Clara narrowed her eyes at him, dreadfully tempted to reveal just precisely what she did in her ordinary life, but she decided it was not worth the effort. The man was a buffoon and he would not listen to her.

"If you ladies are quite done with your fantastic theories, I'll be getting on with some real police business," the inspector tucked his notebook in his pocket, happy that his work was done.

"Mrs Hunt had enemies," Clara tried one last tactic. "She made enemies like some people make friends. She was, if I may say so bluntly, an utterly cruel and heartless creature who took pleasure in the misery of others."

"Doesn't sound like anyone will much be crying over her then," the inspector shrugged, still not interested.

"Inspector, are you really going to ignore all those facts and leave this woman's killer to go free?"

"We don't know she was murdered," the inspector pointed out quite logically. "So far all I see is a sad accident."

Clara wanted to call him a fool, but thought it prudent not to. She merely nodded.

"So be it inspector, but if I happen to come across information that might change your mind how can I contact you?"

The inspector was amused by this suggestion.

"Hop into the nearest police station and ask for Inspector Gateley. They'll probably be able to tell you where I happen to be at the time. But, and I say this for your own best interest, don't start prodding around and making more of this matter than needs be," Inspector Gateley threw aside his cigarette, narrowly missing the coroner's shoe. "There is a reason we don't have female police inspectors. Women are too emotional and too fanciful. They see foul play at every turn. I don't need you playing detective and upsetting people. Get on with your holiday and leave this to us. After all, you didn't know Mrs Hunt very well, did you?"

"We met on this trip," Clara admitted.

"So then you have no reason to worry about the fate of someone who was a virtual stranger to you," Inspector Gateley was satisfied with himself. "There will be an inquest, I imagine, best you ladies don't go disappearing before then. Hopefully it will be all arranged and dealt with before your little holiday is over."

Without another word the inspector walked off behind the coroner. Clara heard him mutter to 'Jock' in the darkness.

"Get the inquest over and done pronto, so I can get rid of those two amateur sleuths."

She silently seethed with outrage. It was one thing to not be taken seriously, but to be so insulted as well! But there was nothing she could do. She was out of her own territory where she knew the police inspector and was a respected detective. Here she was nobody.

Annie slipped her arm through Clara's.

"Let's get back to the meeting spot. The driver said he would drop everyone off at the hotel and come back for us. And don't let that awful inspector upset you."

Clara sighed as she allowed Annie to lead her away from the crime scene.

"I suppose I shouldn't care," Clara said as they walked. "I detested the woman after all. But she had asked for my help and you can't just ignore a person being murdered."

Clara stumbled a little. Her foot felt like a swollen, hot ball on the end of her leg. She was in a lot of pain and only her fury with the inspector was keeping it from overwhelming her. She focused on being angry with him rather than her foot.

"Now you have met this Inspector Gateley, what do you intend to do?" Annie asked, slowing her pace subtly to help Clara.

"I'll have to make my own enquiries," Clara groaned a little, but even she was not clear on whether that was because of the thought of playing detective on her holiday, or because her foot hurt so much. "I can't just let a murderer slip away. Despite what the inspector said, I do think that someone was trying to harm Mrs Hunt. The tin of poisoned sweets was a sophisticated plan, the last two attempts were far more opportunistic."

"But, as far as we know, Mrs Hunt knew no one aboard the charabanc?"

"I start to wonder if that was true," Clara said. "I have a feeling Mrs Hunt was deceitful as well as unpleasant."

They found the charabanc awaiting them at the meeting spot. The driver rushed from his cab to help Clara aboard.

"I fetched the police as fast as I could!" he told her as she grimaced in pain. "I saw them taking the body away."

"They think it was an accident," Clara answered as she was helped onto a seat.

"I'll have to report all this to Mr Hatton," the driver said anxiously. "It's never happened to me before."

He went to his own seat and started to drive off. The charabanc had been left ticking over while he aided Clara aboard.

"Have you back at the hotel shortly!" he promised her.

Clara closed her eyes and cringed. Her foot was a mass of agony and she was very concerned she had made her old injury a good deal worse. Annie pressed a comforting hand on her shoulder, but said nothing. There was nothing to say, after all. Clara tried to blot out the pain as they trundled sedately back to the hotel.

Chapter Ten

Annie helped Clara hobble to her room and set her down in a chair.

"I'm going to find that doctor who saw Mrs Hunt," Annie informed her, disappearing before Clara could argue.

Clara scowled at her foot, as if that would make things better. It throbbed horribly and even acting carefully it was agony to remove her shoe. She was just giving a groan when someone knocked on her door. Annie had left the door slightly open and Clara shot her head up quickly, thinking she would see the doctor. In actual fact it was Mrs Siskin standing on the threshold of her room.

"May I come in?" Mrs Siskin asked politely.

"Yes, if you don't mind my puttering as I try to remove this shoe."

"Can I be of any assistance?" Mrs Siskin came across the room and started to bend down to help Clara.

The last thing Clara wanted was someone else yanking at her foot.

"No, I am just fine. See? The shoe is just about off…" Clara pulled at the heel one last time and the walking boot fell to the floor, revealing her swollen foot.

Clara wanted to say something very rude about the

pain that followed, but bit her tongue in the presence of Mrs Siskin. The woman seemed not to notice her distress and perched herself on Clara's bed without asking. She sat there a moment, toying with her hands.

"Are you all right Mrs Siskin?" Clara asked after a moment.

"Me? Oh yes, dear," Mrs Siskin's anxiety seemed to belie this answer. "I've just been thinking all evening about Mrs Hunt. Lizzy keeps talking about it."

"Has it upset Mrs Palmer?"

"No," Mrs Siskin looked away, trying to decipher the faint pattern in the carpet on the floor rather than speak. "Lizzy seems quite pleased about it, to be honest."

Mrs Siskin sighed.

"It is a peculiar world."

"It is."

"Lizzy took a very strong dislike to Mrs Hunt. Well, you saw what happened. Lizzy is of a delicate mind frame and you can't just go around saying mean-spirited things to people like that," Mrs Siskin shook her head. "I can't say I liked Mrs Hunt either, but I didn't I wish her harm. I suppose I thought the odd unpleasant thing about her. Maybe that is why I feel so guilty."

"Guilty?" Clara said, quite surprised. "What do you have to feel guilty about?"

"I suppose…" Mrs Siskin pressed her lips together. She was a big-hearted woman by nature, who had a tendency to attract the waifs and strays of this world to her. It was how she had come to befriend the lonely and rather batty Mrs Palmer all those years ago. Mrs Siskin liked to help people and there was a part of her that felt she should have helped Mrs Hunt. Only she hadn't because her friend had taken such a strong distaste to the woman. "I saw her walking along the lake. She passed by me and Lizzy. She was on her own and looked very pale. I wanted to ask her to join us, but I felt I couldn't. I still wonder, if I had of done, whether she would have not fainted and fallen into the lake."

"Is that what the driver said? She fainted?"

"He muttered something about it," Mrs Siskin nodded. "He was rather upset. Have you noticed how he wrings his cap dreadfully in his hands when he is anxious? He will need a new cap soon. Well, he came back to the charabanc and said we could all stop looking for Mrs Hunt as she had been found. I believe it was Mr Wignell who asked if she was all right. The driver shook his head and declared, rather quietly, that she had had an accident in the lake. We rather quickly came to the conclusion that she must have felt unwell after her accident yesterday and fallen in."

"That seems very possible," Clara said carefully. "It is certainly the line the police inspector is pursuing."

"How sad. You see, after we realised what must have occurred that was when I began thinking. If only I had asked her to walk with us, then she would not have been alone when she took ill. Perhaps we could have saved her," Mrs Siskin's shoulders slumped at the imagined burden she placed upon them. "Not that Lizzy would have liked that. I can't tell her any of this, she would have a fit. She had this awful smile on her face when we heard. I think she feels the woman received her just deserts!"

"If it is any consolation, I really doubt Mrs Hunt would have walked with you," Clara said gently, hoping to comfort the woman and ease her guilt. "She was a person who liked to be alone."

"Yes, I had noticed that too," Mrs Siskin sighed. "I thought that rather sad. But some people prefer to be alone."

"You should not feel guilty about anything," Clara added firmly. "You caused her no harm, after all."

"No, that is true," Mrs Siskin was looking more relieved by the moment.

There was a tap on the open door and Dr John Masters looked into the room.

"Oh, I best let you be," Mrs Siskin hopped from the bed. "I hope your foot feels better, I don't suppose all that wandering about today did it any good."

"Thank you Mrs Siskin," Clara said as the woman vanished out the door.

Dr John Masters wandered in. He dropped his medical bag on the bed and glanced at Clara's foot.

"What have you been doing?" he asked.

"Discovering dead bodies," Clara said drily, only a moment later realising how awful that sounded.

The doctor didn't seem to notice.

"The news is all about the hotel. No one can keep a secret here for long. Mrs Hunt drowned, or so they say," Dr Masters knelt before Clara. "I'll need that stocking off."

Clara thought he might turn his head as she wrestled to find the top of her stocking under her skirt, but Dr Masters did not. He kept his eyes averted onto her foot, but that was the best she was going to get. Clara felt uncomfortable as she reached under her dress skirt and found the end of her stocking. She rolled it down, adjusting her skirt hem as she went, until the stocking was a rumpled bundle around her ankle. Dr Masters, without a word, removed it from her foot.

"The foot is very swollen," Dr Masters pressed his fingers into the hot flesh of Clara's foot and made her cringe. "I shan't be able to tell for sure whether you have done lasting damage until the swelling goes down. I shall see if the hotel is able to provide some ice in a large bowl that you could rest your foot in. Failing that, I shall have you sent some very cold water."

Dr Masters stood and opened his medical bag.

"Would you like anything else? A sedative, perhaps?"

"The pain is not all that bad," Clara declined. "Unless I move my foot."

"I didn't mean for the foot," Dr Masters cast her a look out of the corner of his eye. He was almost smirking. "I meant for the shock of finding a dead woman."

"Oh, I have seen more than one corpse in my time," Clara said blithely, the pain in her foot was really damaging her normal inhibitions.

"You see dead people a lot, do you?" the doctor asked curiously.

"I was a nurse, during the war," Clara said quickly. "You rather get used to bodies doing something like that."

"Then you should also know better than to walk about on a crushed foot," Dr Masters said more sternly. "I doubt you have seriously damaged it, but you will have certainly impeded the healing."

Clara didn't like being berated, especially as she had had no choice but to walk about. Mrs Hunt wasn't going to find herself.

"I am sure I will live," Clara said stoutly and to deflect further admonishments she added. "How is your patient? The one you were called here to see?"

"Nearly ninety and convinced she is dying," Dr Masters said bluntly, though not without a twinkle in his eye. "She takes a shine to the idea of a holiday, but then she gets here and everything is different and she is not in her usual room or following her usual routine and she becomes unsettled. I tell her to stop the holidays, but she is convinced they are good for health. The irony of it all! She will be right as rain in a couple of days and off collecting postcards for one of her many albums. Then she will be home, telling me all about how marvellous the Lake District is for one's lungs."

Dr Masters gave a shrug.

"Ah, so that explains why she has a room on the ground floor," Clara added.

"Oh no, she is in a suite on the fourth floor. There is a lift…" Dr Masters paused, the realisation that he had just given himself away crept over him, visibly causing the colour to rise in his face.

Clara had seen him coming out of a room on the ground floor the other day. She would have imagined he was visiting his patient in that very room, had he not just revealed otherwise.

"I imagine your patient is one of these people who get rather set in their ways," Clara said thoughtfully, pretending she had not noticed his change in demeanour. "The sort who prefer sheets to quilts, who prefer their food English and overcooked, the sort who dislikes indoor plumbing, fearing it unhygienic."

"You describe my patient well," Dr Masters said quickly, aiming to get out of the room as fast as possible. "I'll see that something is arranged for your foot. Good evening Miss Fitzgerald."

"Good evening," Clara answered, watching him hurry away and wondering what secrets he was trying to hide. Who, after all, was in that room just down the hall?

"Has the doctor been?" Annie was in the doorway now.

"Been and gone. He is arranging some iced water to be sent to me in a bowl that I must rest my foot in."

"That sounds disagreeable," Annie wrinkled her nose. "I hate cold feet. Worse than cold hands in my opinion. I was thinking, I have to arrange for your dinner to be brought to you here, so why not Tommy and I both join you?"

"That is a delightful idea," Clara agreed. "And, under normal circumstances, I would immediately agree. But tonight I want you and Tommy to do something else for me."

Annie gave a small sigh.

"Why do I get the feeling this is going to involve investigating something?"

"You said it yourself Annie, what can I do but investigate? That police inspector has a bee in his bonnet which will blind him to everything else around him. You saw how he spoke to me, he is already convinced that Mrs Hunt fainted and drowned by accident. Perhaps that is the case, but he will not even investigate the possibility of something or someone else being responsible."

"Could Mrs Hunt have really been killed?"

"I don't want to rule out the possibility just yet, not after the two previous attempts on her life," Clara shook her head. There were too many odd ends left over if you just accepted the idea that Mrs Hunt had fainted and drowned. None of the other pieces fitted, unless you began to ask yourself if it was perhaps just possible that she was murdered. "In any case, I would like you and Tommy to go to dinner as normal and listen to what everyone is saying."

"Spy on them?" Annie said.

"It is not spying if they can see you sitting there and listening," Clara assured her, though she thought that excuse would not cut mustard within international politics, but sitting up a dinner table with fellow charabanc passengers was another story. "I just want you to find out their thoughts and feelings on the matter. If someone is a killer, then the odds are we are looking at the charabanc passengers as suspects."

"Well then," Annie said, a little deflated. "I guess that means I will have to get dressed for dinner yet again."

"Sorry, old girl," Clara apologised. "I would much rather you had dinner in here with me, but we have to take this case seriously, since nobody else is inclined to."

Annie nodded.

"Do you think anyone is sorry that Mrs Hunt is dead? I mean, everyone seems quite jolly about it," Annie shook her head and tutted. "It seems rather callous."

"Mrs Hunt was disliked, that's for sure, but in truth most people are not affected by deaths that do not directly relate to them. For most of these people in the hotel Mrs Hunt's death is just another piece of interesting gossip."

"Well that's very sad," Annie said sternly. "The poor woman might have been hard and unpleasant, but I can't think she deserved to die so alone and so suddenly."

Annie had just finished speaking when a hotel porter arrived at the room door with a big, white enamel bowl in his hands. It proved to be, as he lowered it next to Clara, a bowl of iced water. Ice cubes floated on the top like miniature icebergs. Having asked if he could offer them anything else, and being told they were fine, the porter retreated, closing the door behind him.

Clara stared at the iced water.

"I hope that doctor knows what he is talking about," she raised her right foot and plunged it toe-first into the bowl. The water was freezing and made her wince as a new type of pain soared through her foot. She managed to drop her entire foot in before she puffed out her cheeks and swore in pain.

"Bloomin' foot!"

"I'll be off to dinner," Annie smiled at her. "Behave yourself. I'll drop by later if it is not too late in the evening."

Annie left the room. Clara rested back in her chair and tried to forget the new icy fire burning in her foot. At least she could not feel the original pain anymore. Didn't people get frostbite in such cold conditions? She hoped she would not suddenly discovered her foot going black and threatening to drop off. That would be most embarrassing.

Amused by this assessment of the situation, Clara pretended she could not feel her foot at all, which wasn't so hard as it was rapidly going numb. She let out a deep breath. At least while she was alone she had plenty of time to mull over what had occurred to poor Mrs Hunt. Perhaps, for once, she might be lucky and be able to conjure the solution to the mystery without hardly trying. Somehow she rather thought not.

Chapter Eleven

Clara had fallen soundly asleep in her chair when there was a knock on the door. She opened her eyes groggily and automatically went to stand, remembering too late that she had her foot in a bowl of icy water. She stood, slipped, stumbled, kicked the bowl across the room in the process, spilling water everywhere and fell onto the rug before the bed.

"Oh rats!" Clara scowled to herself, more annoyed than hurt.

The door burst open (it was unlocked since Clara had not had the energy to get up and lock it after Annie left) and Dr Masters darted in. He looked at Clara, the wet floor and the bowl lying upside down halfway across the room and relaxed a little.

"You are rather accident prone," he said.

Clara gave him a look that implied he was walking on treacherous ground.

"Other people are accident prone. I suffer from minor mishaps caused by the inanimate objects of this world conspiring against me," she told him firmly.

"You fell over the bowl of water?" Dr Masters interpreted.

"Yes! I fell over the bowl of water," Clara said

grumpily. She was now sitting in an upright position. "Might I add, whose idea was it to place my foot in a bowl of icy water?"

Dr Masters actually smiled at her, which was quite novel.

"I take full responsibility," he said, offering her his hand and helping her back into the armchair. "How does the foot feel?"

"I can't honestly say as it is utterly numb," Clara answered. "Which explains why I fell."

"Were you asleep?"

"Only a little."

Dr Masters nodded.

"Next time I will aim not to disturb you so late," he knelt down before Clara and lifted her foot in his hand.

"Is it late?" Clara asked, her idea of time completely out the window with falling asleep. She could at least see that it was dark outside.

"It is nearly eleven," Dr Masters said, prodding her foot quite hard to feel the bone. "The swelling has gone down considerably. I assume none of this hurts?"

"I don't feel a thing," Clara shrugged. "I didn't realise time had got on so. They brought my dinner at seven and I ate that before setting the dishes on the sideboard…"

"You took your foot out of the bowl?" Dr Masters accused her, one eyebrow raised in a stern look.

"Merely to place the plates and cutlery in a safe place, else there would be more chaos around us about now," Clara pursed her lips, uncertain what to make of the doctor. "I sat back down at once. Then, I suppose, I fell asleep."

"You were probably exhausted from finding bodies," Dr Masters said, displaying an art for black humour. "You are quite the talk of the dining room. I hear tell you are a private detective."

Clara glanced at him, wondering if the statement was accusatory. After all, she had hidden, or rather omitted, the fact she was a detective during their last conversation.

She found Dr Masters impossible to read at that moment. He simply seemed curious.

"I am a private detective," Clara said carefully. "Though currently I am on holiday."

"So you are not investigating Mrs Hunt's death?" Masters asked bluntly.

Clara hesitated again, she wasn't sure how much she wanted Masters to know about her, but she really couldn't hide the fact that she was involved with Mrs Hunt's case. She also wasn't convinced she trusted Dr Masters completely. He had a secret too and it had not eluded her that he came rushing down the stairs shortly after Mrs Hunt was clunked on the head by a falling chamber pot. Potentially Dr Masters had been on the same floor as Mrs Hunt's attacker.

"I am not officially doing anything," Clara said, hedging around the truth. "Mrs Hunt's death is being investigated by the police."

"That is not what everyone else is saying," Dr Masters put down Clara's foot at last and perched himself on her bed. For once he seemed in no hurry to leave. "Mrs Palmer, in particular, seems to be convinced you are investigating this matter as a case of murder. I might add she also thinks that a waste of your time, since she seems to believe Mrs Hunt's demise a case of divine retribution, albeit at the hands of a very mortal soul."

"Mrs Palmer really said that?"

"In a lot more words, of course. She was quite blunt over the affair at dinner. I happened to be late going in and the only seat spare was at the long table where your charabanc party usually dines. It seems I took your place," this apparently amused Dr Masters. "Mrs Palmer had a lot to say on the matter of Mrs Hunt's passing."

"And she thinks it is not an accident?"

"From what she was saying it seems she is quite certain it was not. She had everyone listening as she deported her theories. According to her wisdom Mrs Hunt was pushed into the lake by an attacker, a person from the charabanc perhaps, who she had deeply offended."

Clara pulled a face. Mrs Palmer's lack of tact was appalling and rather distasteful. Mrs Siskin had mentioned how her friend seemed rather pleased by Mrs Hunt's misfortune, almost as if she had plotted it herself. And yet Mrs Palmer was with Mrs Siskin during the entire visit to Windermere, so it couldn't be possible for her to have committed murder. Unless Mrs Siskin was lying?

"Do you think Mrs Hunt was murdered?" Dr Masters' broke Clara's reverie.

"I can't say I know what to think," Clara admitted. "The circumstances suggest an accident. Mrs Hunt was walking alone by the water. She had suffered a head injury the day before which could have rendered her dizzy, you would agree with that?"

"The bump on her head was nasty and it would surprise me if she did not have a concussion from it," the doctor agreed.

"In a condition like that, could it not also be possible that she felt unwell, perhaps fainted, and fell forward into the lake?"

"Severe concussions can lead to blackouts," Dr Masters said cautiously. "But I am not certain Mrs Hunt's was that severe. I suppose she might have fainted and not roused in time to save herself."

"Yet it is still strange," Clara read between the lines. "Dr Masters, what was your opinion on Mrs Hunt's general health?"

"I only examined her briefly and was mostly concerned with her head wound," the doctor hastened to say. "I did listen to her heart and lungs which sounded perfectly healthy for her age. There were no obvious signs of major illness, though she was deeply reluctant to be examined. The wound on her head was wide and shallow. It was a bump rather than a cut, the chamber pot having seemingly hit her on its rounded edge. It was sore, understandably, but not bleeding. I advised her to put a cold compress on it and to take some aspirin, which she promptly refused."

"I had noticed a tremor in her hands that at times appeared quite severe," Clara said. "At one point she seemed to be unable to hold her fork, but masked the attack very well. Which made me imagine this was not a new occurrence."

"I was not asked to examine her hands," Dr Masters reminded her. "I saw no signs of tremors."

"I saw them," Clara said firmly. "She clutched her hands in her lap to hide them, but I know she was suffering from some illness. What can cause uncontrollable shaking of the hands?"

"Many things," Dr Masters became vague again. "Such a simple thing as bad nerves can be the cause."

"I very much doubt Mrs Hunt had bad nerves!" Clara almost laughed at the idea. "Perhaps the police coroner will offer a solution, but I don't hold out a great deal of hope. I thought you might offer some insight."

"I can only go by the symptoms as presented to me and Mrs Hunt did not complain of shaking hands when I saw her," Dr Masters answered, a little hotly, as if he imagined Clara to be accusing him of failing to diagnose Mrs Hunt's condition correctly.

"I don't mean to impinge on your medical reputation," Clara said gently, noticing how easily the doctor became riled. "I was merely musing. As it seems Mrs Hunt met her fate by accident, I was just curious as to what sort of illness might have contributed to her collapse."

Dr Masters seemed a tad mollified. He sat on the bed and drummed his fingers on the bed clothes.

"Am I the only one who finds it odd to imagine a perfect stranger killing Mrs Hunt because she offended them? Particularly one of the perfect strangers I just sat having dinner with?" he said after a moment.

"I find it poor motive too," Clara admitted. "Though people kill for all manner of odd reasons and we can't rule out manslaughter. But we are left with the difficulty that no one saw or heard anything and Mrs Hunt was not so far from the rest of the party to make that seem plausible. Perhaps I must accept the police are right and that she just fell."

"So you are investigating?"

Clara saw she had been caught out. She shrugged her shoulders.

"I didn't care for Mrs Hunt. It rather seems no one cared for her. But I don't care for murderers either, and I can't let the police simply brush aside the possibility that Mrs Hunt met her end by foul means. Two attempts had already been made on her life."

"Two?" Dr Masters asked, but Clara chose to ignore the question.

"I am supposed to be on holiday," she grumbled to herself. "Then again, so was Mrs Hunt, allegedly. Had you ever met her before the evening she was injured?"

"No," Dr Masters clicked the clasps on his medical bag. "I ought to be going. Did you care for any painkillers or a sedative?"

"No, thank you," Clara answered. "And ignore Mrs Palmer, I think she is as ignorant as she is loud-mouthed. She took a dislike to Mrs Hunt and that is that."

"She explained as much to me," Dr Masters nodded. "Said the woman got everything she deserved. Tell me, how did she upset Mrs Palmer so badly in such a short space of time?"

"Mrs Palmer is pining for her grandson lost in the war. Because they were never sent a telegram to say he was dead, she is convinced he is still alive somewhere. Mrs Hunt was rather blunt on the subject."

"That sounds about right. I have many older patients and more than one has an attitude to life like Mrs Hunt. They seem to think belligerence is the secret to survival," Dr Masters shook his head sadly. "They live to spread misery, that is the best way I can describe it."

He stood from the bed.

"The foot seems to be on the mend. Take it easy for a few more days before going on these epic walks of yours."

"I hardly think a stroll around Windermere 'epic'," Clara puttered, though she was not about to ignore the advice.

"Well don't go calling me again if you ignore my prescription and then hurt yourself further. The hotel staff know how to get hold of me. I have a room here until my other patient agrees that I can leave."

"What of your patients back at your surgery?" Clara asked, thinking it odd that a doctor would spend so much of his time with a single person, and to be so indulgent to their whims.

"Other patients?" Dr Masters smirked. "I don't have other patients, only my elderly lady who I run to at her every beck and call. So, you see, it is most prudent of me to keep her very much alive so I can continue to be employed."

Clara sensed this was a joke, though it had been told in Dr Masters' serious voice and was difficult to judge. Clara dreaded to imagine how he broke bad news to his patients.

"I shall be going," Dr Masters said again, wandering to the door.

"I've told no one about what I saw," Clara said softly as he was leaving.

Dr Masters hesitated with his hand just on the door handle.

"What did you see?" he asked.

"Nothing, which is why I have not told anybody about it," Clara said cryptically.

Dr Masters relaxed a little at this explanation. He let himself out of the room without a backwards glance.

What a strange man, Clara mused to herself. He seemed friendlier than at first, but there was still something about him that made her feel uncertain, as if a part of her feared he was untrustworthy. What an odd thing to imagine in a doctor, but she could not shake the feeling. But, if there was a connection between him and Mrs Hunt, Clara could not see it. Mrs Hunt had not apparently recognised him when he came to treat her head, after all. And what of this mysterious room along her corridor that the doctor was visiting? If he had a room in the hotel, which Clara was not sure about, then it would logically be near that of his patient's. But she was on the fourth floor, so what was he doing acting suspiciously on the ground floor and why was he so secretive about it? That was a mystery Clara would like solved.

For the moment, however, she only wanted her bed and the opportunity to sleep for several hours. She limped about the room preparing herself; picking up the knocked bowl, locking the room door and slipping into her night things. It was with a guilty pang that she realised that Mrs Hunt could not now do the same – guilty because she was coming close to giving up on the whole idea of investigating Mrs Hunt's death. She was, after all, on holiday and didn't want to spend the remainder of her fortnight break hunting a murderer. Yet, it looked likely that such a task had fallen on her shoulders. Mrs Palmer was right, Mrs Hunt had been killed, Clara was growing more sure of that by the hour. She kept coming back to one idea – if Mrs Hunt had simply fainted and fallen into Windermere, why had she not woken swiftly enough to save herself? When people faint they are usually only unconscious for a moment or two, not enough time to drown in. Yet that is what Mrs Hunt had done, according to the police.

Clara climbed into bed, this thought on her mind – Mrs Hunt's accident was beginning to look less and less accidental. But where did that leave Clara? Apparently with an awful lot of questions to answer and a charabanc full of suspects. Why was it that even Clara's holidays proved so complicated?

Chapter Twelve

Clara slept soundly that night. Her dreams were not disturbed by visions of floating corpses in lakes. A thought that actually made her feel a tad guilty when she awoke. The trouble was, however hard she tried, it was difficult to feel a great deal of anything for Mrs Hunt. The woman had been so disagreeable in life that feeling sorrow for her passing did not come naturally. That being said, Clara was curious about what had happened to the woman.

Clara rose, washed and dressed. Her foot seemed reasonably restored, if a little tender. She flexed her toes tentatively and cringed at a sharp pain that radiated out from her big toe.

Picking up the brochure provided by Mr Hatton she took a glance at what the arrangements were for the day and saw that a visit was planned to Derwentwater. She had liked the sound of that particular place, especially when she heard it was the home of the exquisite artists' pencils that had been lent their name by the location. She rather liked the idea of seeing how lead was turned into a pencil of various hardness and softness to suit artists. But her foot was not up for walking, so she placed aside the brochure and decided she would have to ask Annie and

Tommy to take notes on her behalf. Maybe they could even buy her a new set of pencils so she could take up sketching again.

Clara was still contemplating her bare foot when there was a knock on the door. She wandered over and unlocked it. Outside were Annie and Tommy.

"We have an hour before the charabanc leaves," Annie informed Clara. "Are you fit to come to breakfast?"

Clara glanced at her wristwatch and was surprised to see it was already nine o-clock. She must have slept a lot longer than she had first imagined.

"Yes. Of course!" Clara quickly squeezed on her softest shoes – the walking boots were out of the question that morning – and followed the others to the dining room.

At least by having a late breakfast they found the dining room quite quiet and they could talk discreetly without being overheard. There was no one from the charabanc party present, the only other guests in the room were an elderly couple quietly working through their bowls of porridge and a young woman Clara had not seen before. She sat all alone nibbling at a small slice of toast without any apparent sign of enjoyment or even of appetite. She was a scrawny thing, with an almost skeletal face, and arms that looked little more than bone covered with skin. She made Clara feel quite fat in comparison, (not that Clara was, she was a girl with curves, that was all) and she rather wished she could persuade the poor mite to dig into a large plate of scrambled egg, sausage and black pudding. She rather felt it would do her some good.

Annie refused to let Clara go to the breakfast table and help herself. Rest was the order of the day and under Annie's strict watch that was precisely what was going to happen. She fetched Clara a plate of food, consisting of a little bit of everything on offer – bacon, lightly fried, scrambled egg, fried kidney, pork sausage, kedgeree, toast and black pudding. Clara took a look at her plate, then glanced at the emaciated girl across the room who had given up on her toast, and felt quite greedy.

"I'll never eat all this Annie!" Clara said.

"You must try," Annie retorted. "You need your strength."

"I don't need this much strength," Clara puttered, but she dug into the bacon anyway. She knew she wasn't going to win against Annie's determination to 'feed her up'. "So, what occurred at dinner last night?"

Tommy rolled his eyes. His plate was equally well loaded with fat and protein, but he was judiciously sharing it with Bramble who sat obediently at his side.

"Mrs Palmer occurred," he said. "That woman positively seemed to revel in Mrs Hunt's demise. It was embarrassing."

"It was disrespectful," Annie butted in sharply. "I thought the woman uncouth and callous. Why, it almost sounded as if she had plotted the thing herself. Though, of course, we all knew she had not. Quite frankly I found her most disagreeable."

"Annie had the misfortune to sit next to Mrs Palmer. We took seats halfway down the table so as to be able to see and hear most of what was going on around us. Annie was on my right, and further along the table sat Mrs Palmer and then Mrs Siskin. Opposite us sat the Wignells. Diagonally to our right sat that Dr Masters, who had joined our table because he was late to dinner and there were no other seats available," Tommy explained all this while loading his fork with sausage and scrambled egg. "Diagonally to my left sat Eleanora Smythe, while next to me sat a pair of ladies I had not met before. The older one was a Miss Plante, I suppose she is in her eighties. Very well turned out, definitely has money. Next to her sat Miss Soloman, a woman in her sixties, I would say. She is Miss Plante's companion."

"Aside from Mrs Palmer, did anyone talk about Mrs Hunt?" Clara asked.

"Mr Wignell spoke about her. He seemed agitated on the matter. Seemed to have quite spoilt his day," Tommy said.

"You would almost imagine he had found the body," Annie tutted. "He seemed quite fallen to pieces over it. Kept reciting some awful fact about how many suicides had occurred at Windermere in the last fifty years. His wife had that look on her face, the one which seems to imply she would rather not be associated with the man. She didn't stop him however."

"Between him and Mrs Palmer it was quite the diabolical discussion!" Tommy laughed. "Mrs Siskin was desperately trying to shush her friend, kept nudging her under the table, but there was no holding her back. That Dr Masters had such a grimace on his face. I think he wanted to tell her to shut up, in fact it was Miss Plante that finally came to our assistance. She was clearly tired of Mrs Palmer's ramblings."

Annie interjected.

"Miss Plante struck me as one of those old ladies who has decided they are now too elderly to bother holding their tongues. She cut through the conversation like my best carving knife!" Annie's eyes twinkled as she recalled the moment. "She turned to her right and leaned forward, so as to see Mrs Palmer better and remarked in a very calm voice that 'people who revel in others' misfortunes are surely very wicked.' Mrs Palmer stopped with her mouth agape and stared at the woman. Miss Plante then said 'if you cannot do anything but find joy in the death of another, then I despair for the health of your immortal soul. For there is an evilness in this gossip, the like of which I have not seen in many a year.' With that Miss Plante sat back in her chair and returned to her dinner."

"What was Mrs Palmer's response?" Clara asked, rather wishing she had been present at this exchange.

"For a while she said nothing," Annie said. "Then she turned her head to look down the table and declared, 'there is nothing wrong with my immortal soul.' And Miss Plante merely answered that she was very glad to hear that."

"That rather brought the conversation to an end," Tommy nodded, tossing the rind off his bacon to Bramble. The little dog danced on its back feet to get it. "Everything went a bit quiet then, until Eleanora Smythe looked up. She asked, in that quiet way of hers, whether anyone else had received a gift from the management? Naturally we all said we had not. For a moment she said nothing more, then she looked up again and I swear directly at myself and Annie, and spoke 'there was tin of marzipan fruits in my room when I arrived. With a little card saying they were a gift for my stay. I thought it rather odd.'"

"Marzipan fruits!" Clara hissed in surprise. "Tell me the woman does not intend to eat them."

"She informed us she had not touched the sweets because she disliked marzipan," Tommy reassured her. "But she was curious about them and wondered if it was commonplace for hotels to leave little gifts for their guests, this being her first charabanc tour and all."

"What did you tell her?"

"I said nothing, Annie was swifter off the mark than myself," Tommy nudged Annie to tell her part of the story.

Annie, who had just started in on her fried kidneys, gave a small sigh and put down her knife and fork.

"It occurred to me that firstly we could not allow another person to fall victim to a poisoner, and secondly that the tin of sweets might have accidentally been delivered to the wrong person," Annie began. "Since I could not see a connection between Mrs Hunt and Miss Smythe, nor why anyone would want them both dead, it struck me as a possibility that someone had thought to make a second attempt to poison Mrs Hunt, only, with Mrs Hunt moving rooms, the tin had been sent to the wrong one.

"I thought of it this way. Mrs Hunt had made no indication of being poisoned, other than her veiled comments in the charabanc. Now, supposing the poisoner thought that their first batch of sweets had failed? Perhaps they did not pick up the significance of Mrs Hunt's comments? So they decided to try again, with a second batch of marzipan, a delicacy they knew Mrs Hunt favoured."

"A good theory," Clara concurred, motioning with her knife her approval. "So what did you say to Miss Smythe?"

"I raised the possibility that the gift was accidental and not intended for her. Seeing as none of the rest of the party had received a tin and she knew no one on the charabanc before our departure, nor anyone at the hotel, this seemed a logical assessment. I proposed that the sweets were destined for someone else, someone who cared for them. After all, most people are clever enough to know that marzipan is the sort of thing people either like or dislike. You don't offer it as a gift without knowing your recipient has a taste for it. Miss Smythe thought that a very reasonable consideration," Annie smiled, rather pleased with herself. "I then suggested that it would be advisable for the tin to be returned to the hotel management, who might then give it to the correct recipient. Presuming that it was one of the hotel staff who placed the gift in Miss Smythe's room. This proposal she took very well and agreed to. Of course, I was thinking that at some point you would have a quiet word with the management about those same sweets."

"A thought I completely agree with," Clara smiled, amused at how well Annie had taken to the detective business. Since Clara had hurt her foot Annie had been serving as her agent and doing a fine job of it, not that she would ever consider a career in investigation. She was much happier in her kitchen making her inimitable cakes and pies. "I don't know about you, but I rather feel our killer grew a little desperate after their first attempt failed."

"The chamber pot was an impulsive act," Tommy agreed without hesitation. "In fact, it was rather clumsy.

They could easily have hit the driver instead, and there was no certainty the blow would kill Mrs Hunt."

"They made their last move at the lake," Clara gave up on her breakfast and laid down her knife and fork. "Still, the 'how' and the 'why' elude me. I shall have a chat with the management first thing and see how accommodating they will be of my curiosity."

"You are not coming to Derwentwater then?" Tommy asked in surprise.

"The old foot needs a good rest," Clara answered apologetically. "For once I plan on being sensible. A novelty, isn't it?"

"Jolly good!" Annie said with stern approval. She could be rather like a head teacher or hospital matron watching over her ninny-headed charges. Occasionally Clara desperately wanted to stick her tongue out at her, but that would be rather childish.

"I insist you tell me all about the place when you return, however," Clara reclaimed the conversation. "And you must buy me some pencils and a sketching book. I shall supply you with some money…"

"Absolutely not, I can treat you to some pencils!" Tommy told her stoutly.

Clara wondered if he realised how expensive artists' pencils could be, but wasn't going to argue with his generosity. They had finished their breakfasts and the charabanc would be leaving shortly. They rose to go their separate ways, Annie telling Clara, with that look of honest intensity in her eyes, that she could rely on them to keep their ears and eyes open. Clara had to smile at her dedication.

The rest of the diners had left, they were the last to go and leave the hotel staff to clean up the place before lunch. They wandered past the table where the emaciated girl had sat. Her toast remained on her plate, the edges slightly nibbled as if got at by a mouse. Annie shook her head sadly.

"The poor thing will waste away like that," she sighed.

Clara had not realised Annie had noticed the girl as she had.

"She made me feel quite the porker eating such a hearty breakfast," she replied lightly.

Annie gave her a very sad look.

"Never complain about a hearty appetite Clara, that girl will be in her grave long before you if she does not learn to eat," Annie, who believed most of the ills of the world fell down to a lack of good food and the stomach to eat it, clearly felt the girl a hopeless case. "There was a girl at school just like that. Looked like a breath of wind would carry her off."

"And did it?" Tommy asked with his usual silliness.

Annie scowled at him.

"No, but pneumonia did one winter. I despair of these magazines promoting stick thin girls. It is dangerous for the health. I shall never understand it," Annie shook her head. "I am just glad both of you know how to eat."

Clara discreetly pinched the skin at her waistline, plucking up a fatty piece between thumb and forefinger. Somehow she rather regretted knowing how to eat.

Chapter Thirteen

Once the charabanc and most of the touring party had departed Clara decided to begin her investigations in earnest. Mrs Hunt had asked for Clara's help and, even deceased, she was going to get it.

Clara made her way to the front desk, intent on pigeon-holing the hotel manager and persuading him that he needed to assist her. Precisely how she was going to do that had yet to fully form in her mind, but she was sure she would come up with something once she was speaking with him.

The receptionist was a bright young thing of about twenty, who had yet to be informed that thick black kohl painted around the eyes was more becoming on film stars than ordinary girls. She blinked fast at Clara, possibly due to her heavy mascara threatening to stick her eyelashes together if she did not.

"Might I help?"

"Is Mr Stover about?"

"Is there anything amiss?" the girl put on a well-practiced look of professional concern. Clara wondered if a hotel guest being found deceased in a lake would count as something amiss.

"Nothing concerning the hotel," Clara reassured her

with a smile. "I am most satisfied with my room."

"That is wonderful to hear," the girl beamed overly brightly and had clearly been told to smile a lot at guests. "We aim to please. Perhaps, when you conclude your stay, you will write something in the guest book we keep?"

Clara assured her she would then impatiently repeated her request to see the manager. The girl had clearly forgotten this in her enthusiasm to remind Clara about the guest book. She now stood and said she would find Mr Stover. Clara found she was most relieved when the girl was gone. Some people were just too jolly by far.

Mr Stover appeared rather like a rainy cloud on a sunny day. Unlike the smiles of his receptionist, he could only offer a worried frown and looked beside himself.

"Is anything the matter?" he asked anxiously.

"Not with the hotel," Clara promised, wishing the girl might have informed him of this so he did not look like someone expecting bad news. "Actually, I had wanted to talk to you about the late Mrs Hunt. Specifically, what you might be intending to do with her belongings?"

"Oh," Mr Stover instantly looked relieved. Such mundanities as dealing with a late guest's belongings he could manage without fear. "These sort of occurrences do happen from time to time and it is hotel policy to return all belongings of the deceased to the nearest family member."

"Then you know who this family member is?"

Mr Stover hesitated, because, in actuality, he didn't.

"I imagine Mrs Hunt might have supplied the charabanc company with her next of kin, for emergencies."

"But she didn't," Clara couldn't be sure that was true, but she needed to persuade Mr Stover of the fact. "Now, Mr Stover, just before Mrs Hunt passed she beseeched me to help her with a problem she was having. I am a private detective, for my sins, and it concerns me greatly that Mrs Hunt has passed so suddenly and without anyone close to her knowing about it."

Clara was being deliberately vague because the receptionist was near enough to hear all, but her tone implied an awful lot to Mr Stover and his own natural tendencies towards pessimism supplied the rest. He decided it was time to speak with Clara alone.

"Might you come into my office to discuss this in more detail?" Mr Stover motioned to the room behind him.

Clara was only too eager to be able to air her concerns in private and followed him to his office.

"I took from your tone that this matter is more complicated than it at first appears?" Mr Stover asked once the door was closed and prying ears could no longer overhear them.

"Before she passed Mrs Hunt confessed to me she feared someone was out to harm her. At her last hotel she believed someone attempted to poison her. Here she was almost killed by a falling chamber pot, and then she found herself dead in a lake. She asked me to investigate and try to discover who meant her harm. Sadly, my efforts were too late to save her," Clara explained briefly and with a hint of sadness in her tone. She regretted having failed Mrs Hunt, even if the woman had been deeply disagreeable. Clara couldn't help thinking that was why she had not put much effort into the case before disaster struck, with the result that she now felt guilty.

"I thought the chamber pot was a fluke accident," Mr Stover said quietly, he adjusted his tie nervously, a sick look coming across his face. It didn't make a man feel good to imagine his hotel was the scene of an attempted murder. "I questioned all my staff and no one admitted to dropping the chamber pot."

"And I don't expect them to," Clara said plainly. "I don't think your staff are to blame."

"Then... who?"

"That is the precise question I am trying to answer. The question Mrs Hunt employed me to answer."

"You must tell this all to the police!" Mr Stover seemed to find this a reassuring idea and one that absolved him of all responsibility in the matter.

"I have attempted to discuss this with them, but they are not interested. Have you met Inspector Gateley?"

"Regrettably, yes," Mr Stover sighed. "We had a spate of robberies at the hotel. Guests were naturally upset. Inspector Gateley arrived and turned my hotel upside down before informing me he could find no evidence of a thief on the premises. What a shame Inspector Wake had to retire, he really was superb."

"As you have met Inspector Gateley, I suspect you can imagine the disbelief with which my suggestions were met," Clara said, lowering herself into a chair as her foot ached considerably. "Inspector Gateley has decided that Mrs Hunt had an accident and nothing but the strongest of evidence will shake that idea from his mind."

"Perhaps it was an accident?" Mr Stover said hopefully.

"Perhaps it was, but the woman asked me to investigate and so I shall. But I must ask for your help. I need to know more about Mrs Hunt and the people closest to her."

"Next of kin," Mr Stover nodded.

"But more than that. I would like to visit Mrs Hunt's room and look for any clues among her belongings as to why someone would wish her harm."

Mr Stover looked duly shocked.

"To let you into another guest's room..."

"The guest is deceased and cannot complain, besides, you can call it a legitimate visit since you need to go to her room and look for details of any next of kin. I will merely be there to act as an impartial witness in the search, if anyone cares to ask."

Mr Stover had that sick look on his face again. He was a man who lived on his nerves and did not handle unusual stresses well. Dead guests he could just about manage, because there was a policy for that, but dead guests who might have been murdered went beyond all his experience.

"I can't let you into another guest's room," he protested weakly.

"You must. I shall not remove anything, merely look. But I really do owe this to Mrs Hunt. She feared for her life and I, like so many others, failed to take that seriously enough," Clara was determined and she made that plain in her voice.

Mr Stover still faffed.

"It would be setting a dangerous precedent."

"Who will know?"

Mr Stover paced about his small office. He was not good at making impulsive decisions.

"Mrs Hunt surely just collapsed?"

"Maybe, but if she did it was as a consequence of being struck by a chamber pot," Clara fixed him with a stern gaze. "Your hotel's chamber pot to be precise."

"Oh dear," Mr Stover said softly, well aware of the consequences now being laid out before him. "Oh dear."

"If nothing else, Mrs Hunt deserves justice. People can't just go around callously murdering each other, no matter how disagreeable their victim might be."

"She was disagreeable," Mr Stover sighed. "That no one can deny."

"Disagreeable people do not deserve to be murdered," Clara reminded him.

Mr Stover puffed out his cheeks and paced again. He didn't like what he was being asked to do, but he also knew he could not avoid it. Mrs Hunt died while technically under his care, and he didn't want to think about the field day the newspapers would have if they caught a whiff of the story. He could imagine the headlines – murder by chamber pot! No, no, he could not face such ignominy. This matter must be resolved swiftly and privately. Finally he turned to Clara.

"I shall let you into Mrs Hunt's room, but nothing must be removed and I shall supervise at all times."

"Naturally," Clara assured him. "And if anyone asks our business we are merely looking for details of Mrs

Hunt's family to send a message to."

"Yes. Quite," Mr Stover did not look convinced, but he was not going to escape Clara's grasp now she had him. He gave another sigh then collected the master key for Mrs Hunt's room from a board next to his desk. "Shall we?"

He held open his office door for Clara, then escorted her to the bank of elevators in the hotel lobby. These were rather new and Mr Stover had yet to fully accustom himself to them. He drew back the iron gates and gave a superior nod to the liftman who operated these contraptions.

"Floor three."

They clattered upwards. Mr Stover grimacing, though it was not clear if this was due to the movement of the elevator's carriage or the task ahead of him. Clara said nothing, appreciating not having to use the stairs today. They arrived on the third floor and Mr Stover led the way to Mrs Hunt's room, toying with the master key in his hand all the time. He said nothing to Clara.

No one was about in the hallway. Most of the guests were either downstairs in the communal lounge and garden room, enjoying the spring sunshine, or had made arrangements to go out. Mr Stover still insisted on glancing up and down the hall before he unlocked Mrs Hunt's door.

The room appeared as Clara had expected it to. Neat, tidy, barely used. Mrs Hunt had hardly left an impression. She was one of those people who cannot make a hotel room their own, and so do not bother to try. She had not even emptied her suitcase, other than to remove a few items that were liable to crease badly and to hang them on the front of the wardrobe. Clara looked about the room, taking in everything and trying to sense if something were out-of-place. Nothing seemed wrong.

"We shan't be long," Mr Stover hinted, closing the room door with a last glance outside. "I only need the name of someone to contact."

He seemed to have conveniently forgotten that they were actually looking for clues of a murder.

Clara went to the dressing table in the room where Mrs Hunt had sat her sponge bag. She had had her handbag with her when she perished and there was no knowing what might have been inside, since the police now had it, but perhaps Mrs Hunt had been good enough to leave behind something important here. Clara emptied the sponge bag. It was a floral thing, oval in shape with a long zip. Inside it had several pockets for holding items. Clara pulled out an assortment of feminine items; nail file, powder box, toothbrush and tooth powder, headache pills, a tortoiseshell comb and an unused flannel. At the very bottom she found a glass bottle, quite small but heavy and tinted in that strange brown colour popular with manufacturers of medicine jars. Clara held it to the light. She could make out a number of small round pills in the bottom, presumably enough for this trip. Next she read the label. During the war Clara had volunteered as a nurse at the local hospital, she had dispensed a lot of drugs in that time (usually the mundane, household sort) and had learned the names of a number of others. The name on Mrs Hunt's bottle was not familiar as any medicine she knew of. She took note of the prescribing doctor's name and wrote it down in her notebook.

"Something important?" Mr Stover asked.

"I can't say," Clara turned the bottle in the light again, trying to fathom out what the pills were and failing. "Perhaps a means to finding her next of kin."

Her comment was meant to settle the hotel manager, and it was quite correct, Mrs Hunt's doctor would be sure to know of her next of kin. Clara restored the contents of the sponge bag to their rightful places and turned her attention to Mrs Hunt's suitcase on the floor. She clicked open the clasps, the case not being locked, and carefully unpacked Mrs Hunt's clothes. There was nothing surprising in the contents, just the usual skirts, blouses, stockings and cardigans a woman of Mrs Hunt's age might be expected to take along with her. Clara checked any pockets in them to be safe, she only found a handkerchief. Mr Stover was peering over her shoulder, until she came to a layer of underwear under a piece of tissue paper, then he darted away as if he had been stung by a bee. There was nothing sinister among these garments either, and Clara returned everything as she had found it.

So far she had found nothing enlightening, but perhaps Mrs Hunt chose to keep important items elsewhere? Clara opened the drawers in the dresser, then went to the bedside table. She opened its drawer and found that Mrs Hunt had stored a romance novel inside – that alone was a surprising find considering the woman! Clara lifted up the book, but it seemed ordinary enough, it was as she went to put it back that the pages fluttered open and a slip of paper fell to the floor. Clara bent and picked the paper up.

"What is that?" Mr Stover asked, though from the safety of the far side of the bed in case Clara started pulling out underwear again.

"A list of names," Clara said, pulling a frown as she read. The people named were all travelling on the charabanc. Was this a suspect list Mrs Hunt had compiled?

"Does it tell us next of kin?" Mr Stover asked hopefully.

"No," Clara answered.

"Then you must put it back," Mr Stover said stoutly.

Clara glowered at him, but he was not to be deterred. She insisted on writing the names down in her own notebook for future reference, then returned the paper to its place between the book pages, and restored the novel to the drawer.

They were done at last and Mr Stover was eager to have Clara out of the room. He shuffled her into the corridor quite brusquely and then locked the room up again. Clara wanted to say something, but decided keeping silent was more prudent. She would likely need more help from Mr Stover as yet. But the list was curious – why had Mrs Hunt listed those names? There was no order to them that Clara could see, but that just meant she did not know the order Mrs Hunt had put to them. But it was a clue, Clara was sure of that, and she would follow it up no matter what Inspector Gateley thought.

Chapter Fourteen

Mr Stover was rather acting like a man with a guilty conscience as they headed back downstairs. He was upset at having to prod around in a guest's bedroom. Clara thought it rather a cowardly way of thinking, after all, it was his hotel and he was fully entitled to enter a deceased guest's room and make arrangements for her belongings. Clara decided that Mr Stover took his guest's privacy a little too seriously and needed to remember that a woman had met her end a lot sooner than she should have. Mr Stover also didn't seem to like the fact that Clara insisted on following him back to the front desk, he rather felt she was putting him in a very difficult position. What if the police did suddenly decide to take an interest in Mrs Hunt's death? He could hardly lie if they asked him if anyone had been in Mrs Hunt's room after her demise, and then he would have to explain his actions. No, he was really most concerned about this pushy woman who seemed to poke her nose into his business. He should never have agreed to let Clara into the room at all.

Mr Stover was hoping to be able to shut himself away in his office, but Clara spoke before he had that chance.

"Might I use your telephone?"

Mr Stover hoped to put her off so he could retreat to

his private office.

"There will be a necessary charge for making a call."

"Naturally," Clara said without hesitation. "Telephone calls do not come cheaply, but this really is important."

Mr Stover still hesitated.

"Perhaps a letter sent overnight…"

"Mr Stover," Clara said sternly. "Are you always this unaccommodating towards your guests? All I am asking is to use the telephone and I am quite willing to pay any charges incurred as a result."

Mr Stover sighed, glancing briefly at his office where he desperately wanted to hide himself away from the world.

"Very well," he gave in and opened the office door to Clara.

"Thank you," Clara said, pointedly shutting the door behind her so her call could be private.

Clara needed to know more about Mrs Hunt's health, because it was just possible that she had been overcome by illness and had fallen into the lake. Equally, as she had no evidence to the contrary, it was also possible that there had been no poison in the tin of marzipan fruits Mrs Hunt received, and that her strange episode had been a result of the same sickness that caused her hands to shake. On the other hand, Mrs Hunt's doctor would be well placed to give Clara the names of next of kin, because someone ought to be contacted and informed of Mrs Hunt's death – there had to be someone who cared even just a little to know about it.

Unfortunately, Clara did not have the number for Mrs Hunt's doctor, all she had was his name and the address of his surgery that had been printed on the label on the pill bottle she had found. Nor were telephones all that common in Brighton as yet. The best houses tended to have them, more as novelty gadgets to demonstrate their owner's largesse than for any practical purpose, and some businesses found them valuable – for instance, Mr Hatton at the Charabanc Company had a telephone and was always using it to prepare arrangements for his latest planned trip. But they were the rarities. Clara would have to think laterally if she was to somehow get Mrs Hunt's doctor on the 'phone.

Her first step was to try and contact Oliver Bankes, Clara's friend and police photographer. Oliver had his own photography shop in Brighton, inherited from his father, but he did not possess a telephone. Therefore Clara would need to find someone who did, who could then pass the message to Oliver, and Oliver could then locate Mrs Hunt's doctor. After a moment of consideration Clara knew who she could ring. She lifted the receiver to her ear and heard the line crackle, as if somewhere a bird had picked that moment to land on the telephone wires. A feminine voice came onto the line.

"Operator speaking. Number please."

"Brighton 16," Clara said, hoping she had correctly remembered the number for Miss Maundy's Post Office. Miss Maundy was a woman with a keen sense of the way the world was turning and had decided to have a telephone installed at her Post Office that the public could use for a small charge. It was not so far-fetched an idea, considering they already had the telegraph for receiving messages and the 'phone was only a more advanced form of communication using wires. Miss Maundy was very accommodating with her telephone, particularly as she charged callers a penny per minute of use.

The line rang for several moments, the operator briefly came back on the line to ask if Clara wished to persist.

"Yes, do," Clara told her. "No doubt Miss Maundy is too busy to answer just yet."

The operator fell silent and the phone continued to ring. Clara was half expecting the operator to return and inform her she should put the 'phone down when Miss Maundy herself answered.

"Brighton Post Office," she declared in her best King's English.

"Miss Maundy, its Clara Fitzgerald."

"Oh Miss Fitzgerald! I have a parcel for you. I sent the boy round to let you know, but no one was at home."

"No, I am currently on holiday in the Lake District."

Miss Maundy made an approving noise.

"About time you took a holiday. You were beginning to look rather pale. How is the foot?"

"Improving daily," Clara lied agreeably. "I wonder Miss Maundy if you might be able to send someone to fetch Oliver Bankes to your 'phone? I must speak with him at once."

"At once, you say?" there was a pause on the line as if Miss Maundy was glancing around to see who was available. "Ah, the boy has just returned. Peter, go fetch Mr Bankes from his shop and tell him I have Miss Fitzgerald on the telephone for him!"

There was another moment of silence.

"Peter's gone to fetch him," Miss Maundy assured Clara. "I hope nothing is seriously amiss."

"Oh, no, no, just trying to help out someone here."

"They aren't taking advantage of you, are they Miss Fitzgerald? You are supposed to be having a nice peaceful holiday," Miss Maundy had adopted a stern tone that sounded altogether too much like Annie for comfort.

Clara wondered why so many people felt the need to fuss around her? Did she really give the impression of someone who failed to take proper care of their health? Clara considered herself quite robust in that sense.

"No, no, just helping someone out by finding a name for them, that's all," Clara promised.

"Hmm, well don't let them monopolise your time. Now, I have a customer and must get on. I shall leave the 'phone off its hook until Mr Bankes arrives."

"Thank you."

The line went quiet and Clara sat idly staring at her fingernails and wondering if she really did look rather pale. Clara felt perfectly fit and healthy, aside from her foot, yet Miss Maundy's comments had given her a pang of worry. Perhaps she was working too hard?

She was spared any further musing by the arrival on the 'phone line of Oliver Bankes, who sounded out-of-breath, as if he had run across from his shop.

"Everything all right Clara?" he asked anxiously.

"Perfectly," Clara told him. "I am fine, Oliver, nothing to worry about."

"Oh good! It was just so strange to hear you had telephoned for me I started to worry you had taken on a case!"

Clara gave a slight cough.

"Supposing I had taken on a case?"

"Clara! You are meant to be on holiday! Do you know what a holiday is? It involves relaxing and reading a book and getting utterly, utterly bored. Not taking on cases!"

Clara rather found the way everyone berated her for doing her job a little offensive. Did everyone in Brighton feel the need to concern themselves with her wellbeing? Did she seem such a hopeless case?

"Look, Oliver, I am relaxing and reading and I am utterly, utterly bored," she said, unable to mask her cross tone. "But a woman died here yesterday and the police are being awfully useless."

"So you are taking over the matter?" Oliver said with a gentle sigh.

"The woman confessed her fears to me only the other night," Clara responded, her voice sharper than she meant it to be. "Now, while I can't say for certain yet that she was murdered, it looks awfully like it and I need to make a few discreet enquiries. If I do not the police will chalk this up to accidental drowning and a killer will escape."

"All right, I understand," Oliver attempted to appease her. "As long as you are also going out to see the sights and getting plenty of fresh air and rest."

"Honestly, you are worse than Annie! I have been out, in fact, I was out so much yesterday my foot is now protesting, so I am taking some time off sight-seeing today. Are you satisfied? I might add they are feeding us as if we just survived a famine, I have never felt so stuffed in my life! And there even happens to be a doctor in the hotel, who has been good enough to look at my foot. So, you see, I am amply taken care of!"

"Steady on, I grasp that you are being well looked after," Oliver chuckled lightly down the line.

"Sorry Oliver," Clara apologised. "I just rather feel that people imagine I am incapable of taking care of myself. I had Miss Maundy lecturing me before you came on the line."

"No more lectures," Oliver promised. "I am sure Annie has those all sorted anyway. Now, what has happened that you need my help? You say a woman has died?"

Oliver whispered the last sentence, not wishing to cause a stir in the Post Office; public telephones were not particularly private, after all.

"Yes, the woman was Mrs Hunt and it seems she fell into a lake yesterday and drowned. No one knows much about her, or at least they won't admit to knowing anything to me. I am hoping to find some next of kin at least, to offer her belongings to. I came across a bottle of pills in her belongings and the doctor named on the label is a Brighton man. I would dearly like to talk to him."

"What is the name?" Oliver asked.

"Dr Day-Bowers," Clara said, referring to the notes she had made. "I didn't recognise the name of the medicine. He has a surgery in the Avenue, number 52."

"I've written that down," Oliver assured her down the line. "Is there anything else?"

"If you could arrange for Dr Day-Bowers to ring me on this telephone, unless he happens to have his own he could use, then that would be perfect," Clara read off the hotel's telephone number from a printed slip of paper stuck on the base of the 'phone.

"I'll get on to it straight away," Oliver told her. "Now go enjoy some sunshine, if you have any."

Clara glanced out of the office window and saw Mr Stover glaring at her and tapping his watch.

"First I have to appease the hotel manager who I appear to have offended."

"Oh Clara!" Oliver laughed.

"He is remarkably sensitive," Clara said stiffly. "Thank you Oliver, in any case."

Oliver said his goodbyes and hung up. Clara put down the receiver before the operator could come back on the line, then rose to speak with Mr Stover again. There was one last thing she needed to discuss with him.

Mr Stover was looking impatient when she exited his office. It was nearly half an hour since she had gone inside to use his telephone and he was not pleased.

"Please place the charges on my bill," Clara said calmly. "And there is one other thing."

Mr Stover seemed to slump a fraction, as if he was convinced he would never get rid of this woman who was determined to torment him.

"Yes?"

"I take it you are not in the habit of leaving gifts for your guests in their rooms?"

"Gifts?" Mr Stover raised his eyebrows in a perfect look of surprise.

"I thought not. Miss Smythe received a box of marzipan fruits in her room, however, she does not care for them and it seems unlikely they were intended for her. In any case, she has been advised to bring them to you."

"Marzipan fruits?" Mr Stover's voice had taken on a comical edge to it, he seemed quite aghast at all this.

"When she brings this tin to you, might I request you advise me of it? I am concerned that the sweets may contain something harmful."

"What…" Mr Stover shook his head and decided further questions would only prolong his torment. "Yes, yes, I'll do that."

Clara nodded.

"Thank you, Mr Stover. I will be expecting a telephone message later on."

Mr Stover grumbled under his breath as he finally

returned to his office, and shut the door firmly behind him. Clara couldn't say how she had managed to so offend him, but clearly she had. She limped her way through to the hotel's sun lounge, her aching foot demanding she sit down. Hopefully Oliver would be able to find the doctor, but whether that would provide any answers was another matter.

Clara sat in a chair that faced the tall windows overlooking the lawn. It was a slightly overcast day and the garden had that damp look about it that only occurs in spring. Clara thought of Mrs Hunt. Who was this woman and why did she imagine someone was so intent to kill her? And what was important about the list of names she had made? Clara glanced at her notebook, but the names seemed to have no rhyme or reason to them. Why would anyone off this list want Mrs Hunt dead? Clara settled into her chair and thought over her own conversations with Mrs Hunt. Nothing particularly revealing. Only that the woman seemed to attract misfortune. Perhaps it was all as simple as that – misfortune? Well, perhaps the doctor could shed some light on the matter, for the moment it was all a mystery. One thing Clara did know, despite Oliver's warnings, investigating the death of Mrs Hunt was proving far more interesting and distracting than any holiday!

Chapter Fifteen

Clara watched the world go by. It was quite therapeutic. Just outside the tall windows of the sun lounge, on the patio, sat Miss Plante and Miss Soloman. They had clearly decided they would rather sit quietly in the sunshine than go on another excursion. Miss Plante was wrapped up in a shawl, just her head protruding from a heavy layer of knitted Arran wool. Miss Soloman was reading to her from an Elizabeth Gaskell novel in a hushed tone. Clara couldn't hear what she said.

"Miss Fitzgerald?"

Clara glanced up and saw Henry Wignell standing at her side, one hand resting on the wing of her chair.

"Did you not go to Derwentwater, Mr Wignell?" Clara was a little surprised to see him. Henry Wignell struck her as a person who would take any opportunity to explore the English countryside.

"Yesterday rather unsettled us," Mr Wignell said very solemnly. He lowered himself into the chair next to Clara's. He did look extremely deflated, his usual exuberance seemingly lost.

"I am sure you must know some interesting facts about Derwentwater," Clara tried to distract him. "I would have loved to have gone, only my foot hurts too much. Possibly you could tell me something of what I am missing?"

Mr Wignell was staring out the window at Miss Plante and Miss Soloman, he didn't seem to have quite heard Clara.

"Lake Windermere is known for its drownings. Most are accidental. Boats overturned, or sudden storms taking swimmers by surprise. And then you have the suicides," Mr Wignell said instead. "The history of it all is quite appalling. Why would anyone ever wish to go near such a place after hearing all that?"

Clara wasn't sure what to say. Mr Wignell seemed unduly distraught by Mrs Hunt's tragic demise the day before. Certainly it was shocking, but not the sort of thing to dwell on.

"I hear Derwentwater has several islands within the lake, one being named after a seventh century priest," Clara said, hoping to lure Mr Wignell off these gloomy thoughts. "Its name may mean 'river with oak trees', or so the booklet Mr Hatton provided states."

"It is three miles long, by one mile wide and 72 feet deep," Mr Wignell joined in, though without losing his morose demeanour. "One of the islands is inhabited and bears an eighteenth century house."

"Now that would be very interesting to see," Clara nodded. "Though I don't suppose it is open to the public."

Mr Wignell gave a very heavy sigh.

"Miss Fitzgerald, might we talk freely? I really need to speak with someone and I rather fancy you are the sort of person who is good at keeping confidences."

Clara was a little surprised, but she certainly was not going to deny Mr Wignell.

"I shall keep all you say between us," she promised him.

"It is not so much that it is a secret, rather, it is such a personal matter, one that caused considerable heartache, I would not have others know about it."

"Mr Wignell, what awful thing has happened? Is your

wife quite well?"

"A little shaken," Mr Wignell admitted. "And we seem to have misplaced her sleeping powders. It has upset her. My wife has not slept unaided these last ten years."

"Oh," Clara found it hard to imagine Mrs Wignell as an insomniac, she looked too determined to have anything to do with such nonsense.

"It is since our great loss," Mr Wignell persisted. "Our daughter, our only child, perished ten years ago. She was a gift from God, given to us late in life, long after we had accepted we would remain childless. She was always a fragile thing, and taken with whims and fancies, but we both loved her dearly."

"I am sorry," Clara said gently. "A loss like that must be hard to bear."

"It is Miss Fitzgerald and I fear my own stubbornness has made matters worse for my wife," Mr Wignell grimaced with his own internal guilt.

"You are entitled to your grief as much as your wife," Clara soothed him. "I am sure you meant no deliberate harm. Sometimes, when our emotions are raw, we do things we later regret."

"You are kind, but you do not really understand," Mr Wignell gave Clara a soft smile. "I was referring to my recent stubbornness, not past matters. You see, my daughter perished on the banks of Lake Windermere, and this journey was supposed to be a means of laying her memory to rest once and for all."

Clara said nothing, she rather felt it was not her place to speak. Mr Wignell had a story to tell and interruptions would not assist. Mr Wignell tapped his fingers on the arm of his chair, with a slight cough he began his story.

"My daughter was prone to melancholy from childhood. These dark moods would come over her out of the blue. We found them hard to predict and harder to manage. She would shut herself away, refuse to eat or talk, become almost a living statue. Doctor after doctor offered hope only to disappoint us. We eventually came to the conclusion that the situation could not be cured, only managed," Mr Wignell blinked slowly, unwanted memories surfacing in his mind. "At first the melancholia was unfortunate, but not harmful. The dark periods would pass and our lively daughter would return. When she was well she was vivacious and delightful. She loved to dance and to play music. She made me so happy, I cannot explain it Miss Fitzgerald, which was why when the dark spells came over her it made me so very sad.

"As she became older the moods became more complicated. She began to talk of harming herself. She despised who she was, she would say, she could not bear to carry on. Naturally we cajoled her and coaxed her through these periods, but we began to be afraid for her wellbeing. One Sunday, after a carriage ride which we had all enjoyed, our daughter attempted to kill herself by drinking a bottle of laudanum she found in the bathroom. There was not enough to kill her, but she was very ill. When she was recovered enough to talk, we asked her why she had done it when she seemed so happy. She looked me straight in the eye and said that was precisely the problem, she had been so very happy that afternoon and she could not imagine ever being that happy again, and the thought had caused her such despair she saw the only solution to be to take her life."

Mr Wignell had to pause. His throat was tight with emotion and the words did not want to come out easily. Tears were threatening in his eyes, but he would not cry in public and certainly not before a young woman. He had to focus on Miss Plante and Miss Soloman, on the latter's steady reading of the novel, to compose himself. He was glad Clara did not interrupt at this point. She just sat quietly and waited. Finally he spoke again.

"After the incident, my wife and I agreed that Susan, our daughter, must never be left alone for even a moment. But how was this to be achieved when I was at work and my wife would at times have to leave the house on errands and visits? We concluded we should find our daughter a companion. She had had tutors in the past and we would say that this was just a continuation of her education. Susan loved to draw and she loved geography. We looked about for a person who could expand on this knowledge. That was how we first came to know Mrs Hunt."

Clara looked up sharply at this statement. There had been no indication during the last few days that the Wignells knew Mrs Hunt, certainly no sign that they had once employed her.

"I can understand your surprise," Mr Wignell said. "Let me continue my story and you will see why we were not inclined to renew our friendship after all this time. Mrs Hunt came to us with very good recommendations. She was a little sharp for my taste, but my wife postulated that this might be just what Susan needed. We were, by our own admission, rather soft. Perhaps someone so practical and lacking in imagination as Mrs Hunt would be of benefit to her. As it happened, Susan liked Mrs Hunt and soon they were spending every day together. In the mornings they would explore Susan's passion for geography by studying atlases and travel guides. In the afternoons Susan would draw while Mrs Hunt read to her. For a time things seemed perfect.

"Then Susan came up with the idea of a visit to the Lake District. She had been studying the lakes, they were a particular passion for her, and she wanted to see them and to sketch them. We all thought it a grand idea and the arrangements were duly made. We came to the Lakes in August, the only time I was able to get away from work. Susan spent the first few days sketching the scenery, seemingly content. On the Wednesday we went to Lake Windermere. Mrs Wignell and I wanted to relax and enjoy the view, Susan wanted to walk around the lake looking for a good sketching spot. Naturally Mrs Hunt went with her. That was the last time I saw my daughter alive. She seemed so happy, so vibrant in that moment. I had no fears for her."

Mr Wignell's voice trembled and he paused.

"What happened?" Clara asked softly, feeling that Mr Wignell needed to hear another voice in the room to save himself from complete distress.

"I only know what Mrs Hunt told me. She and Susan walked the banks a while until Susan saw a spot she liked and set up her easel and paper. Mrs Hunt was feeling rather hot and weary. She sat under a tree and fell asleep. When she woke the easel was still there but Susan was missing. Mrs Hunt rose and walked along the lakeside, looking for Susan. When she could not see her she walked back to the easel and saw that the sketch had been finished and the pencils set down. Confused, she walked towards the lake edge, pushing through a tall patch of reeds, perhaps imagining Susan had decided to wet her feet in the lake water to cool off. Instead, she saw Susan floating face down. She dragged her out and called for help, but it was too late.

"We can only assume one of Susan's dark moods had suddenly overtaken her and she could not resist the lure of the water," Mr Wignell fell quiet, he was thinking. "Naturally there was an inquest. Death by accidental drowning was concluded. Mrs Hunt was dismissed, we had no need of her services. That was the last we saw of her for many years."

"Until you came on this holiday? That must have been a shock."

"Yes, and then again, no. You see, my wife received a letter from Mrs Hunt. It said that the woman was ill and she was trying to resolve matters in her life before the end came. One of the things she wanted to do was return to Lake Windermere and say a final goodbye to Susan. Only, she felt she could not face going alone. She wanted our company," Mr Wignell shook his head. "It seemed absurd at first. We had spent all these years putting the matter behind us. Why now stir it up again? But, after a while, my wife came to think the idea fitting. She thought it might help her to sleep again. So I made the arrangements. But, when it came to it, I could not bring myself to speak with Mrs Hunt. Perhaps, deep down, I blame her for what happened to Susan. We treated each other like strangers."

"And then Mrs Hunt perished in the lake like Susan," Clara added. "Do you think it was a symbolic act?"

"I don't know," Mr Wignell admitted. "As I say, we did not speak with the poor woman. Perhaps, in the end, she felt guilt over Susan too."

Or one of the Wignells had allowed emotion to get the better of their rational senses and Mrs Hunt had been murdered.

"I can understand why your wife is so upset. There is a doctor in the hotel, you know, if she requires more sleeping powders."

"Yes, it may come to that," Mr Wignell nodded. "But not until we are sure she has lost her supply. Probably they are tucked away in a suitcase."

"Probably," Clara assured him.

"It was most good of you to listen to me," Mr Wignell continued. "Yesterday's events stirred up an awful lot of bad memories. I truly regret coming on this holiday. It has made things a dozen times worse. We should have left the past in the past."

Clara wondered if Mrs Hunt had thought the same before her untimely demise.

"Did Mrs Hunt say what illness she was suffering from?"

"No. But I assumed something fatal," Mr Wignell took a handkerchief from his top pocket and dabbed surreptitiously at his eyes. "Is it awful to say sometimes I wish we had never had Susan?"

"No," Clara corrected him. "Sometimes it feels harder to lose a precious thing, than to have never known that thing in the first place. But you must hold on to all the good memories that Susan gave you."

"Thank you, Miss Fitzgerald," Mr Wignell rose. "I have heard your name in Brighton. They say you are a very good investigator."

"That is reassuring to hear," Clara smiled.

"If you happen to come across any information about Susan, while you are examining Mrs Hunt's case…"

Clara looked up sharply.

"I know your name and I know Mrs Hunt spoke to you," Mr Wignell shrugged. "I suspect you are investigating, but you need not confirm it to me. In any case, if you do learn something about Susan, will you please inform me?"

"Naturally," Clara said.

Mr Wignell gave her another nod, then wandered away. Clara sat back in her chair and turned her attention to the two ladies outside. How curious, she thought. Another piece of the puzzle had become visible, but exactly how it fitted the whole eluded her as yet.

Chapter Sixteen

The charabanc returned around 4pm. Tommy and Annie appeared in the hotel lobby. Tommy gave his sister a hug and presented her with a long, flat parcel wrapped in brown paper. It was of a reasonable weight and when she disposed of the paper she saw it was a sketching book and a pack of artist's pencils in a little brass tin.

"Thank you Tommy," she said, giving him another hug.

"Have you had a productive day?" Tommy asked.

"It's hard to say," Clara answered, "It has certainly been interesting."

Eleanora Smythe had just appeared in the lobby and Clara smiled at her. The woman seemed oblivious, though she looked morbidly unhappy.

"That reminds me," Clara wandered to the hotel's front desk where the morning girl had been replaced by a man who was less inclined to smile. When Clara asked to see Mr Stover he frowned at her.

"I can assist you with most queries," he told her bluntly, perhaps inferring from her request that she did not imagine him competent enough to deal with her concerns.

"I am sure you can," Clara smiled. "But this is a private

matter between me and Mr Stover."

Reluctantly the gentleman went to the little office behind the front desk and summoned Mr Stover. He was smiling as he came out of the office door, until he saw Clara.

"Have there been any 'phone messages for me?" Clara asked as soon as he came over.

"If there had been I would have informed you," Mr Stover said coldly.

Clara was unperturbed.

"And if Miss Smythe brings you a tin…"

"I shall put it on one side and inform you, yes, Miss Fitzgerald, I have not forgotten."

Clara pursed her lips, but bit her tongue. She had an important thing to ask and did not want to irritate Mr Stover further.

"You mentioned an Inspector Wake earlier?"

"Yes, he was the inspector around here for many years."

"Was he the inspector ten years ago?"

Mr Stover gave her a strange look, the sort that implied he was not sure where she was heading with this question, nor whether he should be cautious or not.

"I believe so," he said at last.

"Might you be able to tell me how to contact Inspector Wake?"

"Miss Fitzgerald, why might you want that? Inspector Gateley is investigating this case, or so I hear, and I doubt he would want his long retired predecessor poking his nose in," Mr Stover pulled a face. "Whatever his flaws, the powers-that-be have deemed Inspector Gateley sufficient to watch over this district and all enquiries must go to him."

Clara gave Mr Stover a polite smile.

"I actually wanted to talk to Inspector Wake about an historic case. I doubt Inspector Gateley will wish to spare me the time."

Mr Stover gave a long sigh.

"Inspector Wake is a creature of habit. At this very moment he will be wandering along to the Red Lion, to have his supper and enjoy a glass of beer. I shall send a message to him there, asking when you can call on him. Is that to your satisfaction?"

"It is, Mr Stover, it is," Clara assured him. "I promise you I do not do all this to try your patience. I merely wish to see justice done."

Mr Stover's stern façade weakened a little.

"I understand that Miss Fitzgerald," he admitted. "I merely find it inconvenient to be discussing such things. I run a hotel, not an enquiries service."

"Be comforted that by my efforts I might be able to find Mrs Hunt's next of kin and so let you know who her belongings should be sent to. That will save you an effort."

Mr Stover merely shook his head and retreated once more to his office.

Clara, Tommy and Annie made their way to Clara's hotel room to talk over their day and update each other. There were still several hours before dinner and it was a sufficient quiet patch in which they could mull over the latest information. Clara refrained from telling them about her talk with Mr Wignell. For a start it had been a private conversation and Clara had given her word of honour that she would not share the information she was given, secondly she had yet to decide if it had any bearing on the case and thus whether it needed to be revealed. For the moment Mr Wignell was entitled to his secrets.

"Mrs Palmer has talked about nothing else but Mrs Hunt's demise," Annie said before she was even sat down.

Clara sat on her bed and eased off her shoes, much to the relief of her injured foot.

"Mrs Palmer is the sort of person who snatches up an idea then refuses to let it go," Clara said, barely masking the sigh of pleasure that came with easing her discomfort. "Is she still saying Mrs Hunt was murdered?"

"That is the gist of her talk," Tommy answered. "She

really took a dislike to the woman."

"Mrs Hunt had the audacity to criticise a fantasy that has sustained Mrs Palmer these many years. She damaged the fragile cocoon the woman lives in and which protects her from the horrific grief she must suffer if she admitted the truth. That sort of thing lends itself to a vivid hatred," Clara explained. "Mrs Palmer is a very fragile woman under all her bluff."

"That may be, but she is driving us all insane with her chatter," Annie said. "Her friend, Mrs Siskin, keeps telling her to hush."

"Poor Mrs Siskin. What of the others?"

"You saw Miss Smythe coming back into the hotel?" Tommy queried, though without waiting for an answer. "She seems deeply depressed about something, but she has not revealed what. She wandered around Derwentwater quite alone and, I feel sure, at one point she was sobbing to herself."

"I hope she didn't eat any of those marzipan fruits she was sent!" Annie said, a sudden awful thought crossing her mind. "What if she was meant to be sent them and there is a mad man in the hotel, poisoning people at random?"

"I doubt that," Clara tried to still her panic. "Besides, Mrs Hunt received her parcel at our previous hotel. Why would a random killer follow us all here?"

"He could be on the charabanc!" Annie said in horror, the colour draining from her face.

"I think you are getting carried away," Clara told her friend affectionately. "Mrs Hunt's killer, if there is one, was after her and her alone, of that I am sure. The tin sent to Miss Smythe was a mistake or something else."

"Such as?" Tommy asked.

"For the moment I don't know, but I am certain this is not the actions of a person who randomly kills people on charabanc tours. For a start, someone made at least two attempts on Mrs Hunt's life, with possibly a third successful one at Windermere. A random killer is unlikely to have gone to such effort."

Everyone agreed with that, though Annie thought she might look a little more closely at her soup before consuming it at dinner.

"Did anyone seem to take particular offence at Mrs Palmer's talk?" Clara asked.

"There is a young couple," Annie said. "I thought they were newly married at first, but now I don't feel so sure. The man, he kept casting looks over at Mrs Palmer, but he may just have considered her speaking out in poor taste."

"The driver was very nervy today," Tommy added. "Seemed all out of sorts, but then I suppose that comes from having one of your passengers die on you."

"Aside from that, was Derwentwater nice?" Clara decided they had played detective long enough.

"Beautiful!" Annie exclaimed, "I didn't realise any place in England could seem so… ethereal. The mist was still rising off the water and it seemed so fantastical. I can see why artists are so inspired when they come here."

"Mrs Crimp even tried her hand with some pencils she bought in the village shop!" Tommy laughed. "I don't think even she was impressed by her efforts!"

"Then perhaps I shan't risk bringing out my pencils!" Clara chuckled.

"Oh, but you must! They cost enough!" Tommy winked at her. "Now, what did you find in Mrs Hunt's room?"

"Nothing revealing, except for a medicine bottle and a list of names. It seems Mrs Hunt was keeping track of some of her fellow charabanc passengers. But whether she deemed them suspects or was recording their names for another reason I can't say," Clara produced her notebook from a pocket and showed them the names.

"Mrs Unwin sat near us during luncheon," Annie picked out a name from the list. "She talked a bit. She is a widow with three grown daughters and a fondness for hat pins. I can't see her connection to Mrs Hunt, she certainly didn't mention one."

"Mr Hardwich," Tommy pointed a finger at the paper. "He was a dealer in butterflies and beetles, of all things, before he retired. You know, the sort people put in little glass cases or paperweights. I happened to talk to him while at the edge of the lake. He made no mention of Mrs Hunt either.

"And this Captain Blake," Tommy ran down the list further. "He is around my age. Can't really see why he is on this tour, to be honest, he doesn't seem to much care for it, nor the company."

"I suggest those are two people you need to speak with a little more," Clara said to her brother. "They would be more likely to speak to you than me. The rest of the list we can divide among us, and observe the respective individuals."

"Might I make a suggestion?" Annie raised her hand as if in school.

"Of course," Clara told her. "This is a free discussion, after all."

"I think it might be worthwhile talking to the servants within the hotel, they often see or hear things that others don't. They may know more about the chamber pot mystery."

"A valid point," Clara nodded. "Can I leave that in your hands?"

"Naturally."

Annie had barely finished speaking when there was a knock on the door. Clara asked the person to enter. It was the desk clerk.

"Miss Fitzgerald, there is a man by the name of Bankes on the 'phone for you."

Clara rose at once and followed the desk clerk back to Mr Stover's office. The 'phone receiver was resting off its hook on top of a pile of papers and Mr Stover was eyeing it as if it might bite. Clara gave a slight cough as she entered. Mr Stover glanced at her, then gruffly rose and left her alone. Clara picked up the receiver.

"Oliver?"

"Clara! I have Dr Day-Bowers ready to speak with you," Oliver Bankes dropped his voice to a whisper as he said the next bit. "He is rather wary of telephones, thinks they emit electricity. He insisted I ring you first, I suppose he thinks if I don't die, it is safe!"

Clara wanted to chuckled, but she didn't. Quite a number of people were scared of all the new inventions that were flooding into Britain, indeed, there had been accidents involving the new technology, and no one could deny these new-fangled cars had claimed more than one life. But the telephone was not terribly new and, as far as Clara was aware, no one had died from using one.

"Let me speak to him Oliver," Clara said.

The line went quiet a moment, though Clara could hear what sounded like the rustle of clothes on the wire. Finally Dr Day-Bowers came on the line.

"Good afternoon Miss Fitzgerald."

"Good afternoon," Clara responded. "Has my associate explained my concerns?"

"A little. I am deeply distressed to hear the news about Mrs Hunt. She has been my patient these last five years."

"She was not a well woman," Clara pressed.

"She was not," Dr Day-Bowers confirmed. "In my opinion she was suffering from Parkinson's disease. It is a deeply unpleasant condition characterised by uncontrollable tremors, usually in the hands, and muscle weakness. As the condition progresses the gait can be affected, the person may shuffle, be slow to move or, when they do move, do so in a curious fashion as if someone is operating them by strings. It later often develops into a psychiatric condition."

"Is there a cure?"

"No. And the disease progresses extremely rapidly. The majority of patients after eight years with the condition will no longer be able to walk without assistance and, after ten years, we would expect the patient to be bedridden."

"And Mrs Hunt knew this?"

"She was well aware," Dr Day-Bowers gave a gentle sigh. "The condition would ultimately have left her requiring constant care. With no immediate family I imagine this was a great concern to Mrs Hunt."

"You prescribed some pills for her?" Clara asked. "I found the bottle in her belongings."

"Yes. They were a new treatment from America. Still experimental and unproven, but any port in a storm, as they say. It was too early to say if they were working."

"Thank you doctor. Lastly, do you think Mrs Hunt may have considered taking her own life?"

"Many with her condition do," Dr Day-Bowers said thoughtfully. "But I rather felt Mrs Hunt still had hope and the new pills gave her a reason to carry on. I was very upset to hear of her demise."

"And she had no next of kin?"

"None recorded on my files, I'm afraid."

Clara thanked the doctor and ended the call. It was curious, she thought to herself, here was Mrs Hunt clearly very ill and close to suffering a fate many would consider worse than death and yet someone still felt the need to try and dispatch her from this world. Either they did not know how ill she was, or they did not care to wait for the condition to take its course. It was time, Clara decided, to investigate those people on Mrs Hunt's list.

Chapter Seventeen

Dinner proved a quiet affair, even Mrs Palmer refrained from discussions of murder and talk consisted of remarks on the weather and people's varying opinions of Derwentwater. When dessert had been concluded and post-dinner drinks were being offered, Tommy excused himself to go in search for Captain Blake who had departed the table before the last course.

Tommy found the forlorn soldier in one of the hotel's several lounges, this one set aside as a sort of music room with a grand piano and a shelf stacked with music sheets so that any guest might wile away an hour or two playing the ivory keys. Tommy was not altogether sure how to approach Captain Blake, but he had been charged with the task by Clara and refused to fail. He had noticed Blake on the charabanc, one of the few men of his age on the tour and looking distinctly out of place. He travelled alone and had not made any effort to befriend his fellow passengers. Very often he left dinner early and when he was at the table he rarely talked or joined in conversations. He was the sort of person it was terribly easy to overlook.

Tommy had also been a captain in the army during the war, though he long ago gave up using his rank. Tommy preferred not to be reminded of those horrific years and since he had no intention of returning to the military life, what was the point in retaining his title? He was Tommy Fitzgerald, civilian, and that was the way he liked it. But other men were different. Other men felt the need to use their rank as a shield or even a badge of honour – proof that they had served and people should pay them a certain respect for it. Whether that was how Captain Blake felt about his affix Tommy was yet to find out.

Captain Blake was playing out a sad classical tune on the piano. It sounded a little French to Tommy's ears as he limped into the music lounge, using his sturdy walking stick to safely traverse him across the carpet. The discovery that he could walk again after years of being confined to a chair had filled him with elation, but there was still a way to go before Tommy could walk unaided, and he somehow doubted he would ever lose the limp. Perhaps that was his badge of honour? Proof that he served his time and took a bullet for dear old England. This holiday was certainly giving him the chance to stretch his legs, but the ache in his back, thighs and calves suggested he may be overdoing it. He sank into a solid armchair near the piano with some relief. The slight groan he gave as the pressure came off his weary muscles was not feigned.

Captain Blake paused in his playing and looked over. He was a gaunt young man, the sort who look like they need several hearty meals to be considered healthy. He had high cheek bones and a sharp nose that might almost be described as Grecian. His eyes were an icy blue, almost to the point of being colourless, though a ring of indigo circled the pupils. His hair was an ashy brown, trimmed to a military shortness, so that it seemed as if he had only just stepped out of his uniform. He regarded Tommy with a coldness that chilled the heart.

"Don't mind me, old man," Tommy smiled at him lightly. "I just needed somewhere to sit and take the weight off this leg," he tapped his right knee. "Needed to get away from the chatter too."

Captain Blake cocked his head to the side and glanced at the door of the lounge which had been left ajar by Tommy.

"They do go on," he remarked solemnly, then he returned to playing and went through the same piece of music once more.

Tommy noted he was not using a musical score and assumed he knew the melody off by heart. When he finished and the last note died away, Tommy asked;

"Is that a French tune?"

Captain Blake rested his hands on his knees. His eyes were still fixed on the piano keys as if he could still 'see' the music he had just played dancing over the keys.

"Possibly," he said in his quiet, unemotional tone. "I learned it in Belgium."

"I liked the French tunes," Tommy mused. "Though I could never learn them off by heart like that. I'm rather a poor pianist. I remember there was a battered piano in one of the old houses we slept in during rest periods. We had a private who could play beautiful things on it, considering it was missing a key or two and probably hadn't been tuned in years."

"You were in the war?" Captain Blake enquired, watching Tommy out of just the corner of his eye.

"From 1914," Tommy told him. "Until I took a bullet in No Man's Land."

He tapped the knee again.

"That was 1918. I thought I would never walk again, until I met this doctor in Brighton. I only just got back on my feet, quite literally, last month. This holiday is rather kill or cure," Tommy grinned. "I consider myself one of the lucky ones though. Some of the blighters who survived their injuries, well, I imagine they wish they hadn't."

"That is true," Captain Blake tapped one of the piano keys, making it play very softly. "I only served from 1917. I have no scars to speak of."

"It's the scars up here no one talks about," Tommy

rapped a knuckle on his temple. "That's what this doctor has told me. He says it is why so many of the boys who came home have a bad time of it. I didn't believe him at first."

"They treat you with such derision when the pain is in your head," Blake nodded slowly. "No one sees it, so no one believes it exists."

Tommy paused. He sensed that here in Captain Blake he had found a fellow sufferer of what his doctor called 'shell-shock', it was a term many of Tommy's fellow soldiers considered derogatory or a label for cowardice. Only a man who had suffered through it could understand.

"I used to have awful nightmares," Tommy decided to offer Blake a lifeline, maybe that was a way to get him talking about other things. "Only my sister, Clara, really understood them. After I came out of the hospital she made it her duty to look after me."

"You don't have the nightmares now?"

"Only occasionally. Not like before."

They were silent. Captain Blake continued tapping the piano key and playing a soft note. Tommy found it a little irritating.

"I have nightmares too," Blake said very quietly. "I try not to sleep too much."

"Clara thought this holiday would do me good," Tommy said, a white lie since Clara had been offered the holiday as thanks for solving a case. "Is that why you are here?"

"Not precisely," Blake watched his finger pressing the piano key.

"No, you don't quite look right amongst the rest of them. All old ladies and spinsters, well, for the most part. I can't imagine you choosing such a holiday if you had the option."

Blake looked at him sharply, his eyes a little narrowed. Tommy expected a rebuke for his assumption, but it did not come. Finally Blake said;

"No, this was not my choice. It was a gift. A gift I could not turn down."

Tommy nodded.

"People try to be kind. They think they can understand a man just back from war, but... well, they never saw the things we did," Tommy paused because all this talk was stirring up his own memories, most of which were not pleasant.

For a moment he was lost in his thoughts, visions of dead friends flashing through his mind. Horrific battles, bloody messes that were once men, screaming horses, battering guns. A rain storm of shrapnel. A mist of gas. The images swirled up unbidden and Tommy felt the quick tightening of his chest that these memories always brought. He realised, quite suddenly, that Captain Blake and turned to sit sideways on the piano stool and was watching him intensely. Tommy blinked and glanced over at him.

"Sorry," he said, abashed at his sudden lapse.

"That is how it catches me out too," Blake said, his tone warmer than before. "All this around me, all this natural beauty – the lakes, the countryside, even this music, it stirs nothing within me. But those memories, when they come crashing back they remind me I am still alive. Sometimes I even crave them just to remind me I have any feelings at all."

"I would give everything I have to be rid of them," Tommy said wholeheartedly.

"At least you have family to distract you," Blake responded without sympathy.

"You don't?"

"My parents are dead. I have no other living family."

"Then who gifted you this holiday?" Tommy asked, the first real question he had placed before Blake and something of a retaliation for the lack of empathy the latter had shown him just a moment before. Blake was the sort of man who could only feel sorry for himself and no one else could possibly suffer as he did. Tommy would hate to be a man serving under him.

Captain Blake gave a cold smile.

"A late aunt. Her idea of compensation."

"She perhaps imagined it would help," Tommy said. "I am sorry to hear she has departed this world. Presumably it was quite recent?"

Blake returned to tapping the piano key. A long, dreary note echoed over and over about the room.

"Very recently. Only yesterday in fact. But I shan't weep for her. I had not seen or heard from her in over a decade. She cut my mother from her life in a temper over her marrying and subsequently having me," Blake shrugged. "Had she not written to the family address the other month I would have assumed she was dead also."

Tommy was turning this statement over in his mind. The aunt had only died yesterday? Blake did not seem to be grieving for her, rather he seemed amused by it all. There was something about his face that suddenly struck Tommy as familiar. It was the way he smiled condescendingly, he recognised it from someone else's face, but his mind failed to offer him the name of that person.

"Must you go back to arrange her funeral?" he asked, surely a nephew must feel some compassion for a late aunt?

"I am more inclined to leave it to the authorities," Blake said, almost yawning over the answer. "Apparently, my aunt was very secretive about my presence. No one seems aware that I exist!"

Blake found this most amusing and chuckled to himself.

"Surely you will attend though? As the poor woman had no other family." Tommy asked, not liking this man's reaction at all. He could forgive a lot when men admitted to suffering from shell-shock, but such callousness troubled him.

"That was her choosing," Blake said with a sneer. "I shall not weep for such a woman. You should understand, having met the old witch yourself."

Tommy must have looked surprised for Blake laughed, and played a chord loudly on the piano with his left hand. Then he rattled out a brief ditty that sounded rather like the music they played at the pictures to accompany a dramatic moment in a silent movie.

"Dear man! You dined with her the other night! Not that I think you enjoyed her company. You shot daggers at her with your eyes until she relieved you by departing from the table, so don't attempt to come high and mighty with me!"

"Who…?"

"Mrs Hunt, you fool! She was my aunt! She gifted me this trip and I had half a mind not to accept. But I did, and when I get here she is aboard also. She had never said anything about that," Blake clattered the lid down on the piano. "And all she wanted to do was talk to me about my mother. I suspect she wanted to make amends for cutting her from her life, too late for that if you ask me! But she could not change her true nature and every sentence was some criticism of my mother, her only sister. She would say she was sorry and then attempt to justify her actions by pointing out some flaw in my mother, some forgotten sin she had committed that had caused this consternation. As if I cared! I was rather relieved when she wound up dead in Windermere, it saved me the bother of feeling honour-bound to invite her over for Christmas."

Tommy was stunned by what he was hearing. He felt almost sickened by Blake's admissions and the cruel nature of his response. But he also saw so much of Mrs Hunt in that young man, that he found himself also understanding the reaction. They were two grapes off the same vine. Neither could feel compassion, nor ever imagine themselves wrong.

"You look shocked, old man," Blake laughed. "That's what comes from prying into another fellow's business."

Captain Blake stood and strode across the room to the door.

"Don't tell the police what I just told you, there's a good fellow, or I may have to just pay you a visit and sort out that dodgy knee of yours," with that threat Blake was almost out the door.

But he had stirred something in Tommy, rattled a demon that usually lurked safely in its cage. Tommy had a temper and he had never tolerated bullies. He jumped from his chair far faster than he thought possible and raced across the room to Blake, then he snatched the man by the coat collar and dragged him back into the room. Slamming him up against the wall, knocking a picture frame sideways he stared Blake straight in the eyes.

"This isn't the trenches, and I am not one of your men," he hissed at him. "So don't try and threaten me. I didn't spend four years up to my neck in Belgium mud to be intimidated by the likes of you. I survived that war, I fought it. If you want to discover just how tough I am you are going the right way about it."

Blake licked his lips, but had deflated. Like many a bully he was cowed by his victims retaliating. He gave another chuckle, this one more nervous.

"I don't doubt you are tough. Four years is nothing to be sniffed at."

Tommy released him and stepped back. They squared up eye-to-eye, but there was no fight in Blake.

"She wasn't a woman to lose your temper over," Blake said, still a slight smile to his face. He went out the door with no further word.

Tommy gave it a moment, then he stumbled back and had to hastily find a chair to sit down in. His legs had not appreciated his sudden action and felt shaky. He sat and caught his breath, realising he had come very close to striking Captain Blake. Where had that fury come from? Tommy shut his eyes and calmed himself. Blake had triggered something within him, something angry and terrible. But it was gone now and there was no harm done. If anything Blake would think twice about infuriating Tommy again. He took a deep breath. If nothing else he had learned something useful, something that would interest Clara. For if anyone seemed like the sort of person to murder their aunt it was Captain Blake.

Chapter Eighteen

The next morning the charabanc party were due to travel to Coniston Water and to explore the ancient ruins of Furness Abbey. Mr Wignell seemed back on form after his bout of the doldrums the day before. His confession to Clara had clearly eased his mind. He informed everyone at breakfast that Coniston Water was the third largest lake in the Lake District, a good five miles long and half a mile wide. It had two true islands and one partial island. This geographic information excited Mr Wignell a great deal and he delighted in telling anyone who would listen how the lake had been formed during the ice age by a glacier.

Clara had offered instructions to Tommy and Annie that it might be advisable to 'divide and conquer' during the drive to the lake. So they all agreed to discreetly spread themselves out on the charabanc and talk to someone else other than themselves. Tommy was still a little ruffled by his encounter with Captain Blake the night before, but since the Captain had not decided to join their expedition (in fact he had not come down to breakfast) he could try to relax and forget what had occurred. Clara had been quite firm in her assessment of Blake – after Tommy had explained what had happened – as an oaf and a fool. She was quite prepared to tell him so to his face if needs be. Tommy replied he would much rather see his lights knocked out. Clara mused on this and then stated that she was quite prepared to do that as well. Tommy gently informed her that if anyone was going to knock Captain Blake's lights out it would be him. He really didn't need his baby sister fighting his corner.

Clara found herself a seat on the charabanc next to Eleanora Smythe. There was a good reason for choosing to sit next to the bashful spinster – she had claimed to have received a box of marzipan fruits, just as Mrs Hunt had. Clara thought the box could be useful evidence. Untouched it might reveal if the fruits contained poison, and thus would lend substance to Mrs Hunt's earlier claims that someone had tried to poison her. Clara could only assume, as Miss Smythe seemed a very unlikely murder victim, that the poisoner had accidentally delivered the marzipan to the wrong room. It was intriguing to note that before Mrs Hunt insisted on a room change, she had been situated right next door to Miss Smythe.

Clara sat next to the woman who had already acquired the window seat.

"Oh," Miss Smythe glanced up as she sat down. "Miss Fitzgerald."

"You don't mind me sitting near you?" Clara asked with a smile. "We boarded a little late, you see, and have to spread ourselves about the seats."

"No, of course not, but if you would like me to move and allow you a seat for your brother, or friend…"

"Nonsense! I would never ask such a thing. You are clearly quite settled there. Please remain where you are."

The charabanc rolled off and took to its gentle perambulation of the country lanes.

"Are you enjoying your holiday Miss Smythe?" Clara asked her neighbour.

"I thought I would enjoy it more than I am," Miss Smythe admitted with a sigh.

"The tragedy on Monday rather dented the holiday

atmosphere," Clara nodded.

"Oh, it was before that…" Miss Smythe stopped herself and bit her lip. "Yes, Monday was awful."

Clara wondered what she had been about to say, but knew prying would not release the truth from such a cautious soul.

"Still, there are several more days to go and we shall endeavour to make the most of them," Clara said brightly. "I hear tell you had a small gift sent to your room?"

Miss Smythe looked at her blankly.

"Perhaps I was mistaken," Clara said apologetically. "I just wondered how one went about getting presented with a tin of marzipan fruits. I am rather fond of them."

"The fruits!" Miss Smythe suddenly understood, then she blushed furiously at having been so absent-minded in the first place. "I had quite forgotten mentioning it."

"You only seem able to buy them at Christmas usually," Clara continued as if she had not heard. "I really rather fancy some. Were they purchased locally?"

"I couldn't say," Miss Smythe was still blushing. "I really do not eat them."

"Then, might I be awful and ask to buy them off you?" Clara persisted. "I would be quite happy to offer you the value of the tin."

"Ah," Miss Smythe shook her head. "I threw them away, I do apologise. I do not eat them and someone told me that Mrs Hunt had taken ill after receiving a similar gift. I thought perhaps the batch was bad and disposed of them. It happens sometimes."

"What a shame," Clara did not need to feign disappointment, she had hoped the marzipan might have been part of the key to this mystery. "Perhaps the tin would have the name of the shop on it? Or the maker? So I might know where to purchase some."

"I… I gave the tin to one of the maids in the hotel," Miss Smythe said, looking flustered now. "She mentioned something about needing a new container for her pins and needles, so I offered her the tin."

"A very kindly act," Clara assured her.

Miss Smythe looked somewhat distressed by the conversation and Clara wondered if she had perhaps been too forceful with her questions. Perhaps Miss Smythe was one of those people who feel awful when they let others down, even when it is not their fault. Clara hoped she would not feel guilty that she had given away the tin before she could see it.

As it was, Miss Smythe was reluctant to make any more conversation for the rest of the journey and resigned herself to answering anything Clara said with little mumbles of assent or dissent, and nothing further. Clara had gained no further information by the time they reached Coniston Water.

The lake was truly beautiful. It was surrounded by tree covered slopes and glimmered in the sunlight. To the north-west rose the fells, including the one known as the Old Man of Coniston. The party were to spend a couple of hours admiring the lake, then they would reboard the charabanc and travel towards the coast and the ruins of Furness Abbey. It was going to be a long day as the trip to the abbey would take a good couple of hours and then they must travel all the way back. A hearty picnic had been provided by the hotel to sustain their guests' spirits.

Clara took out her new sketching book and found a suitable rock that she could prop herself on and observe the view. Folding back the cover of the sketching book and removing a pencil from the brass tin Tommy had given her, she settled to drawing, after all, this was her holiday too and she was entitled to a little break from investigating. She had been at this activity for about half an hour, and had a reasonable drawing forming on the paper – certainly nothing spectacular but respectable for an amateur – when she sensed that someone was standing behind her. She glanced up and saw Miss Plante staring over her shoulder. The old woman was quite short-sighted and had to peer through a pair of half-moon glasses balanced on the tip of her nose.

"Excuse my curiosity, Miss Fitzgerald," the old woman said, though clearly not in the least fazed by being noticed. "You draw well."

"I have not picked up a pencil in years," Clara responded, not being particularly unsettled by her observer.

"Might I ask how goes your investigation?" Miss Plante said, edging herself around the rock Clara sat on and lowering herself very genteelly to sit upon it. She was a bird-like creature, who looked fit to be blown away by the slightest breeze. She rested both hands, one atop the other, on the handle of her walking cane.

"Investigation?" Clara feigned ignorance.

"Please do not belittle me, Miss Fitzgerald. I know you are investigating the sudden demise of Mrs Hunt."

"What is there to investigate?" Clara answered honestly enough. "The woman appears to have drowned."

"And yet that in itself raises so many questions. Was she suicidal? Did she slip? Why did she not call for help? I was not in any sense fond of the woman, I met her only on Saturday and it struck me that she was one of those individuals who delights in making the world a little more unpleasant for her fellow human being," Miss Plante allowed herself a small smile. "But she was also an old woman, as am I, and I don't like the idea of people going about assuming they can do away with old women, even when they are cantankerous and rude."

"I don't think Mrs Hunt's age was a consideration in the matter," Clara said lightly. "That is, if she was murdered, and I might add the police do not think that the case."

"And of course the police know everything," Miss Plante said with just the right amount of sarcasm in her tone that you could almost have missed it if you had not been paying attention. "You are investigating Miss Fitzgerald, of that I am certain. I witnessed your quiet conversation with Mr Wignell. His daughter's death, so similar to that of Mrs Hunt, was tragic and I could quite understand if he resented the woman."

Clara looked up sharply.

"I am partially deaf, Miss Fitzgerald," Miss Plante waved a hand at her ear. "I lip-read very well and it masks my disability. I watched Mr Wignell's mouth as he talked. He forms his words very precisely and with a great deal of movement of the lips. I gathered the essence of your conversation."

"You will not share the information?" Clara asked her.

"Of course not! I consider such things a private matter, and I am the soul of discretion. But, you see, it made me wonder just who else might have known Mrs Hunt before seeing her on this charabanc."

"That I cannot answer."

"But you are looking into the matter?"

Clara conceded in the face of the woman's determination, even if she said she was not Miss Plante would not believe her, so why lie?

"Yes, I am investigating."

"On whose behalf?"

"Mrs Hunt's," Clara said simply. "She asked for my assistance before she passed. She feared someone intended her harm."

"I see," Miss Plante rested her chin on her hands and stared out over the water. "Strange how life tends to catch up with one. The deeds we perform in our youth and which we forget about so easily, have a tendency to find one again when age has cast its withering spell upon you. No one tells the young this, yet it is a most valuable and worthwhile lesson. Imagine if we lived our younger years with the knowledge that our actions will one day seek us out and pay us back for our sins?"

"That is a sad thought, for the last few years have seen many commit awful sins," Clara noted.

"It is a thought that I think haunted Mrs Hunt constantly," Miss Plante said solemnly. "The old tend to seek each other out. I spoke with her the night before she died. I found her a most disagreeable creature but, at the same time, I sensed that she had a burning desire to make amends. The problem was, her wickedness was so ingrown that she found it hard to prevent it spilling out. So she offended others without even giving it a thought. That is the sadness of it all. I hope she is at peace now, though perhaps many would not."

Miss Plante raised herself stiffly from the rock.

"What makes you seek out the truth, Miss Fitzgerald? It cannot be for a love of the woman."

"It is for a love of justice," Clara said calmly. "Murder, under most circumstances, is a most vile act. Perhaps Mrs Hunt threw herself in the lake, or fell in by accident, but I fear someone wished her harm and harm has now befallen her. I find myself coming to only one conclusion, that a murder has been committed and a woman has perished just at the moment she appears to have been trying to make amends for her past misdeeds. That cannot be allowed to stand."

"And what if you find the murderer was justified? Perhaps performing their own undeniable justice?"

Clara considered this for a while, the water of the lake rippling a short distance away and the birds chattering in the trees.

"I think that unlikely, but, as you know, I am not the police and I can make my own decisions on the subject."

"Very well," Miss Plante gave her a sage smile, one that spoke of indulgence and the amusement of seeing the young work out a problem she had long ago solved. "Very well. Enjoy your drawing. You are, honestly, very good at it."

Miss Plante hobbled away. Clara watched her leave and then tried to turn her mind back to her sketching, but the impetus had gone. She could not find the energy or the concentration to finish. She tapped the pencil on the side of the book and looked away into the distance, at Old Man Coniston and the other fells. Was there a killer among them? Clara feared so. But, if there was, the motive remained a mystery. Why had Mrs Hunt died?

That question rang in Clara's mind and prevented any thought of drawing.

Chapter Nineteen

The tour party turned their attention to the afternoon's excursion. The driver bustled them back aboard the charabanc just on eleven o'clock in the morning, tapping at his watch and clearly concerned that their diversion might take a considerable length of time. He even risked taking the charabanc to 30mph on the long stretches to get them there sooner.

The passengers were less concerned. They had been supplied with ample lunches in individual baskets and contented themselves on enjoying the contents and remarking on the fine nature of the weather. Once lunch was consumed and there was a risk of boredom setting in, the conductor stood up and, while holding on to the support pole just behind the driver's seat, he regaled them with a potted history of Furness Abbey.

"While it may be somewhat out of our way, the abbey is worth our attention as one of the great ancient monuments of Britain," he stated, swaying to the left as the charabanc took a corner. "Furness was established as a monastery in 1123 and passed to the Cistercians in 1147. The ruins are made of sandstone and largely date from the original construction in the twelfth and thirteenth centuries. It became one of the richest monasteries in the country, but was sadly destroyed during Henry VIII's dissolution of the monasteries.

"For those of you partial to folklore, there are legends of a tunnel under the abbey which hides both the Holy Grail and the lost jewels of King John. And, if you are of a sensitive nature, do mind the sandstone arch near the abbey tavern, where the ghost of a headless monk on horseback is said to appear."

The party gave a suitable chuckle of derision at this conclusion to the otherwise factual history. But the brief talk had served its purpose and gave the passengers something to think about and discuss for the remainder of the journey.

Clara had not sat next to Miss Smythe again. The woman seemed to be positively avoiding her and had wedged herself beside Mrs Crimp. Clara found she was restored to her friends and sat on the long bench at the back of the charabanc next to Annie and Tommy. Annie asked after Clara's drawing, and Clara produced the book and the half completed image.

"Miss Plante distracted me," Clara said to excuse her unfinished composition. "She is very curious about this matter."

"Aren't we all?" Tommy noted. "There must be an inquest soon. You and Annie will have to give evidence."

"Oh, tosh!" Annie declared stoutly, being actually utterly appalled by the idea of standing up before a host of strangers and talking. "They won't need that for a drowning, will they?"

"All unexplained deaths are put before an inquest to determine, by jury, the cause, or whether further measures must be taken," Clara broke the news to her gently.

Annie pulled a face.

"I shan't be going to it, in any case," Annie muttered.

"I'm afraid, old love, you won't have a choice," Tommy squeezed her hand and tried to soften the blow. "Hopefully they will have the sense to hold it before we all have to go back to Brighton."

Clara said nothing. She didn't want there to be an inquest before she had a handle on her own investigations.

The charabanc pulled up near the abbey ruins in the early afternoon. The sun was still shining and the party were quite jolly as they disembarked. Clara took up her sketching book, determined to make some drawings of the ruins which were nothing if not picturesque. Tommy and Annie declared they were going to wander around and examine the old stone rooms. Clara set herself on a piece of fallen masonry and eyed up a large arched window that she supposed had once contained medieval stained glass. Now it just gaped open, framing a section of wall and the branches of a tree. Clara stared at it for a while, deciding which angle might make the most attractive drawing, and then set to work.

She had barely constructed the outline of the window in faint strokes of lead when she was disturbed.

"Miss Fitzgerald?"

Clara restrained a sigh and looked up. Beside her stood Madeline Reeve, the pretty girl who looked straight off the page of a fashion magazine. She had her hair crimped in the latest style and was tastefully ornamented with kohl about the eyes. Clara's mind swept back to the receptionist at the hotel who had attempted the same effect and failed dreadfully. Where hers had looked false and gaudy, Madeleine's make-up looked natural and perfectly composed for her face. She was slender enough to carry off the current fashions for straight-waists, and she was wearing a smart green dress and matching shoes. She had white lace gloves on her hands and a parasol open and resting on her shoulder, preventing the sun from colouring her pale as snow skin. In short, Madeleine was the sort of woman who, without apparent effort, was able to look perfect at all times, and who annoyed Clara simply for this.

Clara had to admit she was never going to be the

slenderest of creatures. She was not fat, but she had decided curves which were completely out of fashion. She was not inclined to cut her hair skimpily short and she had never had much mastery of make-up. Clara was never going to be a fashion model and a part of her resented those women who, without a pinch of sacrifice, achieved what she could not and flaunted it. That did not mean she disliked Miss Reeve, far from it. She just desired to feed her cake, a lot of it.

"Miss Reeve," Clara set her sketching book down, she sensed this was going to be a long conversation. As she looked over her shoulder at Madeleine she noticed that Edwin Hope was also present and looking anxious. He was smoking like there was no tomorrow.

"I must speak with you at once," Madeleine Reeve continued. "I overheard Miss Plante talking with you and I think it most important I explain my position to you."

"This isn't necessary, Maddy," Edwin Hope gruffed from behind them.

"It is Teddy. We can't ignore the fact that Mrs Hunt has passed in strange circumstances. I heard that you are investigating the matter Miss Fitzgerald?"

Clara gave an inward sigh. So the cat was out of the bag.

"Before she passed Mrs Hunt asked me to investigate her fears that someone wished her harm," she admitted.

"I suppose it seems she was right," Madeleine said. "And you are looking to see who might have had cause to hurt her?"

"In essence, yes," Clara nodded.

"I thought the police were calling this an accident," Edwin Hope interrupted, sounding most unamused by the whole affair.

"The police can think as they please," Clara said carefully. "My duty is to Mrs Hunt and if it happens I turn up something that changes the circumstances of her death and causes the police to reassess the case, so be it."

It had not slipped Clara's notice that the names of both

Edwin Hope and Madeleine Reeve had featured on Mrs Hunt's list. As much as she would have liked a quiet afternoon to enjoy the vistas of Furness Abbey and her drawing, she could not pass up this opportunity to speak to potential suspects.

"What would you like to talk about, Miss Reeve?" she asked the girl who stood beside her. She was probably no more than twenty or twenty-one, while Hope was a few years her senior. They were perhaps lovers, certainly they seemed an obvious match.

"As I say I overheard Miss Plante talking to you, not that I was eavesdropping, it was simply that I was passing along the bank and there is a little stand of gorse bushes which quite masks a person from sight," Madeleine Reeve hesitated. "I heard you talking about justice and investigating the circumstances of Mrs Hunt's death. I heard you say that while you had no affection for the woman, you still cared to find out the truth. And I heard Miss Plante mention how murder could be justifiable."

"Rarely is murder justifiable," Clara told her calmly. "Self-defence being, perhaps, the only time murder can be considered an option. Might you care to explain why this troubles you so Miss Reeve? Did you happen to know Mrs Hunt before this trip?"

Madeleine Reeve pulled a face, showing that the very name of that woman was disagreeable.

"That is what I wish to discuss. Mrs Hunt was known to both myself and Edwin, in quite unfortunate circumstances. It struck me that were you to become aware of these circumstances you might naturally wonder if either myself or Teddy had reason to murder the woman."

"That is a very serious statement," Clara said, a touch surprised by the declaration. "But, if it helps you to speak, I might add that Mrs Hunt had constructed a list of names and yours was on it."

"A list of suspects?" Edwin Hope spluttered, his

cigarette tumbling from his mouth.

"I did not say that. I just said that Mrs Hunt had written out a list of names that were clearly significant to her. Exactly what that significance was now eludes me."

"Then perhaps I can shed some light on the matter," Madeleine Reeve said, while behind her Hope groped in the grass for his lost cigarette. "Mrs Hunt was known to me and to Teddy, because, many years ago, she was my governess."

Clara nodded. Mrs Hunt had mentioned working in schools and was a tutor to the late daughter of the Wignells. That she had also tutored Miss Reeve came as no real surprise.

"I should here state how much I detested the woman. She was most awful and to a child as young as I was seemed quite a tyrant. She ruled my little schoolroom with a wicked hand. I was not allowed to talk during lessons unless asked a direct question. I was not to fidget. I was to keep a clean workbook and avoid ink smuts and smudges. She would beat my hand with a ruler when I failed in this. Should I falter in any of my lessons, or be slow in my work I was denied meals, which she imagined would cure my tardiness. She took no consideration of the fact that some of the work was beyond me, or that I had failed to understand the lesson. No. All errors on my part were due to idleness or defiance, and so were to be punished," Madeleine Reeve paused, the memories of those dark years filling her with sadness. "I was alone in this torment, though Edwin is my brother, he is older by some years and was already away at school."

Edwin, at this introduction, placed a comforting hand on his sister's shoulder.

"Had I known how my sister suffered I would have done something, Miss Fitzgerald," he said firmly.

Clara thought the sentiment very loyal and honourable, but rather doubted there was much Edwin could have done. There were not so many years between him and his sister, despite Madeleine's words. He would have been but a boy during that time.

"If Mrs Hunt had merely been my despicable governess I don't suppose all these years later I would be giving it much thought," Madeleine continued. "Many girls have awful governesses, but they don't go about killing them. Not that I killed her, but supposing you are looking for motive…"

"I understand," Clara said swiftly, seeing the panic on Madeleine's face.

The girl relaxed.

"Mrs Hunt did far worse to me and Teddy. You see, my mother and father were besotted with one another, so much that they hardly noticed their children. I resented that too as a child, especially when Teddy was at school and I felt very alone. Then, a terrible thing happened, my father was thrown from his horse and died. My mother was beside herself with grief. She had no friends in the county, for her life revolved around my father and her family were far away and not much inclined to come down and mourn with her. After the inevitable funeral she was left alone with her sorrows and turned to the only person in the house who was not precisely a servant – my governess, Mrs Hunt.

"She would ask Mrs Hunt to have tea with her in her room and there she would talk about my father. I sometimes used to slip and sit outside the door and listen to them, for there was nothing else to do in the afternoons and Mrs Hunt would merely set me some reading while she went to tea. I think at first she appreciated the privilege and indulgence of this afternoon ritual. It made her feel above the other servants and special. But she was not a kind woman and gradually my mother's talk of my father and her constant sorrow wore down Mrs Hunt's patience.

"I remember sitting outside the door to the drawing room one day and overhearing them. My mother was weeping and saying that maybe she ought to kill herself too, so she might be with my father, rather than living with her grief. That was one of her regular refrains. She was always talking about killing herself. Usually Mrs Hunt placated her, but on that day she was clearly sick of the talk and, forgetting her station, she informed my mother quite boldly that perhaps it would be best for all of them if she did. Why not, she told my mother, why not do it?

"There was an awful silence after that and I feared someone might be coming to the door, so I ran away. Later that afternoon my mother went to the little pavilion in the garden and hung herself."

Madeleine took a very shaky breath, her words had become heavy with emotion as she spoke.

"I am so very sorry," Clara said gently, meaning every word. Having lost her own parents, she knew the toll it took. Admittedly she had been an adult when they had passed in tragic circumstances, the lost to a child had to be wholly greater.

"You cannot imagine the turmoil it caused," Edwin Hope had taken up the thread of the story. His face was set in a rigid expression of grief. "Mrs Hunt took charge of the proceedings, no doubt people were grateful for that. We had no grandparents, they were deceased, so we had to be sent away to various distant relations. Cousins, and such. Mrs Hunt ensured we were legally adopted by these relatives, perhaps she thought that was her duty. Our names were changed to match our new families. Maddy went to one end of the country, I to the other and for many years we had no knowledge of where the other was. Can you imagine the cruelty? To have just lost both parents and then to be torn from one another?"

Madeleine clutched her fingers to her mouth, as if she might allow a sob to escape otherwise. Her gaze, however, was far from emotional when she looked up at Clara.

"For that we hated Mrs Hunt. It took Teddy months to track me down once he came of age and was allowed the legal freedom to do so. The authorities kept things very hushed and the cousins he had been sent to did not speak with the cousins I was with. It must have seemed nearly impossible."

"It was nearly impossible," Teddy admitted. "The lawyers were cagey because Maddy was under twenty-one and they wanted me to prove who I was. That meant getting the adoption papers off my new parents and having to explain what I was about. They were not best pleased because they had never seen eye-to-eye with the branch of the family who had adopted Maddy. They didn't want anything to do with them and feared me trying to track them down would result in just that. It was a nightmare, and Mrs Hunt was at the heart of it all."

"It must have come as a shock, then, to board the charabanc and see your nemesis sitting there," Clara said, having an idea of the response she would get.

"Not precisely," Madeleine spoke, she had composed herself and was no longer in danger of shedding tears. "You see, Mrs Hunt wrote to us both, actually sent us the tickets for this trip. She said she wanted to make up for her past sins. I thought that an odd word for her to use. Mrs Hunt was never very religious."

"She sent the tickets to our adopted parents' homes. I suppose that was the only means she had of contacting us," Teddy added. "They passed the tickets and the accompanying letters on to us. I must admit I felt very angry reading those letters."

"I was angry too," Madeleine was not to be left out of expressing her feelings on Mrs Hunt. "However, the woman's letter was so pleading and apologetic that I thought we must come. It sounded so much in the letter as if she was dying."

"Only, when we boarded the charabanc, she didn't even seem to recognise us," Teddy shook his head. "Let alone try and apologise. I don't know, maybe when she saw us she no longer felt able to speak."

"Or perhaps she really didn't recognise you. It must have been several years since she last saw either of you, and people change considerably as they grow," Clara suggested.

Edwin Hope and Madeleine Reeve exchanged a look, perhaps trying to assess how much they had changed since all those years ago.

"I imagine the purpose of this conversation was to press upon me your innocence in all matters concerning Mrs Hunt's accident?" Clara decided to take the hunt to them. They were suspects after all and had just made a very strong case for motive.

"Neither of us laid a finger on the woman!" Madeleine said sternly, clearly alarmed by Clara's suggestion.

"We knew you were investigating this matter, and it seemed wiser to own up to our association than to let you discover it and wonder what we had to hide," Edwin quickly interjected. "We were with each other at the time Mrs Hunt died, anyway."

Clara merely smiled, well aware of how insubstantial their alibi was. After all, they were both suspects and any sensible barrister would point out that it was to their advantage to alibi each other. To do anything else would be odd. It didn't prove much. If they had killed Mrs Hunt, they could just as easily have done it together.

"We just wanted to explain," Madeleine reiterated, looking as though she regretted the idea completely. "Mrs Hunt caused us a lot of hurt, but we did not kill her. It would be ridiculous for us to come all this way, to effect a reconciliation, and then to murder her."

Clara said nothing, thinking that she could imagine many things more ridiculous. In some regards, travelling all this way to apparently forgive Mrs Hunt, could easily be a cover for murder. Very easily.

Madeleine Reeve was already walking away. Edwin Hope held Clara's eye a moment longer, as if he was about to speak again, then he too turned and walked away. Clara thought their story curious, but not improbable, especially as Mrs Hunt had attempted to make amends with both the Wignells and Captain Blake in the exact same manner. It was starting to seem as if she had almost organised this charabanc tour as a means of making peace with her past. Had Mrs Hunt suddenly developed a conscience?

Clara went back to her sketching, wondering at how people continued to surprise her. And then again, how they did not…

Chapter Twenty

They were all very tired on the homeward journey. The temptation was to doze and Mr Wignell could not resist. His big head flopped back and he snored loudly. His wife clearly disapproved, but seemed unable to bring herself to rouse him. Clara sat next to Annie. Tommy had taken the seat behind them and, as there was no one to join him on it, had stretched out on it. He had his head wedged between the window and the back of the seat and was seemingly dozing.

Annie offered Clara a fruit flavoured boiled sweet from a packet she had bought back at their very first stop. Clara noted the name on the paper bag.

"I don't suppose you saw tins of marzipan fruits in there?" she said.

"Oh yes," Annie replied. "There was a little display of them."

"And did you see anyone from the charabanc party buying one?"

Annie shook her head.

"Sorry, Clara, I wasn't looking."

"Of course you weren't," Clara smiled at her reassuringly. "No one had been harmed then."

The charabanc took an awfully long time to reach the

hotel and it was dusk when they arrived. The driver pulled the vehicle up into the parking space he had been designated, a short walk from the front door. Clara nudged Tommy awake and they all hopped off the charabanc, quite ready for dinner.

Clara noted that there was another car near the entrance to the hotel. It was a black thing, rather formal looking. It reminded her of the single police car the Brighton Constabulary possessed and used on special occasions – usually crimes which the inspector could not reach swiftly on foot or bicycle. The sight of a car was so unusual that Clara peered into the driver's window as they walked past. She couldn't see much inside, which made her wonder even more.

They strolled into the hotel foyer and at once came to a halt at the scene before them. Inspector Gateley was talking to Mr Stover, while policemen in uniform were loitering around, clearly waiting for an order to be given. On one of the foyer sofas a maid was seated, crying her eyes out, while another put her arm around her and tried to comfort her. Clara took in the spectacle in a glance. It was plain some calamity had occurred, and only recently judging by the maid's demeanour. Clara was about to ask the obvious question when the lift gave off a very tinny ping, and the heavy metal gates were pulled back by a police officer inside. Then, rather awkwardly, for the space was not large, a stretcher was manhandled out of the lift. The body on it – for it could only be a body – was covered from head to foot by a white sheet.

Everyone paused to watch the body being processed out of the hotel. Mr Stover peered around Inspector Gateley, clearly agog. He was probably still in shock that such drama could affect his hotel. The maid looked up and gave a slight shriek. The body was clumsily manoeuvred out the door and towards a police mortuary carriage that was just pulling up outside. Clara decided explanations were in order.

"Mr Stover, who has just been carried out of your

hotel?" she walked over to the hotel manager, completely ignoring the presence of Inspector Gateley.

"And here stands before me another of my woes!" Stover said as he saw Clara. "Perhaps, madam, you would care to leave this crime to the police?"

Clara turned her attention to Inspector Gately.

"Has there been a crime committed? I admit something must have attracted you all here, but are we talking murder?"

"Miss Fitzgerald, as you were not present today while the incident was unfurling, I have no interest in talking with you," Inspector Gateley said with equal bluntness, and a slight hint of a smile.

Clara glanced back at Mr Stover, but his tight lips told her she would get no information from that quarter. It was then she spotted Dr Masters coming down the stairs carrying his medical bag. As the only doctor in the building it seemed a reasonable assumption to imagine he had been called to check over the person who had just left the hotel quite dead. Clara made her way to him.

"What has happened, Dr Masters?" she asked softly, catching the doctor's arm.

He looked strained, as if he had just seen things he would rather not.

"I need a brandy," he told her.

They went into the hotel's lounge where there was a bar. Masters ordered a large brandy and glanced at Clara to see if she wanted anything. She shook her head.

"A little early," she answered.

"It is too early for whisky, not too early for brandy," Dr Masters corrected. He took the drink the barman offered him and drained it in two large gulps. Then he motioned that they should walk to the window where they could talk without being overheard.

The window looked into the gardens and in the dusk Clara could see other guests from the charabanc milling on the lawn, upset by what they had seen and uncertain if they were to be allowed back in for dinner. Clara suspected the latter worry troubled them the most.

"There will be a run on the spirits tonight," Dr Masters mused, watching the clutches of guests wandering around. "I was called to examine the body."

"I guessed as much," Clara said. "Who was it?"

"I didn't know him," Masters shrugged. "Mr Stover had to identify him. He said he was a man named Captain Arthur Blake."

Clara actually jumped at hearing the name. It was so utterly unexpected that it stunned her for an instant.

"Did you know him?" Masters asked.

"Only in connection with the sudden death of Mrs Hunt. Also, he was rather rude to Tommy."

"Well he won't be rude to anyone ever again," Dr Masters said with morbid humour. "I think I need another drink. Only the second time I have attended a suicide."

"Suicide?" Clara said, knowing the colour was draining from her face as she spoke.

"Seems that way," Masters waved his hand at the barman and called out his order for another brandy. "Hanged himself from the light fixing with his own belt. I'd never seen a hanged man before. I had read about the effects on the body, but to see it was so much different."

"I can imagine," Clara's mind flicked back to a recent case where she had come across such a suicide. The image of the man's swollen and reddened face, his tongue jarred out of his mouth and his eyes bulging from their sockets would not leave her in a hurry. "But what an odd thing. Why would that young man take his own life?"

Dr Masters said nothing until his brandy had been placed in his hand and he had drunk half of it.

"That is not my field of knowledge," he said. "I specialise in looking after the living. I imagine those uniforms back there will be the ones solving the riddle."

"If Inspector Gately takes an interest. Was the coroner called?"

"Yes. He came to the room a little while after I arrived and pronounced the man dead. He concurred with my assessment, well, it was hardly difficult. The man had hung there so long he was rigid."

Clara started to think about timescales. The body had perhaps hung there all day, allowing plenty of time for rigour mortis to set in. Blake must have killed himself that morning.

"Did he leave a note?"

"I hardly looked for one," Dr Masters finished his brandy. "Are you seeing his suicide as connected to that of Mrs Hunt?"

Clara did not correct his inference that Mrs Hunt had killed herself.

"From what Tommy told me, Captain Blake was struggling to adjust to civilian life, or at least gave that appearance. He was alone in this world, his parents being dead."

"How depressing," Masters glared at his empty tumbler, but the desire to order another was overridden by his common sense. "The door was locked from the inside, if that means anything to you. I know it is the sort of thing that creates a riddle in a detective novel. How was a man murdered if the door was locked?"

"In general, it usually means there was no murder," Clara said, though she had to admit that on at least one occasion that had proved a misleading conclusion. "Blake was probably just another tortured soul come back from the war. How many of those have we seen?"

"Too many," Dr Masters agreed. "In any case, I really ought to see my genuine patient. She has probably spotted all this excitement from her window and is wondering what is going."

Masters put down his brandy glass with a tut at himself. It had been unprofessional to have two. His patient would smell it on his breath. He left Clara by the window.

What Clara wanted was to get inside Captain Blake's room and see for herself what had occurred. She had no faith in the Inspector, though she was not particularly thinking this was anything but a tragic suicide. She was more curious as to the why, than the how. Was Captain Blake's death connected to that of his aunt? That was always a possibility. Clara mused over her possible moves a moment longer. The one person who might be of use to her, who might actually listen to her concerns, was the local coroner, and it seemed likely he was still up in Captain Blake's room. Clara made up her mind. Before the Inspector had time to banish her from this case, she had to act. She abandoned the lounge and went in search of Captain Blake's room and the scene of the crime.

Chapter Twenty-one

Clara headed upstairs, avoiding the attention of Inspector Gateley. He was busy grilling Mr Stover still, the latter appearing quite distraught. Two of his hotel guests had apparently committed suicide. It was most alarming.

Clara was uncertain which floor Captain Blake's room was on, but as the policemen who had brought down his body had clearly travelled some distance in the elevator, she assumed it was the third, or possibly fourth. She actually had to travel up to the fifth floor before she came upon the source of all the disturbance. It was obvious when she stepped off the landing that this was the correct floor, for a start there was a policeman just heading to the stairs. Clara gave him a polite nod as he passed her. He did not enquire about her business and was soon heading down. The corridor was otherwise empty, presumably all the other guests on this floor had been tactfully removed while the body was being examined and carried away.

Clara walked along the corridor, pausing at the only open doorway. She looked in to see a bedroom, much like all the other bedrooms in the hotel – a large bed slightly offset from the centre of the room, a nice picture window overlooking the beautiful scenery, a substantial armchair, a dresser, a wardrobe and a bedside cabinet, and a small fireplace. It all looked very cosy and comforting. Had Clara not just learned of what had occurred here, she could not have guessed.

The coroner was standing in the centre of the room, thoughtfully studying a three-armed light fixture set in the middle of the ceiling. His black doctor's bag was sitting at his side, still open. The remains of a brown leather belt, that had been recently cut through, lay on the floor beside the coroner's slickly polished black shoes. As Clara watched, he bent down and picked up the fragments and deposited them in a brown paper bag.

"Good afternoon, Miss Fitzgerald," the police surgeon said, glancing at her at last.

"I heard the news," Clara explained. "Was it suicide?"

"An inquest will determine that, but it looks very much like it. Captain Blake had looped his belt about his neck tightly. He stood on the armchair to reach this fitting and unscrewed one of the light shades, as you can see here," the coroner indicated the missing shade. Without it the arm of the light fixture revealed that it was a gas fitting, and the spoke where the gas emerged and could be ignited to light the room was visible. "The wide buckle of the belt was just big enough to slip over this arm. It rested here, where the brass pipe has been clearly crushed. That was from the weight of Captain Blake hanging off it. With his noose arranged, Blake stepped off the armchair and slowly throttled to death."

Clara grimaced, it was not a pretty ending. She imagined how the thick edge of the belt must have cut into the man's chin as he tortuously suffocated.

"How long would it have taken?" she asked, though she rather felt she did not want to know.

"Such slow suffocation takes a considerable time," the coroner was looking at the light fixture again. "Anything from ten minutes to even an hour, though that is quite an extreme case. Most likely he was unconscious within half an hour, and dead a little after."

The coroner gave her a stern look.

"Why are you up here Miss Fitzgerald?"

"Because I am concerned, very concerned," Clara answered. "It may not, as yet, have come to the police's attention that Captain Blake was Mrs Hunt's nephew."

"How extraordinary," the coroner tapped a finger on his lip absent-mindedly. "That does not give you cause to be up here, however."

"I thought it might be possible to talk with you," Clara said, aiming to mollify the man. "Inspector Gateley has no time for me, but I hoped you might. Before she passed Mrs Hunt was concerned someone meant her harm and she had asked me to look into it. I have been following her wishes, even though she is now free of this mortal coil. In that capacity I discovered Captain Blake. And now he is dead too. I really don't like coincidences, do you doctor?"

The coroner smiled at Clara.

"Dr Frederick Macguire," he introduced himself. "I suppose this place has a lounge where one might purchase a drink?"

"Yes. Downstairs."

"Then, I suggest we retire there and I shall see if I can put your mind at ease about these events."

Clara thought that unlikely, but she agreed to his terms. Dr Macguire placed the paper bag of evidence in his medical bag and went downstairs with Clara. They avoided the foyer and ended up back in the room where Clara had just so recently spoken with Dr Masters.

Dr Macguire ordered himself a glass of tonic water and Clara asked for lemonade. They took their drinks and seated themselves near the window. Dr Macguire seemed very jolly for a man who has just witnessed such a hideous scene, quite the contrast from Dr Masters, though Clara supposed he had witnessed a lot worse in his time as coroner.

"It is rather unusual for me to be called upon twice in the same week," Dr Macguire said, taking a sip of water. "I have my own small practice which holds my attention when I am not engaged with the police, which is much of the time. This is a nice, rural district. Very quiet, very little crime."

He seemed to emphasis this last statement as if making a point. Clara decided to ignore it.

"Has there been a post-mortem of Mrs Hunt, as yet?"

"There has. I conducted it. She was drowned. Water in the lungs."

"Any signs she struggled?"

"No."

"You see, that is what concerns me," Clara shook her head. "If you or I were to fall into a lake and start to drown, we would surely try to save ourselves?"

"Unless we wished to drown," Dr Macguire pointed out.

"Or we were unconscious and could not save ourselves," Clara countered. "Mrs Hunt did not strike me as a suicidal woman."

"Many people who take their own lives present as the sort of people who would not do such a thing," Dr Macguire argued. "Always at the inquest the loved ones get up and state that their dearly departed was simply not the sort to do away with themselves."

"Perhaps on occasion they are right?"

"In my experience, those who truly contemplate taking their own lives keep the fact very secret and put on a very normal façade for all around to see."

Clara knew this argument was getting her nowhere, so she changed direction.

"Was anything found on Mrs Hunt's body or nearby?"

"She had her purse in a pocket, so she was not robbed if that is your thinking."

"It was not, but please carry on."

"There was a handkerchief in the other pocket and that was it."

Dr Macguire took a long drink of his tonic water.

"I have never seen a less suspicious death," he concluded.

"But it is curious that attempts had been made on Mrs Hunt's life before she died, and that now her nephew, her sole living relative, is also deceased."

"Remind me again of these 'attempts'," Macguire asked.

"Mrs Hunt was sent poisoned sweets, sadly there are none remaining to examine, but it is apparent that Mrs Hunt briefly 'died' two days before her actual death. If the sweets were poisoned, she had a lucky escape. Mrs Hunt's medical history does not indicate that she should be prone to sudden collapse, in fact her only illness was not a life-threatening one."

"What condition was that?" Macguire interrupted.

"Parkinson's. In the very early stages, so, as I stated before, not currently life-threatening."

"Indeed. You have been actively studying this case. Do go on."

"The second incident had the appearances of an accident, but coupled with the previous night's misadventure it takes on a new light," Clara took a breath. "Mrs Hunt was climbing the stairs in this hotel to go to her room, a room she insisted on changing to from her original one, when a chamber pot came flying down from above and struck her on the head."

Dr Macguire stifled a chortle.

"I apologise, it is not amusing, yet it does rather sound like a skit from a play. Death by chamber pot is a new one on me."

"Mrs Hunt survived this encounter too. But it is rather mysterious, considering the chamber pot is unlikely to have been simply dropped by accident. To fling it down the stairs would require it to be thrown, or lifted over the high bannisters."

"I will admit Mrs Hunt appears to have attracted dreadful luck. But I honestly can say that there is no evidence of foul play at her actual death. If someone had held her down in the water, I would have expected to find bruising where they had gripped her. If they struck her before she went into the water, then I should expect to find a wound or bump on the back of the head. There is nothing of the sort."

"And what if they gave her something that sedated her?" Clara pressed. "Something to render her unconscious before she tumbled in? This killer has demonstrated themselves a poisoner once already."

"Let us pause for a moment and ask ourselves another question," Macguire held up a finger. "Supposing Mrs Hunt was murdered, are we imagining the deed was committed by her nephew who is now also deceased? Perhaps inferring that he suffered from a guilty conscience and hung himself out of regret."

"That possibility has crossed my mind," Clara admitted. "Though Captain Blake had no love-loss for the woman, and nor was he a stranger to death. For his conscience to suddenly get the better of him strikes me as unlikely, though not impossible."

"Well, I shall see what my post-mortem presents to me, but for the moment it seems very straightforward. The room was locked from the inside, after all, the key was on the bedside table. Had not a maid been sent up to change the sheets and let herself in with the master key, no one would have known," Dr Macguire drained his glass. "Unless we propose the killer clambered out of the window, on the fifth floor of this establishment, no less, then I think we can exclude someone else being involved."

Dr Macguire rose and collected his medical bag. He gave her a nod as he departed the lounge. Clara sighed as he went, feeling she had not even come a step further forward. She was about to leave, when the strange, emaciated girl she had noticed at breakfast the other day suddenly appeared.

She looked just as waif-like as before, there seemed not an ounce of flesh on her bones. She was almost painful to look at. She drifted over to the window and looked out at the guests still milling on the lawn of the hotel. Then her eyes drifted to Clara.

"What has happened?" she asked.

"A man has killed himself," Clara answered, realising this was the first time she had heard the waif speak. It was a surprisingly strong voice, not thin nor weak as her appearance might have suggested.

"John looked most distressed," the girl said, almost under her breath, but Clara heard it nonetheless. "At least this means I have a good reason to avoid dinner."

Clara studied the girl for a moment, then an observation sprang into her mind.

"You don't like food, or rather, eating, do you?" she said.

The girl gave her a gentle smile.

"No, not really."

Then she drifted away as silently as she had arrived, exiting out of the door like a ghost that had barely been there at all. Clara watched her go with all her curiosity aroused. Could the John she mentioned be one and the same as Dr Masters? What an intriguing thought. Perhaps the good doctor had more than one patient in the hotel?

Chapter Twenty-two

Upon seeing the calamity in the hotel foyer, Annie had quickly shuffled herself and Tommy out of the way. Clara was clearly going to take an interest, but that did not mean they all had to get involved. Tommy had protested, but Annie hushed him, reminding him that sometimes it was more prudent to sit back and observe rather than ask questions.

"Let Clara poke her nose in," she said. "While we watch what happens from the side lines."

Annie had one thought in particular on her mind, and it involved the little maid who was clearly distressed by whatever had gone on while they were out. The girl was being comforted by another maid, but it wasn't long before Mr Stover could no longer abide seeing his hotel in an uproar, and told the other maid to return to her duties. Dinner had to be served on time. Rooms had to be swept, dusted, and the bed sheets changed. There were living people to worry about.

The distressed maid was left all alone, virtually ignored, even by the police who had already dragged a sobbing statement out of her about how she had opened the room door and seen Captain Blake hanging. She howled pathetically into her hanky. It was now Annie 'poked her nose in'.

"There, there, hush now," she sat herself next to the girl and put a very gentle hand on her shoulder. "It's been an awful shock. Has anyone brought you tea?"

The maid shook her head. She was about sixteen, a stocky little thing, working class and with only a limited charity school education to tide her over. The events of that afternoon were all rather beyond her.

"Right, you are coming with me. You need hot tea and something to eat, nothing worse than shock for the appetite," Annie told her robustly. Annie believed that a good meal was the cure for almost all ailments. "Direct me to the kitchens and don't worry about a guest helping you, now. In everyday life I am more like you than one of these charabanc folk."

Bridging no objection, she had the girl show her towards the servants' quarters. She put her arm through that of the little maid's and half-supported her as they stumbled towards the hotel kitchens where it would be possible to make tea.

"So sorry, miss," the maid sniffled. "My legs has quite gone to jelly."

"No matter," Annie reassured her. "That is why I am here."

Like most big buildings where catering and other services were required, the servants' area of the hotel was vast and labyrinthine. Pointless little sets of stairs let down two paces into a corridor before, further along, another short set let back up again. Doors led off into rooms or more hallways, many had internal glass windows to allow natural light to filter into otherwise unlit rooms.

The little maid directed their progress in-between taking little sniffles, for she was still on the verge of tears. Annie managed to extract her name from her as they were traversing a long corridor with a heavy door set at the end. It was Mary Sharp. The girl was from Windermere and came in everyday to clean rooms and make the beds. She had never seen someone dead before.

"Once I caught this little old lady naked," Mary said as they moved along, talking about herself was distracting and the tears threatened less. "Mr Stover was cross. But I knocked on the door as I'm supposed to, and I called out to see if anyone was in. When no one answered I opened the door myself. It was mid-afternoon. It states quite clearly in a little notice in each room that between the hours of ten and four the maids will be going around cleaning the rooms and a guest should give special notice if they don't wish to be disturbed."

Annie had seen that notice herself and had made a point of ensuring her room was spotless each morning by nine o'clock before any maid came to clean it. Annie had standards and no one was going to have to clean up after her. She even made the bed, though she knew the maids would change the sheets.

They finally made it to the kitchen, where Annie deposited her charge in a large wooden chair. Quite a number of servants were in the kitchen and it appeared they were holding a discussion concerning the events of the day. They all looked up in surprise at Annie's arrival with Mary. No one moved to go to the girl's aid, however. Annie cast her eye around at them, feeling annoyed by their lack of movement. Surely one of them was concerned about the hapless Mary and the shock she had suffered?

"Well?" Annie asked them sternly. "Do none of you know how to make a strong cup of tea for someone who has suffered a nasty shock?"

The room seemed to jump back into action. A French chef, wearing a stiffly starched white hat (that looked rather pretentious to Annie) lifted up a heavy copper kettle and passed it to a girl who filled it at the sink. Other people excused themselves, muttering about work they had to attend to. Rather rapidly the kitchen emptied, apart from those people who found it necessary to their work to be there.

Sweet tea was at last placed before Mary, and the French chef went into the vast pantry and returned with a small piece of chocolate torte, which he set before the maid and reassured her that she must eat it all.

"Sweet things for shock, yes?" he cast a wary eye at Annie, who was still standing, hands on hips, in the doorway looking rather tyrannical.

Annie had taken a good look at the kitchen during the tea making, and was satisfied it was ship-shape enough for her. There was an enormous dresser along one wall, probably purpose built, which contained vast numbers of pans, copper moulds and serving platters. On the opposite wall, almost as huge, was a coal range, brightly polished and black-leaded. Next to it was a smaller gas range, clearly very newly installed. Mr Stover did like his modernisations, but whether his chef agreed with him was another matter.

"I suppose you have all heard what has happened?" Annie asked those few left in the room.

Everyone looked sheepish. One maid muttered something about a suicide. A young man near the sink, clearly the pot boy destined to scrub plates all evening, prodded a stack of breakfast bowls on the draining board and grumbled that he never got sweet tea. He was scowled at by the maid.

"Have none of you got a tongue in your head?" Annie was annoyed with them all. She had forgotten that she was a guest here and not a fellow servant. No one was sure quite how to address her.

"It is horrible!" the French chef declared at last, in his rugged accent. He collapsed into a chair. "How can I cook tonight with thoughts of this dead man on my mind."

"How will I sleep?" the maid added.

"I'll never feel safe opening a door in this place again," Mary sniffled.

"Dear me," Annie shook her head at them all. "Surely you lot saw worse in the war? I know I did. If you work in a hotel, with all these people coming through, all with their own woes, eventually you will have someone pop their clogs on you. It stands to reason."

"But two people?" Mary said. "That woman was first."

"Mrs Hunt," Annie replied.

"Yes, her," Mary nodded. "I know that weren't at the hotel, but she died anyways."

"And there was all that fuss about someone throwing a chamber pot at her," the young man at the sink clattered the dishes again. "Us servants got the blame for that."

"But none of you threw it?" Annie asked.

They all shook their heads.

"Why would we?" the maid spoke. "We have better things to do than throw chamber pots around."

"This has all been very queer," Annie agreed with them, deciding it was time to do a little probing. "And I think it very important that Mr Stover realises his servants aren't to blame in this matter. That is why I came down to talk with you all. I have a few questions for you, would you be prepared to answer them?"

The servants glanced about at each other.

"If we can," the maid shrugged. "We have nothing to hide."

"Good. Perhaps we can begin with a strange story I have heard. Do you all know Miss Smythe?"

"Her!" Mary almost spluttered her tea over herself. "Don't talk to me about her!"

"Why ever not?" Annie asked.

"I went into her room to change the beds, like I always do, and while I was about it I knocked over her suitcase with my foot…"

"You should be more careful Mary!" the other maid interrupted to scold her.

Mary stuck her tongue out at her, clearly feeling greatly recovered from her shock.

"I knocked her suitcase over because it was hidden behind the armchair in the room and it fell down and the catch sprung up. Now, when someone's suitcase falls over you expect to see clothes and private articles. I saw a bloody big rat!"

"Rats!" the French chef almost jumped out of his chair in horror at the thought.

"How did a rat get in Miss Smythe's suitcase?" Annie asked in astonishment. That was the last thing anyone wanted in a smart hotel – even the merest hint of rats roaming around would have everyone leaving.

"It were in a cage," Mary said, enjoying having everyone's attention on her. "Like it were a pet."

The other maid made a gagging noise. The pot boy laughed. Annie had heard of stranger creatures being kept as pets and decided to store this information up for Clara.

"What about a tin? Did anyone see such a thing in Miss Smythe's room? She stated to someone that she had given this tin to a servant," Annie changed the subject.

Again her query was greeted by shaking heads.

"None of the girls has a new tin as far as I know," the maid said. "Unless she is hiding it, and why would anyone do that? We all keep little trinkets about us."

"I never saw a tin in Miss Smythe's room," Mary agreed.

"What about in anyone else's room? Has anyone else received a tin containing marzipan fruits that you know of?" Annie speculated that maids in a hotel were best placed for seeing a person's belongings and for noticing new things. They went into all the rooms and tidied up. When you did that you were bound to see things. But no one had seen tins of sweets in guests' rooms.

"You only get marzipan fruits at Christmas, don't you?" Mary said to no one in particular.

Everything was becoming more and more curious by the moment.

"What about Mrs Hunt? Did any of you meet her?"

The potboy pulled a face which implied he rarely set foot in the main hotel, being chained (metaphorically speaking) to his sink. Mary shook her head, but the other maid seemed to be thinking very hard. At last she spoke.

"I had to take Mrs Hunt her meal after she was hurt,"

she said. "I took it up to her room. She was rather sharp, but perhaps she was just in pain. She complained the food had taken a long while to come and I apologised because I was sent to her original room by mistake at first, not knowing that she had moved rooms."

"I understand it was an abrupt change," Annie said. "She took a dislike to her room."

"I rather thought it more a dislike to the person in the room opposite," Mary said bluntly.

"Why do you say that?" Annie swung her full attention on her.

Mary gave a shrug.

"I had just finished the last room on the ground floor. That is my last floor to do each day, as I always start at the top floor and work down. Not me alone, of course, there are other girls. But we all follow the same pattern," Mary felt this explanation most necessary to justify her knowledge of Mrs Hunt's room change. "Anyway, I was picking up my things when I saw Mrs Hunt being led to her room by Mr Stover. Now Mr Stover hates maids being seen by guests when it isn't necessary, so I darted back into the room I had just cleaned. I heard Mr Stover opening the door to the next room and letting Mrs Hunt in, and she saying it seemed a reasonable enough room.

"I was just slipping away, thinking they were all distracted, when the door to the room opposite Mrs Hunt's opens and a man walks out, and he looked straight across the corridor and for a moment nothing happened, and then his head jerked up as if he recognised someone. I was poised in the middle of the hall, and I could look across and see exactly what, or rather who, he was looking at. Mr Stover had his back to the door, but Mrs Hunt was facing it and I saw her eyes meet those of the man.

"Then the man pulled the door of his room firmly closed behind him, gave Mrs Hunt a filthy look, the sort you give to someone you hate, and left. No sooner had that happened then Mrs Hunt was demanding she have a different room, that the one she was in was not suitable and she could not abide staying in it. Mr Stover had a trying time calming her."

Mary grinned at them all, pleased to be able to impart this information.

"Who was the man?" Annie asked, feeling that this was something important.

Mary had to pause and think for a moment.

"I do know who it is," she said, twirling a strand of hair around her calloused fingers. Too many hours of scrubbing had given her rough, raw hands. "What is the name of that man on the ground floor who is a doctor?"

She had directed this question at the other maid, but Annie didn't need any further hint. At virtually the same time as the maid spoke, so did Annie, and they both said the same name.

"Dr Masters!"

Annie was stunned. The name meant a good deal to her. But so far there had been no hint of Dr Masters knowing Mrs Hunt, for that matter he had tended to her when she was hurt. Could it be that he was really her murderer? But why? Well, there were enough people in this hotel with motives against her, why should Dr Masters be any different?

"I thought Captain Blake very handsome," the older maid sighed mournfully.

"He weren't when I saw him," Mary shuddered.

"Mon dieu! Do not say such things!" the French chef squealed. "How will these hands make fine filo pastry tonight when they shake so? My mind revolts at all this business."

"Why would anyone kill themselves?" the pot boy puttered. "I mean, what's so wrong with this life, anyway?"

Even a life spent washing dishes, apparently, was not one to despair of. Annie did not have the energy to begin explaining the fickleness of the human mind. She, herself, had stood on the precipice and had almost fallen. Clara had saved her and now the days when she wished herself dead were just a distant memory. But that did not mean she had forgotten how it felt or the awful despair that had come over her. But what was Captain Blake's demon? Had he killed his aunt? The thought was not so improbable, surely?

She was about to say something more when Mr Stover suddenly appeared in the kitchen.

"What is all this?" he declared at once, scowling at the few servants scattered around. "Shouldn't you all be preparing dinner? Or are we all going to simply fall apart because a guest has chosen to leave us early?"

Mr Stover's gaze fell on Mary.

"Have you finished all the beds?" he demanded of her.

Annie intervened sharply, determined to make her presence felt. She was not the boldest of creatures, but she would not have someone intimidated, especially when they had suffered a rather nasty shock.

"Mary is recovering herself," she told Mr Stover firmly. "At my command."

For the first time Mr Stover realised there was a guest in the hotel kitchen. He puffed out his cheeks, clearly wanting to shriek at the impropriety of such a thing, but restrained by his decorum from doing so.

"Perhaps you will escort me back upstairs so I need interrupt the running of your kitchens no further?" Annie suggested. "I don't remember the way back up, as I was busy helping Mary when I came down."

Mr Stover continued to puff his cheeks, like he had just run a race and was catching his breath. Finally, with one last glance at Mary, he conceded to Annie's request. He barked one last time at his staff to get on with dinner and then led the way back through the various hallways and up into the body of the hotel. He was agitated, that was plain, but who would not be after the events of the last few days. When they reached the foot of the main staircase and Annie went to depart, Mr Stover turned on her quickly;

"Tell Miss Fitzgerald this is none of her business!" he said stoutly before marching off.

Annie merely smirked at his back. No one ever told Clara what was, or what wasn't her business.

Chapter Twenty-three

Clara convened a council of war. It was clear things had taken a serious turn and there was no more time to waste. She had the list she had found in Mrs Hunt's room and she had written a second list that detailed the suspects on Mrs Hunt's list that were also on the charabanc excursion to Windermere. The list consisted of eight names, including Mr and Mrs Wignell, Edwin Hope and Madeleine Reeve. That left four suspects yet to be questioned to ascertain what connection they had to Mrs Hunt and where they had been at the time of her death. The Wignells stated they were together at the time, as did Hope and Reeve, without further evidence Clara could not pick apart their statements. But the other names might offer a clue.

And then there was the strange Miss Smythe and Dr Masters, both of whom did not appear on the list, but had some connection with Mrs Hunt. Clara couldn't help thinking of that peculiar incident at the stopping point where Mrs Hunt had insisted that a rat had run over her feet, and Miss Smythe had crouched to pick something up. The discovery of a pet rat in her luggage gave Clara pause for thought.

She set out her plans to Tommy and Annie after

dinner.

"We have a list of names of people who may have had a motive to harm Mrs Hunt. So far we don't know if they had the wherewithal to actually do so, or if they had the opportunity. Excluding the possibility that those on the list who stayed behind at the hotel during the Windermere trip actually made their own way there, we are left with six individuals who were at the scene of the crime, and four of those we have yet to speak to."

Clara passed the list to Tommy, who examined it and then gave it to Annie.

"Are we excluding Blake as the killer?" Tommy queried.

"No one is excluded," Clara made plain. "But now you mention Captain Blake, I do have a second prong of attack planned. I want to get into his room and take a look around. There may be evidence of his guilt if he was the killer of his aunt. I am not inclined to consider his death at this stage as anything other than what it looks like. Suicide."

"How are you going to get into his room?" Annie asked.

"That is a little more complicated," Clara conceded. In fact it was very complicated since Mr Stover seemed to have quite taken against her. "I will need the master key for Captain Blake's room."

This statement was greeted with uncertain silence from her friends.

"All the rooms have a master key for use by the maids and Mr Stover," Clara explained. "If Mr Stover won't let me in himself, and I very much doubt I can persuade him to do so a second time, then I will need the master key. Or rather, a copy of it."

"You realise you are stepping rather into the territory of illegal activities, old girl," Tommy said steadily, his face very serious.

"A dreadful crime has been committed and everyone is ignoring it," Clara countered. "I know I am stretching even my own limits, but if a search of Captain Blake's room can produce the evidence either to his guilt or innocence, then it must surely be undertaken."

They were all silent again for a while, then Annie piped up.

"You won't be able to have hold of the master key for long, maybe just for moments before a maid or someone else misses it."

"No, that is plain. I have to figure out a way to make a copy."

"I know how," Annie said.

The other two looked at her curiously, as if she had just revealed herself as a housebreaker.

"I know how you make copies of keys for a perfectly ordinary reason," Annie declared to them stoutly, offended that they thought she might have ever done anything illegal. "I once had such a situation with the old pantry key. You know that little tiny key with a ribbon on the end."

Tommy looked blank, having never been required to unlock the pantry, but Clara knew precisely what Annie meant.

"The key had become rather worn and one day as I went to unlock the pantry it snapped in the lock. Fortunately I was able to use a pair of small tweezers to remove the head of the key from the lock, but now I had a broken key and no replacement…"

"Wait a moment, you keep the pantry locked?" Tommy interrupted with a perfect look of bafflement. "Since when?"

"Since always. In case of rats wandering in, or burglars. Burglars steal sugar just as readily as jewels you know. Not to mention Bramble," Annie was proud of the level of protection she maintained over her kitchen and its supplies. It was like Fort Knox without the ammunition stores. "In any case, the key broke and I needed the potatoes. So I hurried into town and went to the gentleman on the corner who mends shoes and also cuts keys. I showed him the problem and he very carefully fixed the key with a little solder, but he agreed that I would need a copy because the original would ultimately break again.

"If I left him the key he could make me a copy, but as it was quite late in the day and he already had work waiting, it would not be ready before tomorrow. I needed the key back so I could open my pantry, so that was simply impractical, but I also needed the copy as soon as possible. So we came to an arrangement. He made an impression of the key in some clay he kept for such works. He took impressions of both sides and said he would use them as moulds for the two halves of the key. It would not be a perfect copy, not as good as if he could use the original, but it would serve to make a spare I could use while he took the real key to make a true copy. And thus I was able to open the pantry once more and dinner was saved."

Annie sat back in her chair and folded her arms over her chest looking satisfied. Tommy glanced at Clara.

"Sounds like a plan."

"I don't have any clay," Clara replied. "What else could I use?"

"I do believe soft soap can be used for these purposes," Annie informed them, proving herself a fount of knowledge on the subject. "They always use soap in the stories about escaping prisons in the magazines I read. The woman are always being kidnapped and having to find novel ways of releasing themselves."

"Soap," Clara nodded. "Well at least now I have a plan. I shall slip down into the servants' quarters tonight."

"Hold fire one more moment," Tommy interjected again. "You are marvellous in many ways, old thing, but when it comes to stealthy operations you are not renowned."

Clara took this completely the wrong way and scowled at her brother.

"Now, don't take that to heart," Tommy tried to appease her. "I have my failings too. I'm not much cut out for interviewing suspects. The last one I spoke to killed himself."

"I hardly think that is your fault," Annie told him loyally.

"That's not the point, what I am saying is that Clara is best for interviewing people and the tricky, slightly illegal stuff, is much more suited to me. I'll go get that key impression. I would much rather that than interview anymore poor souls who might take the huff and top themselves afterwards."

Clara was mollified, mostly.

"If you are prepared to do this Tommy I won't argue with you," she said. "But, even if we make an impression, how will we get it made?"

"Take it to the local key cutter," Annie answered immediately.

"And tell him what, precisely? He will wonder why I don't just bring him the original," Clara pointed out.

Tommy had a smirk on his face as he said.

"I rather imagine Annie will tell him her pantry key story."

Annie narrowed her eyes at him.

"And what is wrong with the pantry key story? Perfectly logical, as it is," she demanded.

"Nothing is wrong with it!" Tommy said quickly. "It is very… distracting."

Annie thumped him lightly on the arm and Tommy grinned even more.

"Now don't fight you two," Clara interceded. "Do we all know what we are about? There are suspects to interview and keys to steal, we should get to it."

"I really hope, after all this fuss, that Mrs Hunt truly was murdered," Annie muttered as the council of war was disbanded and they set about their tasks.

"The more I learn, the more I am certain her death was not of her own doing," Clara assured her.

Chapter Twenty-four

Clara had two people to try and interview before the evening was out and one of them was Mrs Unwin. Clara only had a vague idea of the woman, having not really crossed paths with her as yet. She was in her late fifties, widowed, her children grown up and living their own lives. That was as much as Clara knew.

She found the widow browsing through a varied selection of books on a bookcase in the hotel's main lounge (the hotel had three, excluding the music room). She seemed to be intrigued by titles about British fauna and flora and had just selected a guide to British wildflowers to peruse when Clara came upon her. Clara stood beside her at the bookcase and pretended to be looking for some to read.

"Dreadful events today," she said lightly, giving the necessary 'tut' at the end of the statement. "I feel too shocked to sleep. I thought a little reading might help."

"As did I," Mrs Unwin indicated the book in her hands. "Though, I am an avid reader most of the time."

"I rarely can find the time," Clara admitted quite honestly. "But, I suppose that is what holidays are for."

"Indeed," Mrs Unwin departed from the bookcase and went to a vacant armchair to sit.

Clara hastily grabbed a book from the shelves and followed her. Once she was sat in a chair beside her, she tried to restart the conversation.

"Did you go on the trip to Windermere? There were some beautiful flowers out along the banks," she nodded to the book Mrs Unwin was endeavouring to read.

"Yes," Mrs Unwin answered, hardly looking up.

"I wish I knew the names of all of them. I rather feel I let such pretty flowers down by not knowing what they are called. Are you much of a botanist?"

"No," Mrs Unwin replied, in that same monosyllabic tone. She seemed determined to avoid conversation.

"I sat by Mrs Hunt that day, poor woman. She was good enough to tell me the names of the plants. She seemed quite knowledgeable."

"She was not," Mrs Unwin had suddenly looked up from her book and there was a darkness about her features that suggested a dreadful, hidden anger.

Clara was naturally surprised.

"She was not?"

"Mrs Hunt knew nothing about the flora or fauna of these fair isles, but was not against brandishing her ignorance and stoking it in others," Mrs Unwin said crisply.

"I'm afraid you rather take me aback," Clara declared. "I thought Mrs Hunt a very intelligent woman."

"She was the sort of woman who reads, but fails to understand. Who learns one fact," Mrs Unwin held up a single finger to emphasise her words. "and then imagines she knows all about a subject. I would not allow her to teach a dog, let alone my children. Though I am aware that many people thought her a masterful tutor in all subjects."

"Then you knew her?" Clara persisted, not wanting to stopper this very productive train of conversation. "I mean, prior to this holiday, you knew her."

"I have known her more years than I am comfortable to admit. Myself and Mrs Hunt are both associates of the

Brighton Horticultural Society. A position I take very seriously, but one which she did not. She masked her ignorance well enough, but for the experienced hand it was plain to see."

The bitterness in Mrs Unwin's tone was also very plain to see. Clara was intrigued.

"Surely a woman's ignorance is not enough to warrant such dislike?" she said. "You almost sound as if you hated her."

"Not far from the truth, indeed," Mrs Unwin was so engaged in the conversation that she had put down her book. "Mrs Hunt charmed her way into the society, possibly through flattering certain members of the society's board. We are an elite group of amateurs who are fascinated by plants and take our fascination very seriously. To allow such a poor excuse for a gardener into our ranks, one who could not tell her pansies from her primroses, was an affront to all we stood for!"

Clara still felt that the utter detestation Mrs Unwin showed for Mrs Hunt had to be based on more than just the latter's failure with plant names.

"Surely Mrs Hunt had to prove herself once in the society?" she hinted, hoping to elucidate the real cause for this anger. "She would have been undone at the first meeting she attended and spoke at."

"Not when you have friends on the committee," Mrs Unwin scowled furiously. "It makes my blood boil to think about it. She waltzed in with little more knowledge than a toddler and paraded her ignorance unashamedly. Then the annual flower show came up and she presented this pathetic little pot of lavender, which she claimed to have grown from seed. It looked straight out of a shop to me, but she was presented with the award for best newcomer! Can you imagine. She received a whole £5 and a certificate! And all the time, I was there with my beautiful Busy Lizzies, and no one even acknowledged them! I should have won that award! It was truly unfair!"

Clara began to understand. The dislike Mrs Unwin

felt for Mrs Hunt was due to jealousy over an award and not a great deal else.

"You must have been upset to see her on the charabanc?" Clara said.

"Not really," Mrs Unwin moped, her anger disintegrating into tepid misery. "She had written me a letter, suggesting the trip. She implied we could use it to build friendship, over flowers and such. I might not have accepted, except she mentioned she was unwell and might not be able to do the trip again. She wrote a lot of stuff about wanting to make amends."

Clara spotted a familiar trend in all this.

"And when you got aboard the charabanc?"

"Why! She didn't seem to even know me!" Mrs Unwin paused, looking hurt as much as angered by the woman. "Leopards do not change their spots, I suppose."

Mrs Unwin suddenly looked down at the book on Clara's lap.

"Are you much interested in the repair and maintenance of steam engines?"

Clara sharply looked down herself at the book she had taken off the shelf with little consideration to its title. It turned out to be a workman's guide to steam engines, probably thirty years old or more. How it had ended up in the hotel's library was anyone's guess.

"A little research," Clara said quickly, feeling deeply embarrassed by her obvious effort to talk to Mrs Unwin. "I rather fancy it is a topic beyond me."

Excusing herself thus, Clara returned the book to the shelf and hastened out of the lounge, leaving Mrs Unwin to her perusal of wildflowers. The woman seemed a dead end. No one took the lengths someone had gone to to murder Mrs Hunt over a flower competition. Or, at least, so Clara hoped, else the world would be an awful lot more sinister a place to exist in.

Clara had one last person to interview before the evening was out. Mr Hardwich, who had appeared midway down Mrs Hunt's list, though with no greater emphasis to his name than any of the rest. Clara might almost imagine the list merely an aide de memoir, had it not been for the fact that all those upon it knew Mrs Hunt and had been mysteriously asked to join her on this holiday. What had the woman been planning?

Clara tracked down Mr Hardwich in the music room, which also served as a smoking room when required. Someone was tapping out a half-hearted tune on the baby grand, while Mr Hardwich sat on a sofa with Mr Wignell and another man Clara did not know. They appeared engrossed in conversation and, at first, Clara had to wonder how she could infiltrate this little group without appearing too obvious. Most people were still unaware she was investigating the death of Mrs Hunt, and she preferred to keep it that way. Simply interrupting the trio's conversation and blustering out questions would never do.

Clara wandered to the fireplace, which was lit and roaring nicely since the Spring evenings were still quite chilly, and pretended to warm her hands to buy time to think. The room appeared to be dominated by men that evening. There was not another woman in sight. Clara felt she would have to do something decisive to break into this informal men's club.

She came to a decision. As unpleasant a prospect as she found it, Clara decided that the only way to slip herself obliquely into Mr Hardwich's presence was to play on the fact that she was the only woman in the room. In short, Clara was about to go against the grain and pretend to be the flighty type of woman she had always loathed. If her plan worked, then Mr Hardwich, who was a gentleman of a certain age, sitting with other gentlemen of a certain age, would come to her aid in the moment of need she was about to have and she would be provided with the ideal opener for conversation.

Clara spun around from the fire, a little faster than she meant to, so the movement actually caught the eye of Mr Wignell. He looked up and smiled at her most benevolently.

"Oh dear," Clara declared, flopping the back of one hand against her forehead as if she was feeling rather clumsily for a temperature. "I feel rather faint."

She took a pace towards Mr Wignell who was sitting right next to Mr Hardwich. He stopped listening to the conversation of the other two and had all his attention on Clara.

"Are you all right, Miss Fitzgerald?"

"I rather think today's events have overcome me. That, or the blancmange at dinner did not agree with me," Clara gave a slight sway to emphasise her discomfort. "I feel quite queer."

Mr Wignell jumped to his feet, his gentlemanly duty more than apparent. Offering Clara a seat in an armchair right next to the sofa, he lowered her into it gently and then went to fetch her a stiff drink.

"Do you feel unwell?" Mr Hardwich was duly distracted from his conversation with the third gentleman. Precisely as Clara had hoped.

"A little," Clara explained.

Mr Hardwich was in his sixties, comfortably retired and with all the time in the world to do as he pleased. So, naturally, he was bored quite a lot of the time. He had come away on the excursion for a change of scene, and had certainly received that. He was a robust gentleman, but more muscular than fat. His slight paunch failing to accurately portray the large quantities of food he was capable of putting away. He was a kindly enough man, not one for spending a lot of time in company, but perfectly capable of presenting himself adroitly when he did so. Now he smiled lightly at Clara.

"It has certainly been a most remarkable day," he ventured. Then he turned to the man at his side. "Miss Fitzgerald is part of my charabanc party. As you may imagine our peaceful jaunt has turned rather dramatic."

The gentleman at his side nodded in understanding and then turned to Clara.

"Stanley Jones," he introduced himself.

"Clara Fitzgerald," Clara answered, just as Mr Wignell returned with her drink.

It was a large glass of brandy and Clara took a diligent sip, trying to mask her distaste for the strong alcohol which had a rather chemical tang to it.

"You mustn't upset yourself over Captain Blake," Mr Wignell told her firmly. "As tragic as it is."

"I have been telling Mr Jones all about it," said Hardwich, giving Clara a fine opportunity to bring the subject around to Mrs Hunt.

"It is just such a shock to have two suicides among one group of people," Clara shook her head, pretending to still be in a state of anxiety over the trouble. "I really can't comprehend it all."

"Mrs Hunt was surely an accident?" Hardwich commented.

"Perhaps, but the police have made inferences," Clara decided to push her luck. "Her health concerns have made them consider the possibility that she was depressed and might have taken the opportunity to…"

Clara purposely tailed off and sipped her brandy. There was silence a moment and then Mr Jones spoke.

"I don't hold with people topping themselves. Cowardice in my book."

This statement flattened the conversation as soundly as if someone had called for silence in the room. Mr Wignell excused himself quite abruptly, his mind already on his daughter and her death all those years ago. He didn't need Mr Jones' comments. Clara felt bad that it was her attempt to start a conversation with Mr Hardwich that had sparked the statement. She didn't like to see Mr Wignell so morose.

"What's up with him?" Jones muttered, watching Mr Wignell disappear.

Clara said nothing. She had been sworn to secrecy and did not break a confidence so easily. She masked her anger at Jones well enough too. Even so, the little party had clearly broken up.

"I suppose I ought to away to my bed," Jones glanced at his watch. "Unlike you souls, I am here on business and must be awake in the morning."

He rose and departed the room. Mr Hardwich sat still, staring at the end of his cigarette and deep in his own thoughts. Clara could not miss her chance.

"Mr Jones was rather abrupt."

"He was."

"I don't agree with him, you know," Clara waited until Mr Hardwich looked up at her before finishing that statement. "Suicide is not cowardice. It is the cry of a soul in deep distress."

"Fortunately, I have never found myself in such a position," Hardwich replied with the slightest of smiles.

"Nor I," Clara admitted. "But that does not mean I fail to understand the situation in others. I can't say what drove Captain Blake over the edge, but with Mrs Hunt I rather feel her illness was weighing heavily on her mind."

"Mrs Hunt never struck me as the sort of person to self-harm," Hardwich said rather flatly, then he hesitated as if he knew he had said too much.

"You knew Mrs Hunt? I mean, before this holiday?" Clara asked, giving him no quarter.

"I knew her vaguely," Mr Hardwich shrugged.

"You know, you must be the sixth person I have met who knew Mrs Hunt before this trip. I rather fancy she arranged this excursion for all her friends."

"Mrs Hunt did not have friends," Hardwich said coldly. "Mrs Hunt despised friendship."

"Oh," Clara let the word fall from her lips, hoping it might drag forth a little more information. When it did not, she added, "I only got to know her aboard the charabanc. She was prone to saying the most offensive things, or at least that is how it struck me."

"You are quite correct," Hardwich told her. "Mrs Hunt had mastered the art of cutting a person to the very bone with her words."

"It sounds rather as if you knew her very well?"

"I did. Once," Mr Hardwich sighed. "Mrs Hunt was a cold creature. Selfish, even. She was only inclined to do things that pleased her or were to her gain. She made enemies rather than friends and she seemed happy with this."

Mr Hardwich stubbed out his cigarette. The room had grown quieter. The amateur pianist had given up his attempts at Mozart and Beethoven, and the room had fallen into a lull as conversation dipped away and people began to feel weariness overtaking their tongues.

"Was she really very ill?" Mr Hardwich asked in a level tone.

"I have been told, reliably, that she was indeed very poorly and that her condition would ultimately prove fatal."

Hardwich pulled a face. Clara could not tell if it was one of misery or fury, perhaps it was neither.

"I thought she looked ill on the charabanc," he said at last.

"How did you know her?" Clara asked. "I assumed she was not a friend."

"No, never!" Mr Hardwich laughed this time, though not very loudly. "Mrs Hunt came into your life and turned it upside down. She left when things were at their worst, it was her knack, and things only seemed to get better after she was gone. I knew her far too well and for far too long."

"Were you surprised she was on the same charabanc?"

"Hardly, though I suppose I was amused to think of her taking such a trip. I knew about it beforehand," Mr Hardwich explained. "She wrote me a letter, saying she was thinking of taking the trip and would appreciate my company and an opportunity to speak with me. To make amends."

"What had she done to require her to make amends?" Clara asked.

Mr Hardwich ducked his head a little and smiled to

himself, but it was a bitter smile.

"I prefer not to say, but she hurt me deeply."

"And now she wrote to you to ask if you would join her on holiday?"

"Yes. I did think it was extravagant for her. She was not the type to normally care if she hurt you," Mr Hardwich started to roll a new cigarette between his fingers, fishing in his pocket for matches. "The letter did seem a little odd, but I put it down to her getting older and, of course, the illness she hinted at. The urgency in her tone came across in her words. I rather felt as if coming on this trip would be an act of compassion, as much as anything else."

"Was she pleased to see you?" Clara asked, thinking that this letter business had to be key to this matter.

"Not precisely," Hardwich admitted. "I think her exact words were 'what are you doing here?' and when I explained she looked at me as if I was quite mad and denied she had ever written any letter. I assumed she had perhaps forgotten about it, some illnesses can make you very forgetful."

"They can indeed. But apart from that, did you ever speak with Mrs Hunt?"

"She didn't want to talk to me," Mr Hardwich shrugged again. "She was embarrassed, I imagine. Mrs Hunt was always a very, very proud woman."

"Not the sort to throw herself into Lake Windermere?" Clara suggested.

Mr Hardwich thought about this a moment, then finally said.

"No, not the sort, but yet she did throw herself in, didn't she?"

"Presumably," Clara did not want to argue the point too much. "Of course she might have slipped, or…"

Clara didn't finish that statement as it needed no conclusion to make it obvious. Mr Hardwich had that wistful smile on his face again, almost as if laughing at his own private joke.

"I think if Mrs Hunt set her mind to it she could do anything. But, no, I never suspected her of contemplating suicide. I can't say a lot about her, not without bringing up her faults, for there were a lot of them, but she did have her principles, that you could not deny."

"Principles can be very double-edged," Clara noted. "I hope she realised that."

"Perhaps she did, perhaps she didn't," Mr Hardwich stubbed out his second cigarette. "Do you feel better now Miss Fitzgerald, as I would like to get to my room?"

"I feel most recovered," Clara assured him. "Hopefully tomorrow will be a very peaceful day."

Mr Hardwich gave a snort, perhaps to imply that he considered that a vain hope.

"Take care," he rose and gave an old-fashioned bow, then sauntered away.

Clara remained in her seat, waiting to see if Mr Wignell would come back. When he didn't she decided it was time for her bed as well. Hopefully Annie had been equally successful with her interviews and they would have something to work with, not that anyone was shaping up to be a murderer so far, but they had to be on the right track. This letter business, for instance, what was that all about? Had Mrs Hunt written the letters and simply forgotten about them? But, if so, she had also spent a lot of money on charabanc tickets. Something was off about all this business, and Clara was going to discover it.

Chapter Twenty-five

Annie appeared at Clara's room just before nine o'clock.

"Would you like a summary of my investigations?" she enquired.

Clara ushered her into the room and sat her in the armchair, then she proceeded to pour her a cup of cocoa from a little pot she had sitting by the fire.

"I ordered a prodigious amount," Clara said as she handed over a pretty pink china cup. "Assuming you would need nourishment after your evening. I certainly required some. And we must wait up for Tommy, of course."

"Tommy has the worst of it tonight," Annie nodded thoughtfully. "Did you discover anything interesting."

"With Mrs Unwin, no. She was jealous of Mrs Hunt over flowers of all things, but I don't peg her for a murderer. Mr Hardwich was more complicated, in fact, he rather failed to tell me anything. I rather feel he is hiding something."

"Well, I went to see Miss Delaware, who was the first name from the list you gave me," Annie took a sip of cocoa and pulled a face. "This is very strong!"

"I asked for extra warm milk, here it is sitting by the fire, pour a little in," Clara proffered the milk jug which was indeed nicely warm and helped to dilute the thick chocolate. "Now, Miss Delaware?"

Annie stirred her cocoa.

"Miss Delaware is soon to be Mrs Strathmore, and my word is she pleased to tell anyone who is nearby about it. I spent a vast amount of the evening hearing about her husband-to-be. Apparently he is in stocks and shares, its sounds rather shifty to me, but I suppose it is legitimate."

"It is a popular occupation these days," Clara nodded. "Buying and selling stocks. Profitable too if you know what you are doing. Personally it seems rather too much like gambling for my taste, but some people find it hugely satisfying. I assume Mr Strathmore is one of those."

"I imagine," Annie shrugged her shoulders with the implication that this was all rather preposterous to her. "Anyway, she could not stop talking about him. As it happened I found her at a table in the small lounge with Miss Smythe. I found it most awkward to look at that woman knowing she carries a pet rat in her suitcase."

"That is a matter for tomorrow," Clara mused, reminding herself that she must discover if Miss Smythe had let her rat loose earlier in their trip. "People have all manner of creatures for pets. After all, Tommy has Bramble."

"But at least Bramble is a dog," Annie muttered. "A shaggy, disobedient dog, yes, but still a domesticated beast. Thankfully, Miss Smythe had not brought her pet downstairs. I asked if I might sit with the ladies, as the lounge was rather crowded and this they agreed to. Before I knew it we were ordering a fresh pot of tea for three. It soon became apparent that Miss Delaware was delighted to have anyone new to tell all about her wedding plans."

"She is one of those, then?" Clara said, meaning that the woman was the sort who could not restrain themselves from talking constantly over their own affairs.

"Most definitely. I must have spent the best part of an hour listening to her detailed arrangements, from the type of lace she was to have on her dress sleeves, to the style of buckle on her shoes, oh, and a full fifteen minutes was devoted to the description of her wedding bouquet," Annie took a long drink of chocolate, finding the sweetness helping her recover from her ordeal. "This improves with extra milk."

"When is Miss Delaware due to be married?"

"That is quite the thing. Her wedding is set for early next month."

"Then what is she doing going on a holiday just before, when there must be so much still to arrange and prepare? Dress fittings alone take up ridiculous amounts of time," Clara had attended several weddings of friends, and knew the frantic preparations that seemed to be required beforehand. She could not imagine any woman choosing to depart from these for over a week so near to the event.

"I wondered the same, and I mentioned it," Annie agreed. "Miss Delaware admitted that she had not taken this journey lightly, as it did cut into her time for planning the wedding, and she still had so much to do. But, she had been asked to come on this holiday, or rather begged to come, by her old governess and she had not the heart to decline."

"Wait a moment," Clara held up her hand to pause Annie. "Let me guess who the governess was."

"If you cannot you must have a head full of straw," Annie smirked.

"I surmise that Miss Delaware was taught by Mrs Hunt and she recently received a letter from her old governess declaring that the latter wished to make amends for, presumably, being an awful tyrant in the schoolroom and Miss Delaware felt required to come away at such a busy time?"

"That is precisely it, in fact, she had the letter on her. Miss Delaware is the sort to keep these things about her and also the letter contained the name of the hotel and the time to catch the charabanc," Annie's smile broadened. "I asked to borrow it. I remarked that it was written on a certain paper I have been trying to get a hold of, as it reminds me so much of some my grandmother used. I asked if I might borrow the letter and see if I could make out the watermark, or even take it to a local shop and see if they had the same. Miss Delaware was barely listening, half-intent on returning to the subject of her wedding, and she gave me the letter without thinking."

Annie reached down to her handbag and pulled out a pale blue envelope, that had been opened along the top with a sharp letter knife. She removed the contents which consisted of a slip of thick paper, the same colour as the envelope, and handed it to Clara.

"There is nothing insightful in the contents," Annie shrugged.

"Oh, I wouldn't say that," Clara had unfolded the letter and was glancing at the writing. "For a start, this is not the hand of Mrs Hunt."

Clara rose from her chair and limped over to her bedside table. From the drawer she removed the list Mrs Hunt had written and brought it back to where Annie was sitting. She compared the list with the letter for a moment then, satisfied with her analysis, handed them both to Annie. It was not difficult to see the two pieces of paper had been composed by very different writers.

Mrs Hunt wrote in a tight, sharp style, her letters very angular and with a hint of shakiness about them, which was presumably caused by her condition. The letter to Miss Delaware, on the other hand, was in a rounded, flowing style.

"They are not the same," Annie said in surprise. "Why, that means Mrs Hunt did not write this."

"And that explains why she appears to have shown such disdain to those people boarding the charabanc who assumed she had commanded them to."

"Why didn't any one of her recipients notice?" Annie stared at the letters again, the difference was too plain to be ignored.

"A few reasons spring to mind," Clara replied. "In certain instances the recipients probably did not know her handwriting anyway. In others many years have passed since they last heard from Mrs Hunt and people forget these little things, such as the way a person writes, unless it is exceptionally distinctive. And lastly, we must recall, that all the recipients were under the impression that Mrs Hunt was very ill, perhaps terminally so. They might assume her handwriting had altered as a result. After all, even the list we know she wrote shows clear signs of deterioration in the writing."

"That leaves the question of who did write this letter, and all the others?" Annie shook her head at the pieces of paper. "What a preposterous thing!"

"I feel I have seen handwriting such as this before," Clara mused. "But I can't bring it to mind where. Never mind, it shall come to me. Tell me why Mrs Hunt might feel the need to make amends to Miss Delaware?"

Clara helped herself to more cocoa as Annie started her story again.

"Miss Delaware was not really interested to talk on the subject, but what little I did extract sounds rather typical of Mrs Hunt. Certainly her story is not very original among all the others we have heard. Mrs Hunt was Miss Delaware's governess from the time the latter was eleven, up until she was sixteen. They never saw eye-to-eye. Miss Delaware is not an academic sort and I could see this might niggle Mrs Hunt. But, more to the point, Miss Delaware, as a child, suffered from the problem affectionately described as 'puppy fat'. In short she was plump and Mrs Hunt railed at her on the subject on a daily basis until Miss Delaware was driven to the brink of depression over the matter."

Annie found herself looking at her cocoa and thinking of her own waistline, not a common habit in Annie who considered food her lifeblood, especially when preparing it.

"Miss Delaware was rather tacit on the topic, but I feel

certain that Mrs Hunt bullied her over her weight issue from the first day she arrived, until the very last. Miss Delaware, as you might recall, is still not the slightest of creatures, but she makes up for her weight by a certain gracefulness about her presence."

"So the letter implied to Miss Delaware that Mrs Hunt wanted to apologise for her behaviour and, considering the impression it had had on the young woman, she probably felt it would be reassuring to have that apology. Thus she was prepared to take time out of her plans to make this trip."

"Using the ticket Mrs Hunt sent her, yes," Annie concluded. "The problem I see is that, as much as bullying can be a painful experience, I can't imagine it as a reason for murder."

"Oh I can," Clara corrected. Having been bullied herself at school for being rather a gawky child, too long in leg and arm, and rather ungraceful at sports and dancing, she could well imagine it. "But Miss Delaware has clearly moved on with her life and these hurts are in the past. Unless Mrs Hunt resurrected them during the brief two days they were in each other's company, then I can't see Miss Delaware as bothering to murder her."

"Then that just leaves Mrs Farthingdale, who was the other person you asked me to talk with. She was a little more interesting, but rather in a sad way."

"How so?"

"Mrs Farthingdale is the widow of a schoolmaster. She seems rather lonely, but then again she does not attempt to make company for herself."

"Is she the tall woman with spectacles, in a black dress and white hair swept up in a bun?" Clara asked.

Annie nodded as she took more hot cocoa.

"Mrs Farthingdale was rather challenging to track down, as she does not haunt the lounges like the others. In the end I found her on the terrace outside, staring up at the stars, wrapped in a shawl. It turns out she used to be an amateur astronomer and for several moments I sat beside her as she told me the names of the constellations. She seems a very intelligent woman, though she is also very frail," Annie sighed. "I wasn't sure how I was going to bring up the subject of Mrs Hunt, but as it happened I didn't need to. Mrs Farthingdale asked if it were true you were a detective and when I said it was she simply smiled. It seems word has spread that we are investigating this business of the letters."

"It was bound to," Clara said, unfazed by this.

"Mrs Farthingdale said she wondered when someone would talk to her, seeing, as she said in her own words, how she had a good motive for killing Mrs Hunt."

Clara pricked up her ears.

"The woman said that?"

"She did indeed, without hesitation. I must have looked shocked and she laughed gently. 'Why,' she said, 'I thought everyone knew how much I hated that woman.' I was as baffled as before and she shook her head at me. 'Mrs Hunt asking for forgiveness was truly novel,' Mrs Farthingdale continued, 'I had to see for myself if she meant it. She did me a grave disservice, one I shall not forget until my dying day.' And then she gave me the strangest smile."

"What was this disservice?" Clara asked.

"She was circumspect at first. She went back to talking about the stars, then she asked if I knew Mrs Hunt had worked as a teacher in a school. I said, I thought I had heard something about that. She remarked that the woman had to leave in the middle of the school year under the cloud of a scandal. She gave that strange smile again," Annie felt a shiver at remembering the woman's look which had seemed part satisfied and part vengeful. "Mrs Hunt, she said, had been having an affair with one of the members of staff and it had been brought to the attention of the board of governors. The gentleman she was having an affair with was married, but even if he was not it was strictly forbidden for staff members to form romantic liaisons with each other. Mrs Hunt was dismissed.

"I asked if the gentleman was dismissed also. Mrs Farthingdale said that was more problematic, seeing as he was the schoolmaster and not so easy to replace as one of the teachers."

"Ah!" Clara said, understanding at once. "And Mrs Farthingdale was the wife of the schoolmaster. Yes, I see why she would hate Mrs Hunt so. In that case, why did she respond to the letter?"

"I doubt the woman knows herself," Annie shrugged. "Perhaps it was just so she could gloat at seeing Mrs Hunt fallen, or perhaps she really wanted to hear her apology. Whichever it might be, the problem I see with her being our murderer is the frailness of the woman. She walks with a stick and looks about fit to fall over at the slightest breeze. I would say she is not long for this world either."

"How sad," Clara said, genuinely feeling sorry for the woman's situation. "And yet she has such a strong motive! Betrayal is a bitter crime, and it has clearly festered inside her all these years."

"Motive, yes. But Clara, this woman could not lift a chamber pot and throw it, she barely lifts her glass of water to her lips without seeming ready to crumple up by the effort. I can't see how she could hold a struggling woman under water either."

"No," Clara had to agree that both acts would require if not precisely strength, certainly a good sense of balance and a steady hand. "Then we are no further forward. But that is not to worry. I have an idea that it is time we discovered something more about Mrs Hunt's life in Brighton and that might provide the clue. I shall make a phone call in the morning to Inspector Park-Coombs."

"And in the meantime?" Annie asked.

Clara glanced at her cup of cocoa.

"In the meantime I suggest we make ourselves comfortable and await Tommy. Let us hope he is as stealthy as he claims to be."

Annie pulled another face.

Chapter Twenty-Six

Tommy pondered how ironic it was that here he stood about to use his newfound ability to walk to commit an act of theft. He wondered what his doctor would say? Probably he would argue it was not what he meant when he extolled Tommy to use every opportunity he could find to exercise his legs. It had not been a lie when Tommy had declared he knew how to be stealthy, all those years on the western front had not been just about going over the top and trying to avoid Trench Foot. He had been on his fair share of reconnaissance missions, scoping out the enemy line, while knowing that the enemy was doing precisely the same. On occasion two scouting parties from the opposing sides would bump into each other. Usually this resulted in a little confusion, a few very gentlemanly excuses for happening to be wandering in No Man's Land and then a pretence that nothing had actually happened. On the odd occasion, when an over-enthusiastic officer happened to be in the party, there might be a shoot-out, which never ended well for either side. Yes, four years of muddy, bitter warfare had taught Tommy how to tread lightly and avoid being spotted. That was one reason (the other being luck) that he had survived.

Of course, when he had been confined to his wheelchair, such secret expeditions as he was about to perform would have been impossible. Probably that was why he was relishing this opportunity. There is nothing quite like knowing you have the legs and the wherewithal to get into mischief, to cheer a man's soul.

Tommy slipped quietly through the door marked 'employees only' that he had spotted at the end of a long corridor. There was no one about on the other side, though the light in the hallway was on. He checked his watch. It was close to midnight, with any luck only a skeleton team of staff would remain on duty. Tommy traipsed down the hall, trying to keep his steps soft on the wooden floor, which was not so easy. He came upon a line of multi-paned windows that looked out over an internal courtyard. It was too dark to see anything through them.

Tommy had no real idea where he was going, though he assumed the master keys would be kept somewhere obvious for the maids, possibly in a cupboard near the laundry where they collected fresh sheets to change the beds. He had toyed with the idea of getting an impression of Blake's room key from those hanging behind the reception desk, but this idea had two problems; first the desk was manned all day and night, so that there might be someone on call for any guest emergencies; second, because it seemed the police had been dastardly enough to remove the key themselves. Rumour had it they were testing the key for fingerprints, to convince themselves that no one else had somehow miraculously used it to lock Blake's room from the inside after hanging him. Tommy supposed that two related suicides by guests from the same hotel was a little much even for them to overlook. Good luck to them, he didn't think it likely they would get anything more than smudges off the key.

He followed the corridor until it came to a junction. There were no signs to guide him, so he opted to go right, assuming this would take him deeper into the warren of rooms belonging to the staff of the hotel.

Everything was painted very white – the walls, the doorframes, the skirting boards. It was rather like wandering through a hospital. He came to another junction and made the perfunctory decision to turn left. He could be at this all night.

Abruptly he turned a corner and nearly bumped into a maid carrying a stack of towels.

"Ooh, sorry!" the maid spluttered, almost dropping her load.

Tommy steadied her and gave her his most winning smile.

"Old girl, I am dreadfully lost. Seems I went wrong somewhere back there. I came after some fresh bed sheets, fool that I was I spilled a cup of tea over mine as I was heading for bed."

The maid, who was probably little more than seventeen, looked up at Tommy. She was small and mouse-like, he was tall and strikingly handsome. Tommy had always been the looker in the family, with his well-proportioned face, hazel eyes and dark hair carefully slicked back. And he had a charm about him that had always made him popular with women.

"You should have asked at reception, and someone would have brought them up," the maid said, a tad flustered. She rearranged her load of towels so she could get a better look at the handsome stranger before her.

"I didn't like to bother you all over such silliness," Tommy grinned at her. "Four years at the front at least taught me how to change my own bed linen."

"Ooh, you was in the war?"

"I was. I made captain."

The little maid's eyes widened a fraction, she was clearly envisaging Tommy in a uniform with medals on his chest. Tommy imagined she was one of those girls who read magazines full of romantic stories about dashing men in uniform. He had seen the sought of thing they contained when he had come across a pile in Annie's kitchen. She had denied all knowledge of them, which had made him laugh. He endeavoured to look as dashing as a character from one of those stories.

"If you could just show me where the laundry is, I'll get out of your hair, you are clearly busy."

"These are some of the clean towels for putting fresh in the rooms tomorrow. We have a hundred and one rooms here, and each has three towels. That's three hundred and three towels to wash each night ready to change with the ones that are being used in the rooms. All I seem to do is wash towels," the maid juggled the towels in her arms again.

"Then I shall not disturb you further, just point me in the right direction."

"Ooh, I better take you. This place is a right jumble of rooms. You'll get lost again all alone."

Tommy didn't argue, just followed the maid as she bustled along one corridor after another until she stopped outside a door. She motioned for Tommy to pause, almost dropping her load, and then opened the door and peered inside.

"No one about, you can get your sheets," she moved back. "I'll wait for you and show you the way out."

That was the last thing Tommy wanted.

"No need," he smiled. "You are far too busy to worry about me. I insist you carry on with what you were doing, I have already wasted your time long enough. I have the feel of the place now. I can find my way out."

The maid looked disheartened, but she was used to being told what to do and didn't argue. She would get into trouble if the towels were not all clean, dried, pressed and folded on time. She reluctantly departed.

Tommy went into the laundry, being struck by a strong smell of washing soap. He glanced about, but his assumption that a cupboard full of keys may be here was in error. There were no keys to be seen. Not to be defeated, Tommy exited the room and headed further down the corridor, there must be an office or something where they were kept. He noticed that in this part of the service area the doors were labelled with their respective functions. He came upon a cupboard full of cleaning materials, and a boot room where guests' shoes were polished ready to be left at their doors in the morning, but there were no keys.

He had come to another junction and was about to cut straight across and hope to find what he was looking for, when he heard voices to his right. He slipped back down the corridor he had come from and hid in the boot room, keeping the door open a fraction so he could see where the people behind the voices went.

"It's a queer business. I don't like it. Can't be working in a place where people keep killing themselves," a woman said. She sounded older than most of the maids, so possibly was some sort of housekeeper.

"Get some sleep in you and it will seem better in the morning," a male voice responded.

The two people came into view at the junction of the corridors, where they both paused. One was indeed an older woman, dressed smartly. She caught Tommy's attention because she had a large ring of keys in her hand. The man was dressed in a suit and seemed to be some sort of under manager.

"Try not to think on it, Mrs Mackin," he said to the woman. "These things happen. He was plainly a very disturbed young man."

"No call to go hanging yourself off light fittings," Mrs Mackin muttered. "Scared that maid half to death. People have no thought for others."

"Quite Mrs Mackin, but really it is very late…"

"Yes, yes, Mr Lake, I know you are fit for your bed."

The pair said their respective goodnights and Mr Lake turned down the corridor one way, while Mrs Mackin carried on straight. Tommy gave it a moment, then slipped from the boot room and hurried to the end of his corridor. He peeped around the corner and saw Mrs Mackin entering a room. She was only inside it a few moments, before she exited, now minus her bunch of keys, and walked further along the corridor to another room. She went inside and Tommy waited impatiently to see if she reappeared. She did not.

Tommy glanced around. All was silent. He crept quietly to the door she had first entered. It bore a sign that read 'Mrs Mackin's office'. Tommy tried the door handle and found that the room was unlocked. He entered and shut the door behind him. The room was unlit and in complete darkness. There was no window as it was an internal room, and an electric light was required at all times to enable anyone to work here. Tommy didn't like to switch on the main light in case it drew attention to him, so he fumbled in his pocket for some matches. Lighting one he glanced around in its dim glow and saw that there was a desk straight ahead. The match burned down to his fingers and he hastily blew it out, returning to the pitch black.

Tommy edged his way forward, trying to feel for the desk before he bumped into it. He failed and his knee caught the corner with a thud. A sudden tremor went through his leg and it gave way beneath him. He fell to the floor on one knee. Tommy had to still a sense of panic that suddenly raged within him. For one awful moment he thought the knock had instantly removed the ability to walk he had just regained. He had to forcefully calm himself. As the panic subsided, he realised he could feel the throb in his knee, not the frightening numbness that had once overcome him. Gingerly he used his hands on the edge of the desk to lever himself upright, then he was standing and he took his hands off the desk. His leg did not give way under him.

Tommy sighed in relief. He lit another match and was relieved to see there was a desk lamp. He flicked on its switch and it cast enough light for him to look around the room without the aid of matches.

The keys were hanging on the wall in several big bunches on rings. They were mounted on small hooks on a board, with labels above that indicated which floor they were for or if they were keys for use below stairs. Tommy stood before the board and picked off the bunch for Captain Blake's floor. Each key had the room number it referred to embossed on its end. Tommy flicked through the bunch until he reached the correct one.

From his pocket he produced a large bar of soft soap provided by Annie. It had become warm in his pocket and he hoped this would aid it to take a good impression. He rested the bar on the desk and pressed the key end into it, first one side, and then the other. He checked the impressions. They seemed satisfactory. Making sure there was no soap left on the key, he replaced it in the correct place and restored the soap to his pocket. He turned off the desk lamp and carefully opened the door to Mrs Mackin's office. There appeared to be no one around.

Tommy slipped out and headed back the way he had come, passing by the boot room and the cupboard of cleaning materials. He was just passing the laundry when he heard footsteps approaching and he darted into the room to avoid being seen. He had only a moment to enjoy his relief, before he realised the footsteps were coming directly to the door and suddenly it was swung back. He was ready with an excuse, anything he could think of, when he realised the new arrival was the little maid with the towels.

"Are you still here?" she declared, looking surprised.

"I… ah… exactly which sheets are bed sheets?" Tommy put on his best impression of being a helpless male.

The maid gave a giggle.

"See, you should have let me help."

"I should have, yes," Tommy looked duly abashed.

The maid went to a shelf and picked off a pile of linen.

"Come on, I'll show you out. Else you'll be lost down here all night."

Tommy was not resistant to her help now his mission was concluded. He followed her out of the labyrinth and had some trouble persuading her not to come with him to his room to change the bed herself. He eventually was rid of her and went to seek out Clara, pleased with his success. There was only one issue as far as he could see – what was he going to do with the extra set of bed linen he had just acquired?

Chapter Twenty-Seven

Clara declined to go on the excursion the next day with the rest of the party, she had things to attend to. In truth, many of the holiday makers were rather depressed about the whole affair – two deaths among their company had somewhat diminished their spirits – and it seemed quite a sombre procession that left the hotel that morning. The driver and his conductor mirrored their passengers' grim demeanours and it seemed no one was much up for sightseeing, but it was better than staying indoors.

The fine weather that had so far graced their adventure had also chosen to depart. A particularly unpleasant drizzle was lacing down outside as the charabanc rattled its engine into life and left the hotel behind. Clara watched the departure from the hotel foyer and then went to the hotel's double front doors and stared out into the rain. She intended to go into town that morning and that would mean walking out into this weather. Resigned to her fate, Clara borrowed a hotel umbrella from a stand of them near the door and set forth.

There were, fortunately, not too many turnings along the road that led into town, so she did not go astray as she left the confines of the hotel grounds and dodged puddles. The town nearest the hotel was rather quaint.

The houses consisted of grey stone cottages, many of them looking fairly ancient, though newer builds in a modern style were springing up around the perimeter. Clara walked past the town's common, where one or two determined dog walkers were bracing themselves against the weather. Otherwise people were opting to remain indoors, unless they had to go outside.

Clara found her way to the locksmith's shop. He had a splendid array of shiny brass padlocks in his narrow window and a few shop models of locks that he might install on doors. A large poster stuck to one of the windowpanes declared that he cut keys and would come out day or night (even on Sundays) to deal with a troublesome lock. Clara wandered in and found she had to ring a bell on a counter to attract the proprietor of the premises.

The locksmith was a robust young man who looked like he spent a good deal of time sitting around and eating. In fact, he appeared on his shop floor with an apple in his hand, which he was munching away on. When he observed that it was a young woman who had entered his shop – and not a bad looking one at that – he hastily put the apple to one side and wiped his fingers on his shop apron.

"How can I help?" he enquired, putting on a breezy smile.

"I am having a problem with a key," Clara informed him. "It is such a nuisance and I thought you might be able to help."

The young locksmith beamed at her. He liked being helpful to pretty young women, especially as his usual customers tended to either be farmers after new padlocks for their barns or old women who had lost their house key while out shopping.

"Tell me the problem and I shall see if I can fix it," he said.

Clara produced the lump of soap Tommy had taken the key impression with. She had wrapped it in a handkerchief and now laid it on the shop counter and carefully unfolded the hanky. The locksmith initially thought she had a large padlock in the parcel, but as the soap bar emerged he looked perplexed.

"I have an old pantry key," Clara explained hastily, seeing his face. "It broke this morning, right before my cook was due to unlock the pantry and begin preparing dinner for a special party I have on tonight. It was most vexing. The shaft has quite sheared in two. I was able to make this impression of the key, in the hope that you would be able to use it to make a temporary replacement. I could not bring the original as my poor cook is endeavouring to use it to unlock the pantry and I feared you would need it some time to make a copy."

The locksmith stared at the bar of soap and scratched his head.

"I could fix the key, perhaps," he said. "If not, I could make a perfect copy from the original. But from a bar of soap…"

"We have to get the pantry open," Clara told him. "It was simply impossible to bring the original. It took me an hour to walk here as it is. By the time you had fixed the key and I had walked back the morning would be lost and some of the dishes I had intended for my party require a day of preparation. At the same time, I did not dare wait around to see if they could find a way to work the broken key to open the pantry, so I might bring it here once they were done, in case they failed and needed a replacement after all. I decided my best option was to make an impression and come at once. At least then I might get a spare, and if they can't open the pantry, all might not be lost."

The locksmith was still staring at the bar of soap.

"It won't be perfect," he said, poking the soap with a finger. "There will be little defects."

"But can you make a working key?" Clara demanded.

"Probably," the locksmith continued to prod the soap as though it was a foreign substance to him. "But I don't like doing a half-hearted job."

"This will be purely temporary. Once I have a working spare, I can bring the original down to you without worry."

The locksmith nodded, gnawing on his lip with a hint of anxiety. He was beginning to regret that the woman had walked into his shop at all that morning.

"I've never made a key from an impression in a bar of soap before."

"But, you must have used impressions to make keys before?" Clara said, a pang of doubt entering her mind. After all, what you read about in magazines was not necessarily what was practical, or even possible, in the real world. Tommy might have gone to all this effort for nothing.

"Usually I take a key blank, like one of these," the locksmith opened a draw behind his counter and took out what looked like a key but with no teeth cut into its end. "Now, I will take my little files and my saw and make a copy of the pattern of the original key. I am very precise and my duplicates are never faulty. But here you are asking me to work from a bar of soap."

The locksmith scratched his chin.

"The soap is too pale for me to get a good idea of the pattern," he peered very closely at the impression in the soap. "Hmm, maybe if I…"

He wandered absentmindedly out to the back of his shop, leaving Clara and her bar of soap at the counter. He seemed to be gone a long time, but when he returned he had a small crucible in his hand, like something a chemist would use.

"This is lead solder," he told Clara, waving the crucible at her. "I keep it about for fixing keys and making repairs. It isn't a permanent fix, too soft, but it is useful when I need to put a key back together and then copy it. Had you brought your original with you, I would have fixed it with lead solder and then worked from it. As it is, I think I can use this another way."

There was a little stove at the corner of the counter. The locksmith lit it with some matches and stood the crucible on top. The lead slowly began to melt.

"I make lead soldiers too," the locksmith added, glancing at Clara to see if this would interest her. "Proper ones, using moulds I buy from catalogues. And then I paint then in the correct colours. People buy them for their children, they are educational because the uniforms are all precise. Some of these toy ones you see in the shops are so poor and the colours all wrong. Its unthinkable!"

"I can imagine," Clara said politely.

"How is a child to learn anything from a toy soldier in the wrong uniform," the locksmith suddenly became rather shy and could not quite meet Clara's eyes. "I have a full regiment of the King's Royal Artillery in my workshop, all correctly painted and with proper insignia, if you would like to see it…"

"Maybe another time," Clara said, trying not to show her amusement at his gentle attempt to impress her. Probably he didn't meet a lot of women and had not yet discovered most could care less about lead soldiers, whether in proper uniform or not. Most women, if taken by such outfits, rather preferred their soldiers living and breathing.

The lead had melted and the locksmith carefully poured it into the impression in the soap bar. It formed a glistening pool, with a shimmer on its surface that resemble the pretty pattern of oil on water.

"It will take a moment to harden," the locksmith went back to his drawer and pulled out a key blank. "Who are you having to your party?"

"Old friends of my husband," Clara said quickly.

"Oh, you are married then?" the locksmith looked disappointed.

"I am," Clara lied.

"But you are not wearing a wedding ring?"

Clara pretended to bristle with affront, when really she

was cursing herself for her foolishness.

"This is the Twentieth Century, a girl need not wear a wedding ring to be married. The wedding ring is a form of shackle declaring a woman tied to a man, much like the ring in a bull's nose. I am not shackled to my husband. I chose to marry him."

The locksmith was further confused by this outburst, but, like many of his generation, he had come to learn that women thought a lot differently these days to how they had done in his mother's or grandmother's time. He accepted Clara's statement with a nod.

"I reckon that should be hard enough now," he said, distracting himself with the cast of the key. He carefully plucked it from the soap and set it by his blank, then he began to work cutting a new key.

Clara felt she had been rather forthright and maybe a little rude. She regretted her little rant, even if it had been to cover her own faux pas. She decided to make amends.

"Might you have an example in your collection of a cavalry man?" she asked.

"I do," the locksmith looked up brightly. "On horseback and carrying a sabre."

"Might I purchase it?" Clara continued. "For my nephew, who is very fond of such things."

The locksmith smiled.

"With pleasure. Let me just do the key."

He worked for half an hour getting the key blank to resemble perfectly the impression Clara had given him. When he was done he went out the back of his shop and returned with a little figurine. It proved to be a very fine cavalry man on a white horse, carrying his sabre aloft. The detail was extraordinary and Clara found herself bending down to stare at it.

"Most remarkable!" she declared as she handed over the money for key and soldier.

"I like them to be just right," the locksmith smiled proudly.

"They are indeed just that. Thank you for your help. I

am sure my nephew will be delighted by the figure."

"I hope he is," the locksmith was grinning at her with the delight only a consummate artisan can get from having his work admired, all the time as she left the shop.

Clara stood on the pavement outside and first studied the cavalry man, whose detail was truly breath-taking, then she looked at her new key which was equally finely cut. Pocketing them at last, she went about her next task.

Chapter Twenty-eight

Clara spotted the local grocer's lad just leaving a house where he had delivered their weekly order of tinned goods. He had one of those big shop bicycles with a huge wicker basket on the front where he could carry his deliveries. He already looked soaked and, judging by the number of parcels in his basket, he had a fair way to go as yet before he was done. Clara paused him to ask if there was a telephone in town.

"Mrs Pemble at the Post Office has one," the boy informed her. "She will let anyone use it for tuppence, unless you want to call outside the country. She won't let you do that. Won't even let you ring someone in Wales. Says that is foreign soil and she won't have her 'phone used in such a manner. Which is a shame, 'cos I have an aunt in Wales and ma would like to ring her from time to time."

Clara thanked him for this unnecessary amount of information and he set off on his way once more.

The Post Office was easy enough to find. Like most such places it was well signposted, with a prominent board outside declaring its purpose. It was set in one of the cottages, with a pretty bay window made of lots of small panes of glass. Clara entered and found that it was quite busy with people. It seemed this was the place to come to get out of the rain and have a natter, for most of the customers (if they could be described as such) were talking among themselves rather than actually buying anything. Mrs Pemble was behind the counter, a lady in her fifties with thick greying hair she tied back in a plait. She had half-moon spectacles and had her hands wrapped around a mug of warm tea as she listened to one of her regulars debating the falling quality of black boot polish.

Mrs Pemble adjusted her attention to Clara as she entered, spying a potential customer at long last.

"May I help?" she asked in her best impression of a well-spoken lady. Mrs Pemble worked on the theory that most of the customers who she did not recognise when they came into her Post Office were tourists and, therefore, (to a woman who had never taken a holiday because she could not afford it) very well-off and well-spoken.

"May I use your telephone?" Clara enquired.

"Why yes. It is tuppence for a short call, threepence for longer. I must insist you only place your call within England, however."

"That is not a problem," Clara assured her. "I want to call Brighton."

"Then do come this way, I keep the 'phone in a little back room, so customers using it may have their privacy."

Mrs Pemble ushered Clara through the hatch in her counter and down a short corridor. The telephone had been placed in what once might have been a tiny pantry. It stood on a narrow, tall table in one corner, while a wooden chair took up the remaining space.

"Will you be requiring the telephone directory?" Mrs Pemble asked.

"Not for the moment," Clara responded, and the woman departed.

Clara knew the number for the Brighton Constabulary off by heart. When the girl at the exchange came onto the line Clara gave her the number and then waited as the 'phone rang. It seemed to take a long time before it was answered.

"Brighton Police Station. Desk Sergeant Hargreaves speaking."

Clara gave a silent groan. She was not on the best terms with the Desk Sergeant and had rather hoped a constable might have picked up instead.

"I would like to speak with Inspector Park-Coombs," Clara said into the narrow receiver that rather looked like the trumpet of a black daffodil.

"The Inspector does not speak to random people, miss."

"I am far from random," Clara informed him. "I am Clara Fitzgerald…"

"Oh, you," The Desk Sergeant interrupted her. "I thought you had gone on holiday and wouldn't be disturbing us for a while."

"I am on holiday," Clara said, managing to keep her temper. "But something has come up and I must speak with the Inspector."

"I think he might be busy," Desk Sergeant Hargreaves told her bluntly.

"Perhaps you might ask him, rather than just assume that?" Clara responded tetchily. "It is rather important."

"It always is with you."

"You might remember that I am a taxpayer and thus pay your wages along with the Inspector's. Thus, as a taxpayer…"

"I'll fetch him, shall I?" the Desk Sergeant said sourly, abandoning the telephone before Clara could finish her rant.

She waited impatiently for what seemed like ages, before a new voice came on the line.

"Miss Fitzgerald? Everything all right? I thought you were on holiday?"

Clara recognised the sage tone of Inspector Park-Coombs and relaxed a little.

"I am perfectly all right, Inspector. Sadly the same

cannot be said for two of my fellow charabanc tourers. One in particular has passed away in rather troubling circumstances."

"Oh?" Inspector Park-Coombs managed to fit a lot of implication into that one word.

"I wondered if you could do a little bit of what Tommy refers to as 'background work' on her. I fear she has been murdered, but the local police are refusing to listen to me. They are quite content to consider her death a suicide."

"And you are not?"

"The woman was attacked twice before her death in a suspicious fashion. She was concerned someone wished her harm. Would you, Inspector, when given such facts, ignore them?"

"I take your point," Inspector Park-Coombs said. "But I am a rather busy man and not, I might remind you, at your beck and call."

Clara felt rebuffed, though, she supposed, she had rather just assumed the Inspector would drop everything and help her.

"I apologise," Clara said. "I am just rather at a dead end and hoped for your help. The woman was called Mrs Hunt and she was resident in Brighton. She compiled her own list of suspects in the case, but so far none have presented themselves as obvious killers. I thought you might be able to find something out about her, or at least perhaps her husband, Mr Hunt. Mrs Hunt was involved in a death herself, of a Brighton girl. The case was deemed suicide also."

"Quite a tangle," Inspector Park-Coombs sighed down the phoneline. "But I shall only have records on her if she was ever involved in something criminal in Brighton."

"I appreciate that, but I rather need some fresh ideas. She seemed to dislike a good many people, but whether there was cause for that I cannot say."

Park-Coombs gave another professional sigh.

"I'll take a look and see if anything turns up."

"Thank you, Inspector. I shall owe you dinner, or

something when I return."

The Inspector gave a harrumph and the 'phone went dead. Park-Coombs did not much hold with saying goodbye. Clara put down the little bell shaped receiver she had held to her ear, and went to find Mrs Pemble to pay for her call. The Post Office had emptied somewhat since there had been a break in the rain and people had piled out to hurry home. Clara handed over her thruppence, for it had been a long call.

"Do you have a street directory for the area?" she enquired.

"Naturally!" Mrs Pemble bobbed down behind her counter and reappeared with a neatly bound red book. "Now who might one be looking for?"

Clara paused, not sure if she wanted the whole Post Office to overhear her, but Mrs Pemble had her hands firmly placed on the directory and it rather looked like she was not going to simply give it to Clara. After a moment of annoyance, Clara answered.

"Inspector Wake, retired."

"Oh, that my dear is simple!" Mrs Pemble dropped her pretentiousness for an instant in her delight. "He lives at No.12 The Street. It's a quaint old cottage, several centuries old and kept in good repair. Inspector Wake is very popular in these parts and a keen fisherman. Why, he once investigated a break-in in this very Post Office, and apprehended the criminals too! More than can be said for this modern lot of policemen. They just don't seem interested in crime, unless its particularly violent or involves someone important."

"How might I find The Street?" Clara asked.

"You'll need to go down the road a way, until you see Church Lane, and then, just beyond that is Surrey Street, turn down there, following Clay Road and The Street is right in front of you."

The directions were shot at Clara rather swiftly and she had to process them for a moment before they made sense. She thanked Mrs Pemble and sauntered out of the

Post Office, feeling that a dozen pairs of eyes were upon her.

The weather had turned again and heavy rain fell down as Clara hastened along, following the directions Mrs Pemble had given her. After one or two false turns she eventually came upon The Street and found, as Mrs Pemble had stated, that it consisted of a number of older cottages. Probably these were some of the original homes that had first sprung up in the town, they certainly had an ancient look about them. Clara found No.12 and rapped on the door with her umbrella handle. It was a while before anyone answered.

"Yes?" an elderly man in carpet slippers and with a walrus moustache opened the door and addressed her. He was wearing a brown cardigan with the sleeves rolled up, and the soap suds on his hands suggested he had been doing the washing up.

"Inspector Wake?"

"Indeed. But no one comes calling on me these days who I don't know. Who are you?"

"Clara Fitzgerald," Clara introduced herself. "Private detective, for my sins. I am here about an old case that I believe you worked on?"

Inspector Wake observed her carefully. He might have retired to a life of rural quiet, but he had not lost his policing instincts.

"You best come in. I suspect you have a lot to explain to me," he said, reverting to his inspector demeanour.

Clara followed him into a small front room, where the ceiling was low enough to crack skulls and consisted of white plaster and dark brown beams. A fire was burning in the fireplace and chasing out the damp chill of the day. Inspector Wake showed her to a comfortable sofa and offered her tea. Clara accepted and some time was wasted as the formalities of tea-making and the bringing forth of the tea tray were observed. When they were both settled, Clara opened proceedings.

"I have been asked to look into the circumstances

surrounding the death of a lady at lake Windermere," Clara said, acting as if her client was still alive, which she was most definitely not. "The lady in question was connected with a case I think you may have looked into, and I was curious whether that past case might have any bearing on the current one."

"Who is this lady?" Inspector Wake asked, handing over a plate of biscuits.

"Her name was Mrs Mildred Hunt, late of Brighton. She drowned in Lake Windermere just the other day. The strangeness of the matter is that ten years ago she was here acting as tutor and chaperone to a young lady who also drowned in the lake. Mrs Hunt had returned after all these years to pay her respects to her former pupil."

"And who was the girl?" Inspector Wake asked.

"Miss Wignell. As far as I can ascertain it was believed at the time that she had drowned herself. The circumstances were not suspicious."

"And now they are?"

"Now I am concerned that someone is blaming Mrs Hunt for the girl's death. Or it may be all coincidence. But she drowned in the same spot as her pupil did, and there had been attempts on her life beforehand."

"Now, Miss Fitzgerald, you have aroused my curiosity," Inspector Wake smiled. "I am, obviously, no longer able to reference files in the police station, but I do recall certain cases."

"Do you recall the case of Miss Wignell? It can't have been long before you retired."

"Miss Wignell," Inspector Wake mused. "I do recall the death of a girl in the lake, but not the name. She was a slip of a thing, had been out painting when the incident occurred. My impression from the parents was that she was prone to dark moods and might have taken her life while in one of these."

"Yes, that is the case I am referring to," Clara agreed, feeling hopeful. "Was there anything suspicious about it?"

Inspector Wake thought for a while, trawling through

his memories on the subject.

"Not particularly," he said at last. "Though it was rather sudden, and there was the odd fact that when she was dragged from the water she was still holding her paintbrush. That stuck with me. Why take a paintbrush with you to commit suicide?"

That was an odd detail.

"Perhaps she was so overcome she didn't think to drop it before she threw herself in?" Clara suggested, though she felt it a rather flimsy notion.

"I have attended a lot of suicides over the years, Miss Fitzgerald," Inspector Wake said, pulling together his white eyebrows until they formed a snowy ridge over his eyes. "I have found, in most cases, that the urge is neither sudden nor without serious forethought. In general, there is a thoroughness to the preparations, a certain sense of finality comes over the person and they aim to finish their affairs before they depart. I have never know one to be suddenly taken on a whim to kill themselves, nor to depart so rapidly from this earthly plane that they did not conclude their affairs first. I have known people to pay their bills, cancel the milk and tidy the house before killing themselves, but not the other way around."

"The paintbrush in her hand implies Miss Wignell was not expecting to die, in your opinion?" Clara pressed.

"Everything pointed to suicide, Miss Fitzgerald, a stray paintbrush is nothing to make a case on. But it did strike me that everyone was rather too swift to rule out an accident. Perhaps the girl, trying to get a better view of the lake for her painting, had stumbled through the reeds at the bank and tumbled in? Perhaps her tutor, who I might add I found to be extremely hard of hearing, did not hear her in time? Or perhaps she simply did not rouse from her sleep?"

"In either case, it would be easy to lay the blame at Mrs Hunt's feet."

"It would indeed. I only recollect the woman vaguely, but she was not someone who was particularly likeable, and the death of an only child is a deeply distressing thing. I ask myself, in cases like this, how would I have felt? How would I have reacted? I dare say I would not have been as gracious as the Wignells were."

Clara thought that a very good point. But there was one question she had to ask.

"Did anything suggest to you that Miss Wignell had been murdered by her tutor?"

Inspector Wake gave a rather dramatic sigh and puffed out his cheeks as he contemplated the question.

"If memory serves me rightly, I thought the tutor rather cold over the whole affair. I mean, she hardly seemed distressed by her charge being found drowned. Yet, I rather suspected that was her nature. No. I don't think I was concerned it was murder."

"Thank you Inspector Wake, this has been most helpful," Clara rose and the retired inspector showed her to the front door.

"I assume you have had the debatable pleasure of meeting my replacement at the station," Inspector Wake rose those snowy eyebrows of his as he opened the door for her.

"Inspector Gateley? Yes, I have."

"I didn't choose him," Wake said with a look of satisfaction. "All policemen have their flaws, but he is exceptionally pig-headed. I doubt you will get very far with him."

"That I have already concluded," Clara nodded, adding her own sigh.

"If you do happen to find anything suspicious about the Wignell case I would appreciate being told. Unlike my successor, I am not opposed to being gently told I was wrong."

"If I discover anything new I shall let you know," Clara promised before she said goodbye.

While she had not discovered anything revelatory from Inspector Wake, she had enjoyed their conversation and it was good to know she was not alone in feeling that

Inspector Gateley was allowing his arrogance to blind him to facts. She headed back to the hotel, making a brief stop in a local bookshop where she found a pamphlet that would serve her purposes very well.

Chapter Twenty-nine

Clara shook out her umbrella on the hotel's large doorstep and then strode into the foyer. She was a little sodden around the edges and rain drops splattered from her folded umbrella as she returned it to the stand. She was glad to be indoors and out of the dismal weather.

"Miss Fitzgerald."

Clara glanced up and saw that Mr Stover was glaring at her in the fine way he alone was capable of. Clara wondered what she had done to annoy him now.

"Mr Stover, do you require something?" Clara asked in her most pleasant manner, there was no point infuriating the man further while she remained under his roof.

"Dr Macguire has called for you," Mr Stover said, still looking irritated by her presence. "He is awaiting you in the main lounge. He would not tell me what it was about and insisted on waiting despite my telling him that I had no idea how long you would be."

Clara smiled at the hotel manager, formal to the last, and headed for the main lounge. It was fuller than it had been on past days, since many of the hotel guests had opted to stay indoors out of the rain. A fire had been stoked in the large fireplace and several guests were loitering around it. Including, Clara noted, the strange girl who looked only a meal or two away from starvation. She seemed to feel the cold dreadfully and was wrapped up in a thick shawl by the fire. Dr Macguire, on the other hand, was sitting by the window, drinking tea and watching rain fall down the panes of glass.

"I hear you have been waiting for me?" Clara came to his chair and took the one opposite.

"I have, Miss Fitzgerald. Would you care for tea?" he indicated that he had a second cup at the ready. "You look a little damp, if I might say so."

"I have walked into town and back," Clara explained. "And yes I would like tea."

Dr Macguire went through the processes of pouring milk into the porcelain cup followed by steaming tea. He offered the sugar bowl, but Clara declined.

"Have you been waiting long?" Clara asked as she took her cup.

"No, hardly a moment really. I felt it important to come and see you," Dr Macguire paused. "I fear I owe you an apology, Miss Fitzgerald."

"Oh?" Clara said, intrigued.

"When last we spoke I was rather dismissive about your concerns. However, your suspicions had me intrigued and I conducted a few further tests on the remains of Mrs Hunt. In particular I looked at her stomach contents, a most enlightening part of the human body I oft find."

"Quite," Clara said, trying not to think of such things while drinking her tea.

"I tested the contents and the results were surprising, well, to me at least. Mrs Hunt was positively full of sleeping powder, the strong stuff doctors prescribe."

Clara clattered her teacup into its saucer as she jumped in excitement at this news.

"Mrs Hunt was drugged?"

"Most certainly. The quantity would have rendered her unconscious, that was how she could be dumped into the lake alive without making any commotion. It seems I and the Inspector were wrong to dismiss your concerns so out of hand."

Clara was taking in this revelation. Trying to fit it together with the other pieces of information she held.

"A hotel guest has reported her sleeping powders stolen," Clara said, thinking of Mrs Wignell. "It just so happens she has motive to want revenge on Mrs Hunt."

"Care to tell me the name of this person?" Dr Macguire asked.

"Not just yet, for I have several other suspects as well. But this is the information I needed. Now I know how it was done, the why is not so complicated, I have enough people with motive about this place, all that is left is 'who'. Who had the opportunity and the means to drug Mrs Hunt?"

"The only other item in Mrs Hunt's stomach was strong tea," Dr Macguire added. "I would say that is how the deadly dose was administered. By the way, there was enough of the sleeping powders in her stomach to be dangerous in itself. Even if she had not been thrown into the lake, she might well have died. I assume the killer offered her tea, much as I did to you."

Dr Macguire gave a morbid smile and Clara cast an eye at her teacup.

"That is not amusing," she told him.

"But quite the way it was done. The powders would have taken effect quite rapidly, say half-an-hour at the most? That must narrow your field of suspects. Judging by Mrs Hunt's temperature and condition when we arrived on the scene she must have been dead around four to six hours."

"Meaning she was killed around lunchtime," Clara nodded. "The murderer offered her fresh tea with her sandwiches. The question is who had the facilities to brew up a pot?"

"Tea can be carried in one of those German Thermos flasks," Macguire pointed out. "I have had hot coffee from such a thing."

"Have you tried tea from a Thermos? It tastes ghastly," Clara shook her head. "I can't see Mrs Hunt being persuaded to drink that. No, it was freshly made, I am sure of it. So someone must have brought a portable stove along with them on our trip to Windermere. It would be the only way to brew a pot of tea by the side of the lake. But I can't think of anyone who was carrying a bag that might have contained it."

"I shall leave the idea with you," Dr Macguire slurped the last of his tea from his cup. "I wanted to let you know my findings first, because I had been so crass before. But now I must go to Inspector Gateley and tell him."

"Thank you, Dr Macguire, this has been much appreciated," Clara stood and shook his hand.

He departed with that curious smile of his on his face.

Clara was excited, this news finally justified her suspicions, but there was more to be done as yet. As she went to replace her teacup on the tray with the teapot, she felt something heavy in her pocket and she was reminded of the key she had had made. There was no time like the present to see if it worked. She took one last look about the lounge, (no one was paying her the slightest attention) and headed upstairs.

The corridors were deserted at this time of day, except for the odd maid going about her chores. Clara doubted anyone would pay attention to her opening a room with a key, even if they were around, she would look much like any other guest entering their room. She slipped the new key from her pocket and hoped the locksmith's work was as good as his lead soldiers.

The key fitted into the lock on Blake's door smoothly, but that was not surprising, she was more concerned about whether it turned. She took a look first left then right, up and down the corridor, to ensure no one was about and then she turned the key. There was a click in the lock and the door opened easily. Clara was impressed, the locksmith had truly been a master of his craft, but she did not have time to dawdle. She entered the room and shut the door behind her.

Because Blake's death was deemed an obvious suicide (and because Inspector Gateley took very little interest in such cases) the police had not even bothered to search through his belongings as yet, and the room was exactly the same as it had been on the day Blake had hung himself from the light fixture.

Clara inspected the three-armed brass light that was installed in the ceiling. One arm was distinctly bent out of shape from bearing Captain Blake's weight. It was not hard to visualise the man hanging there and Clara grimaced to herself. If she was going to kill herself, she would not choose to slowly throttle to death at the end of a leather belt.

Captain Blake had kept his room in neat order, having formed a habit in the army for disciplined tidiness. Even two years after he had returned to civilian life (he had been formerly discharged in 1919) he had retained an almost obsessive need for cleanliness. Clara found herself looking at a room that was well-ordered, a room where chaos was not to be tolerated. It seemed remarkable, in a way, that Captain Blake had chosen to hang himself here and create disorder in his formal little world.

Clara started to search about. The drawers of the dresser were empty and the wardrobe contained three shirts, one pair of trousers, a smart jacket and a tie. Captain Blake had been wearing his remaining clothes and his shoes when he went to meet his maker. Clara searched the pockets of the jacket and trousers, and came upon a small velvet covered box that looked extremely familiar. She opened it to see a medal, identical to one that resided in a drawer at their home in Brighton. Just like Tommy, Captain Blake had been issued with the medals that commemorated the end of the war and all those who had served in it. Unlike Tommy, Captain Blake clearly took a pride in his trinket. Tommy could not even look at his. Clara returned the medal to its hiding place and moved on.

Captain Blake's suitcase was under the bed and virtually empty, though there was a book lying in it, a novel that appeared completely unread. The bedside cabinet proved more fruitful; Captain Blake had kept his diary in it. Clara took up the book with its black leather cover and flicked it open. It was one for this year, 1921, and it seemed Blake had been consistent about filling it in every day. Clara flicked the pages until they became blank, then she scrolled backwards to the very last entry;

"May 6th. Tuesday. Can't bear this place much more. People walk around pretending there wasn't a war and that everything is just the way it was. I despise them all. I am sick and tired of everything. The pain continues, despite the doctors telling me it should be gone by now. I don't think I can take it anymore. I met another ex-soldier in the music lounge. He wanted to talk about the war, about how we all felt afterwards. Couldn't stand it, wanted to tell him to shut up! Talked about this new-fangled idea called 'shell shock'. Maybe I have that. I certainly don't feel the same as I used to anymore. Sometimes I don't even feel sane. He made me angry with him, with myself, with everything. The anger makes me reckless. When it comes over me I start to think of ways to hurt myself. That is the only thing that sates it."

"Oh dear," Clara said, knowing full well who the ex-soldier Blake had talked to was. She didn't like to think that something Tommy had said during their conversation had resolved Blake to suicide.

She was flicking back through the pages when something fell out of the diary. It was a loose page that had been ripped free and wedged at the front. It dropped to the floor and Clara scooped it up.

"May 7th. Wednesday. To whoever reads this, though it does not matter now and I am in no position to suffer further I want to make one thing plain. My aunt's death was not at my hand. My aunt was Mrs Hunt, a woman I loathed for the way she treated my late mother, and yet, at the same time, as the sole remaining member (aside from myself) of my family, a woman I wanted to know better. I had hoped this holiday would enable that, but I found her a cold, shallow creature who took no more interest in me than she had when I was a boy.

"Her disdain made me angry, reminded me of all the hurts she had caused my mother. Some nights my mother would weep over the sister she would never see again, who had turned against her so bitterly. Her dying words were not for me, but for Mrs Hunt, a woman who did not deserve them. She expressed her longing one last time to be reconciled with her sister. I could not fulfil my mother's final wish, but I had thought to try and make peace with my aunt as a compromise. But the more I saw of my aunt, the more my hatred grew for her. She was wicked and had broken my mother's heart, and she did not even care.

"On our first evening in this hotel, having shared far too many hours on a charabanc with Mrs Hunt, my hatred overwhelmed me. I saw Mrs Hunt coming up the stairs and, in a thoughtless fury, I grabbed the nearest thing to hand – a chamber pot – and threw it down at her. She was struck and fell on the stairs. I thought I had killed her and instantly regretted my actions. Thankfully she survived. This is then my confession, I tried to kill my aunt but I did not succeed and the failed attempt shook me enough to deter me from trying again.

"I know some wonder if I might have murdered her. I did not. She died in the lake for a reason I don't know, but it was not at my hand. Still, I now find myself utterly and totally alone in this world, my one connection to my past is gone. There is a pain in my chest, my doctors tell me it is not my heart, at least not in any medical sense. But there is still that pain. I wake with it. I go to sleep with it. It has left me so weary. I cannot see anything ahead for me. For months now I have contemplated my own death, I don't know what stopped me, but finally I am resolved. I just wished it to be known, before I leave this life, that I am not a murderer and I did not kill my aunt.

"Captain Robert Blake, Berkshire Regiment. 1921"

Clara restored the letter to the diary so that a policeman might find it, if ever any came to look for such a thing. At least she now knew she was not dealing with two murders. Captain Blake had taken his own life. And now she knew who was behind the chamber pot affair. She found herself looking sadly at the bent light fitting once again. How awful, and how utterly pointless.

She replaced the diary and let herself out of the room. She had learned what she needed to, after all. Blake had not hung himself from a guilty conscience, and there was still a killer on the loose, and she had to find them. As she locked Captain Blake's door she found herself thinking over how so many people had been touched in a negative way by Mrs Hunt's presence in their lives. What sort of person goes through the world aiming to hurt others? And could someone be blamed for wanting to stop such a creature from causing more harm?

Chapter Thirty

Clara had some hours to spare before the charabanc party returned and she was temporarily at a loose end. She certainly had lots to think over, but that did not lend itself to action just yet. She retired to the dining room to see if luncheon was being served and to mull over what she had learned so far today.

Dr Masters was at a table looking very sombre, when he saw Clara he waved her over and though she would have rather sat alone so she might think, Clara felt it was only polite to join him.

"Do you care for ham salad?" Dr Masters asked as she sat down. "Or does it strike you as a tad Continental all this cold meat and lettuce leaves? I was inclined toward a more hearty ploughman's, personally."

He handed her over the luncheon menu and Clara browsed it for a moment then settled on an assorted platter of miniature sandwiches. They did not have to wait long for a waiter to appear at their table and take their order.

"How is your patient?" Clara asked Dr Masters.

For a moment he looked bemused and then he smiled.

"Thriving. She has another decade in her at least."

"Does she not leave her room at all? I have never seen

her about. I would have noticed an extra elderly lady at dinner, aside from Miss Plante, of course."

"She is reclusive," Dr Masters said swiftly. "She sits with the windows open and takes the air."

"It seems a long way to come to just sit by a window," Clara shook her head at the vagaries of some people. "Does she care for visitors? I am at a loose end myself this afternoon and I would gladly pay her a call."

"That won't be necessary."

Dr Masters spoke swiftly, too swiftly and gave the answer Clara had anticipated he would. She was beginning to have serious doubts about the reality of this 'elderly patient' of his.

"You did not go on the charabanc excursion today?" Dr Masters asked to change the subject.

"No. I had some business to attend to. Captain Blake's suicide has rather put the cat among the pigeons."

"Indeed, it has," Dr Masters paused as their pot of tea arrived. "I didn't really know the fellow, but from what I saw of him he struck me as the morbid sort. Not that you can always tell by looking at a man if he is inclined to suicidal thoughts."

"He was Mrs Hunt's nephew," Clara threw in the statement to see what it stirred up.

"Oh. I didn't realise," Masters engaged himself in pouring tea. "I suppose the shock of it all overcame him."

"I don't think he cared for his aunt in the slightest," Clara corrected. "I think it is just coincidence. He had had enough of life."

"Tragic," Dr Masters seemed sincere enough in this assessment. "Perhaps there was a tendency in the family? Suicide can be like that, you see it all the time. A person kills themselves and the next thing someone is mentioning that their late father, or brother, or uncle did exactly the same. Certain families seem to inherit a fascination with self-murder like others inherit flat feet or hooked noses."

"While I have no doubt there might be validity in that

claim, in this case it is not tenable. Mrs Hunt was murdered and I now have the proof."

"Really?" Dr Masters had gone a touch pale and he had to put his teacup down before it rattled in his hand.

Clara was stopped for a moment from carrying on as their luncheon arrived. Dr Masters looked down at his hearty Ploughman's grimly, his appetite had evaporated.

"Mrs Hunt was drugged on sleeping powders before she drowned. Since she could not drug and then drag herself into the lake, we have to assume she was murdered. Someone gave her a last cup of deadly tea and then waited for it to take effect. The sleeping powders it contained were close to being a fatal dose as it was, but to make certain and to fool everyone into thinking she had committed suicide and drowned, Mrs Hunt was thrown into the waters of Windermere while still alive," Clara picked up a triangular egg and cress sandwich. "Positively wicked, don't you think?"

"It is certainly very calculating," Dr Masters agreed, finding himself suddenly absorbed in cutting the chunk of cheese on his plate into small cubes.

"The powders were stolen from Mrs Wignell, at least I think they were," Clara sighed. "It is entirely possible that the Wignells invented the story of the powders being stolen to mask their own actions. If so, they were far too honest with me about their relationship with Mrs Hunt. It would have been far better to say nothing and leave me in the dark concerning their grievance. Of course, Mrs Wignell's powders might have genuinely been misplaced and those used to drug Mrs Hunt's tea could have come from another source. A doctor's bag, for instance."

Dr Masters looked up sharply.

"I hope you are not accusing me?"

"Is there reason to?" Clara asked, feigning an innocent smile. "What cause would you have to harm Mrs Hunt?"

"None," Dr Masters said stoutly. "None at all. The woman was a stranger to me and I to her. It would be an act of madness for me to kill a person I did not know."

Clara investigated another of the sandwiches on her plate and discovered it was cold chicken before she spoke.

"How odd."

"What is?" Dr Masters sounded anxious.

"That you say Mrs Hunt did not know you, when she made such a fuss about being put in a room opposite yours. I am reliably informed that it was seeing you in the room across the hall that made her insist on being moved."

Dr Masters gave a grunt as he prodded at the ham on his plate.

"I am rather regretting asking you to join me," he said.

"I am sorry for that," Clara said and meaning it. "But when a woman is dead and people are keeping secrets from me I become somewhat aggressive in my curiosity."

"Just because a person has secrets, does not mean they are a killer," Dr Masters pointed out sharply.

"No, it doesn't. But I would like to know why Mrs Hunt was so averse to you, especially considering you later were called to attend to her injuries."

"I did not throw a chamber pot at her," Dr Masters pointed his fork at Clara.

"That I know for certain," Clara assured him.

Dr Masters looked at her curiously.

"You know who did, then?"

"Yes," Clara admitted without expanding on the subject.

"I was genuinely coming down the stairs when Mrs Hunt was injured," Dr Masters relaxed a little, coming to the conclusion Clara did not intend a fearsome inquisition. "Everything I said about the woman's injuries and the treatment I gave her was purely professional. There is no secret in that."

"Mrs Hunt did not treat you well, even then," Clara noted. "She was a spiteful woman."

"Mrs Hunt, no doubt, was less than pleased to see my face again. You are right, Clara, we did know each other. But my being in this hotel at the same time as her is pure coincidence."

"How did you know Mrs Hunt?"

"Through my mother, God rest her soul. Since you are well aware of Mrs Hunt's nature it should not surprise you that her connection to my mother was neither kind nor honest. Mrs Hunt became embroiled in a sordid affair with my father, a man who I refuse to have anything further to do with."

"How did Mrs Hunt meet your father, if I might ask?"

"My father is a doctor, like myself. Mrs Hunt was one of his patients while she was teaching at a girls school. It seems they began to see each other quite regularly soon after. The affair broke my mother's heart and I swear led to her decline in health. My father had enough conscience left in him to break off the relationship with Mrs Hunt when my mother became fatally ill. By then it was too late," Dr Masters gave a sigh and shook his head. "My father was not discreet. The entire neighbourhood knew of what he was doing. The shame of it all strained my mother's heart. I was a lad then, just coming to my first exams and wondering what to make of my life. I chose to become a doctor in the hope that I might be able to save my mother's life with my knowledge. It was a foolish whim, but I was desperate. Sadly, I had barely begun my studies when she passed. I continued on, however, finding the subject more fascinating than I had expected."

"And with no more thought of Mrs Hunt than you could help," Clara nodded, understanding Dr Masters slightly better. "And then, out of the blue, she is here."

"I haven't seen that woman in ten years, but I could not forget her. I know she recognised me when I came out of my room. This rather makes me distinctive," Dr Masters pointed at the scar of his hare lip.

"It is well mended," Clara said consolingly. "It certainly doesn't mar your looks."

Dr Masters smiled and almost blushed.

"My father fixed it for me when I was a baby. He always wanted to be a surgeon," Dr Masters shook his head. "When I saw Mrs Hunt I was surprised, but I was even more astonished when she insisted on being moved away from my room. I was a little offended at how she took against me. Though, now I understand that she was afraid someone was out to harm her and my presence so near must have scared her."

"In her last days Mrs Hunt was plagued by paranoia, and much of it was not without validity," Clara explained to him. "She knew someone was out to kill her and suddenly she was surrounded by a number of people she had hurt or offended. She must have thought herself in the middle of a nest of vipers. The question, of course, is why she chose to invite them all here in the first place."

Clara threw in the last comment, knowing it to be untrue, to test the doctor's reaction. He was surprised, which she had somewhat expected, or rather hoped for.

"She invited all her enemies to one place?" Dr Masters found the idea astounding. "It sounds like a fine way to get oneself killed."

"A sort of suicide, you mean?" Clara found the idea interesting, if not very plausible. "Sit yourself among your enemies and see which one tries to kill you? No, she was too worried about herself for that to have been the case. Still, she did rather set herself up for harm."

"Am I off your suspect list?" Dr Masters asked slyly, raising one eyebrow as he broached the question.

"No one is off my suspect list until I know who killed Mrs Hunt, but you do have one point in your favour."

"Which is?"

"I cannot place you at Windermere. You were not on the charabanc, unless you somehow made your own way there. It is quite a distance on foot, though not implausible by bicycle, but I can't see how you would have had the opportunity to kill her."

"How very reassuring," Dr Masters laughed. "Now, perhaps I shall offer some information in return? Mrs Wignell came to my room and asked if I could prescribe her some sleeping powders temporarily until she could return home and see her own doctor. The ones she was taking are particularly strong and addictive, not the sort I would willingly supply. I prescribed something much weaker, but which would hopefully help."

"Was this before or after Mrs Hunt died?"

"After. So it would seem that Mrs Wignell was genuinely missing her sleeping powders, else she would not have asked for more."

"It does not excuse her from the crime," Clara countered. "But, would a woman waste something so precious to her on a person she hated?"

"More to the point, Mrs Wignell was well aware of the right dosage for the medication. She would have known how much, or rather, how little was needed in a person unused to them to induce sleepiness."

"So, she could have avoided unnecessary wastage?" Clara nodded. "That would make sense. It does seem whoever used the powders was heavy-handed with them."

Clara finished her lunch and poured herself another cup of tea. Dr Masters had hardly touched his meal. Clara suddenly felt guilty, she had rather probed him and it was not as if he had a great deal of evidence against him to justify all her questions. She had stirred up the past once again.

"I'm sorry. I do get carried away sometimes," she said. "I would offer to buy you cake as consolation, if you still have an appetite?"

"I understand you are trying to solve a crime," Dr Masters answered. "That means asking a lot of impolite questions."

He finally started on his Ploughman's, his appetite having a resurge. Clara let him eat for a few moments uninterrupted, letting her eye wander about the dining room.

"Have you noticed that girl about the hotel? Thin as a rake and looks a frail little thing," Clara said casually.

Dr Masters seemed to choke on his food.

"Good heavens!" Clara cried out, about to assist him.

Dr Masters hammered a fist onto his chest, the noise he was making alerting the entire room to his drama. He suddenly gave a sharper cough and began to breathe again.

"Are you all right?" Clara asked, watching as his face went from a horrid reddish colour back to pink.

"You do know how to ask all the wrong questions," Dr Masters said as his breath returned to him.

"What do you mean?"

Dr Masters shook his head.

"It seems my secret has been wandering about the place," he coughed. "And trust you to have spotted her."

"The girl? She is your patient?" Clara suddenly grasped what had caused the drama. "But why is that a secret? Surely you are just helping the girl back to health?"

Dr Masters chuckled at her.

"For the moment I shall leave you wondering, that is one secret I refuse to disclose," Dr Masters rose from the table. "Thank you for an interesting dinner, Clara, but perhaps we shall not repeat it too soon."

Dr Masters left the dining, and Clara was left wondering what new revelation she had just stumbled upon.

Chapter Thirty-one

That evening, after dinner, Clara quietly went about the hotel looking for Miss Smythe. She eventually spotted her in the music lounge, listening to another guest attempting to play a tune on the piano. There were a lot of dud notes and pauses as the player worked his way through the piece. Miss Smythe didn't seem to notice, she was watching the rain falling down through the open French Windows that led onto the terrace. Clara sat in an armchair near her, making sure she was in Miss Smythe's line of vision and then retrieved the pamphlet she had bought earlier that day from her bag. It was plainly entitled on the front cover Practical Husbandry for the Owners of Fancy Rats.

Though not a subject Clara was much attracted to, she had a feeling that it would interest Miss Smythe and hopefully draw her into a productive conversation. It was in fact several moments before Miss Smythe observed the pamphlet in Clara's hands.

"Oh," she said at first, her eyes widening with surprise. "Why, Miss Fitzgerald, do you keep rats?"

"Not at the moment," Clara glanced up from her reading. "That is to say, I am considering the possibility. They don't appeal to everyone, naturally."

"That is true," Miss Smythe nodded a little sadly. "Which is a shame considering they are truly remarkable creatures. Quite as intelligent as a dog and a jolly good deal cleaner. Rats are fastidious groomers."

"Then my reading interests do not trouble you?"

"Quite the opposite, I am glad to see another woman taking an interest in the subject of fancy rats. I, myself, have kept them for a number of years."

"Well I never," Clara remarked with apparent astonishment. "What a coincidence!"

"It really is," Miss Smythe moved to an armchair closer to Clara. "Let me see what guide you have there, ah, Mr Thwaite's informative tome!"

"Is it a good choice?"

"Indeed, Mr Thwaite is very knowledgeable on the subject and president of the British Fancy Rat Society," Miss Smythe was very satisfied with Clara's choice of pamphlet. "Why, I have met him on more than one occasion. The Society holds an annual conference in Brighton. Everyone brings their pet rats. The little creatures appreciate the sea air."

"People take their rats on their travels?"

"Why yes! No different to taking a dog after all. Though, admittedly, hotels are far less accommodating of rats than the average dog," Miss Smythe gave a small sigh. "We live in a very unenlightened world, Miss Fitzgerald. A man sees a rat and he sees vermin and nothing else. But if only he took a moment to understand this creature who is so successful in our cities and towns, he might come to realise what a remarkable beast it was. We put such effort into exterminating rats from our streets and homes, and yet they continue to flourish. They are survivors, Miss Fitzgerald, in a world were almost every person they encounter will attempt to eradicate them."

Miss Smythe was certainly passionate on her subject and it made Clara stop and think. She too was one of those who saw rats as merely vermin. Seeing them through Miss Smythe's eyes turned them into a completely different prospect.

"In fact," Miss Smythe continued, dropping her tone to a whisper. "I brought my rats along on this holiday. I couldn't bear to be apart from them, and my mother detests them and would have ignored them the entire time I was away. She would have left them to starve. So I smuggled them along. No one knows, the hotel manager would get rather upset about them, I fear."

"Yes, Mr Stover is rather that way inclined."

"Would you care to meet my rat Augustus? It is always best to meet the real thing when you are considering them for pets."

"I would be delighted," Clara replied, not sure she actually was delighted, but seeing this as a good way to speak with Miss Smythe privately.

Miss Smythe led the way to her room and opened the door for her guest. Clara entered but saw no sign of any rats. She caught herself glancing about the room.

"Ah, you are wondering where I hide them!" Miss Smythe laughed lightly. "Let me close the door and I shall show you."

The door duly shut, Miss Smythe went to one of the suitcases under her bed, (she had two residing there) and flicked open its catches. As the lid unlocked and Miss Smythe pulled it open there was a squeak of greeting from inside. Nearly the entire space of the second suitcase was taken up by a steel wire cage. It was a deep case which meant the rat that resided in the cage could move around freely and there was room for a dish containing rat food and another for water. Miss Smythe popped open the door of the cage and the rat hopped out onto her hand. It was a grey and white creature, with large pink ears and a scaly tail that it wrapped automatically around Miss Smythe's hand. It sat in her palm busily cleaning its whiskers.

"This is Augustus," Miss Smythe held out the rat to Clara.

Clara did not consider herself squeamish, still it took her some effort to calmly reach out and stroke the rat's head with a finger. Augustus stopped washing his whiskers and looked up at her, his little nose twitching in the air and his eyes looking at her brightly. Despite her reservations, Clara had to admit there was something endearing about the way the rat looked at her.

"Your travelling arrangements are certainly ingenious," Clara noted, turning her attention to the suitcase. Something caught her eye. There was a little tin plaque on the cage and it was embossed with the name Augustus, next to it was a second plaque with the name Caesar.

"Where is your second rat?" Clara asked, pointing to the name.

Miss Smythe pulled a face and then sat rather heavily on the bed. The movement bounced Augustus in her hand and the rat looked up, affronted.

"I lost Caesar on the very first night of our travels."

"Lost?" Clara asked.

"In both senses of the word. He slipped out of his cage that evening. It turns out the cage door was not locking properly. I was leaving the suitcase lid open so they could have some air. Caesar opened the door of the cage and vanished. I imagine he ventured out of my room window which was open at the time. Rats are full of curiosity. I came back to my room and found him missing. Augustus had slipped out too but he was in the bathroom devouring a bar of soap," Miss Smythe stroked the rat's grey head. "I looked everywhere for Caesar, but I only found him the next morning and he was deceased, unfortunately. He had been poisoned."

Clara had a flash of insight.

"Was Caesar brown, perchance?"

"Why yes, how did you guess? Most fancy rats are white with blotches of colour like Augustus here, but Caesar was a throwback to wild rat colourings."

"I think I saw Caesar," Clara nodded. "Under a bush

outside the hotel. He had consumed poisoned marzipan fruits, hadn't he?"

"Oh!" Miss Smythe gasped. "Oh, it was awful, and yes, you are right. At the time I could not think where he had found them, but then later I learned about Mrs Hunt's strange gift and realised what had happened. She had thrown them out the window and Caesar had come across them. I hate thinking about him eating that poison."

"And you had no knowledge of the poisoned sweets before that?"

"No! Why would you even ask such a thing?" Miss Smythe was offended.

"Because you spoke of receiving a similar gift," Clara said hastily. "But, there is no evidence you ever did and certainly no reason why you would considering Mrs Hunt was the target. So I find myself wondering why you would say such a thing."

Miss Smythe pulled her lips together in a pout. Tears had formed in her eyes and one glistened as it trickled down her cheek.

"No one was taking the poisoned marzipan seriously," Miss Smythe said. "After Mrs Hunt died it seemed as though the matter would be completely forgotten. The police seemed not to care. But my poor Caesar had been murdered and I wanted to know by whom. I thought, if I made it seem that I had received a similar gift and there were fears that a poisoner was at large, then the police would take an interest again. Mrs Hunt was poisoned, wasn't she? Those sweets were contaminated?"

"They were," Clara assured her. "Caesar was an unfortunate consequential victim in this affair."

Miss Smythe sniffled softly.

"Let no one ever tell you that the death of a pet is not deeply upsetting," she said.

"I don't suppose…" Clara had had another idea. "Did Augustus happen to escape again? During one of our stops on the way here?"

Miss Smythe blushed.

"You have caught me out, Miss Fitzgerald, you are very observant. He did indeed escape, but not from his cage. I had brought him out in my handbag for a little air and knowing that he would be pining for Caesar. I became distracted pouring my tea and when I glanced down Augustus had slipped out. I spotted him running under the tables picking up cake crumbs. He ran over the waitress' foot!"

"And she spilt tea on Mrs Hunt," Clara saw how the pieces fell together. "And then you caught him."

"Yes, but not before Mrs Hunt spotted Augustus. She must have seen me pick him up too for later on she sought me out and ranted at me. She said some awful things, accused me of trying to cause her harm of all things!" Miss Smythe shook her head. "It took a lot of persuading to stop her telling the hotel management about Augustus and I don't think she believed me when I said I meant her no ill. It had been a pure accident."

"You must have been concerned what would happen if she reported your pet?"

"The worst that would have occurred is that I would be asked to leave the hotel," Miss Smythe shrugged. "If such was the case, then I would have caught the first train home. I didn't push Mrs Hunt into Lake Windermere because she knew I had a pet rat!"

Miss Smythe was smarter on the uptake than Clara had given her credit for, but she also had a very flimsy motive for wishing Mrs Hunt dead.

"You did not know Mrs Hunt before this trip?" Clara checked, just to be safe.

"No, she was a stranger to me," Miss Smythe said firmly. "I know you are investigating her death, but you need not look to me for your killer. I have never harmed anyone."

"I had to ask," Clara said, attempting to placate her. "Mrs Hunt had written out a list of names of people she thought might wish her ill. Your name was on it. But I will also quickly add that Mrs Hunt had become deeply paranoid and any slight incident would place a person under her suspicious attention."

"She had nothing to fear from me," Miss Smythe sighed. "Miss Fitzgerald, you do think that Mrs Hunt was murdered, don't you?"

"Yes," Clara agreed, there was no need to hide that fact.

"And, the person who pushed her into the water, probably also tried to poison her?"

"It's very possible," Clara nodded. The idea that two people would both attempt to kill Mrs Hunt independent of each other was not one she cared to dwell on.

"Then, will you do me the great kindness of keeping me abreast of all you discover? I can expect no justice for little Caesar, but I would like to give his killer a piece of my mind. His death may have been accidental, but he was still murdered."

Miss Smythe looked determined through her tears. Clara patted her arm gently.

"I shall do my best," she promised.

Miss Smythe gave her a difficult smile.

"I do hope you will enjoy keeping fancy rats, Miss Fitzgerald."

"They are certainly fascinating creatures," Clara answered, feeling brave enough to gently stroke Augustus on his small head.

Clara left Miss Smythe along with her surviving pet and was about to call it a night, when the hotel porter suddenly came upon her.

"Miss Fitzgerald, telephone call for you," he informed her.

Clara was intrigued, had Inspector Park-Coombs dug up something in his investigations already? She followed the porter to Mr Stover's office (the hotel manager being fortunately absent) and picked up the 'phone.

"Hello?"

"Miss Fitzgerald."

She recognised the voice of Dr Day-Bowers at once.

"Good evening, doctor."

"I apologise for the lateness of this call," Dr Day-Bowers said rather breathlessly down the phone line, "but I have had much on my mind and I could not bear to keep it secret any longer."

"Whatever can you mean?" Clara asked, wondering if there was something more to Mrs Hunt's illness than he had first let on.

"I feel an awful guilt that I might have unwittingly placed Mrs Hunt in a dangerous position," Dr Day-Bowers explained, his voice beginning to tremble. "You see, it seemed a kindly idea at the time. A chance for Mrs Hunt to make peace with her past."

"What did you do?" Clara asked, intrigued by this mysterious statement.

Dr Day-Bowers puffed and sighed at the end of the phone line, then finally he admitted his folly.

"I wrote the letters to all those people inviting them to join Mrs Hunt on the charabanc. I even paid for their tickets in certain cases."

"Why would you do a thing like that?" Clara was astonished. The outlay for the tickets alone must have been immense.

"Mrs Hunt and I," Dr Day-Bowers hesitated. "We had an understanding. We were both lonely, you see. But it is not right for a doctor to become involved with a patient, it is unethical. So we kept things very staid between us. But I truly adored that woman, Miss Fitzgerald and, believe it or not, I wanted to do something for her before she became too ill to appreciate it. She would talk, quite often, about people she had wronged and how she wished she could make things right. But she was too proud to do anything herself, so I took up the idea. It was meant to be a gift, a way for her to make peace with herself. I thought it might help her condition to take the weight of her sins from her."

Dr Day-Bowers' voice broke into a tremble and it was plain he was close to weeping.

"Instead, I surrounded her with people who wished her ill," Dr Day-Bowers choked on a sob. "I shall never forgive myself for causing her death."

"I am so sorry," Clara said gently as the man cried softly. "You could not have known. It was perhaps not the wisest of ideas, but I am sure it seemed at the time to be the right one."

"That is just the thing," Dr Day-Bowers held back his tears long enough to speak. "It wasn't even my idea. It was suggested to me."

"By who?" Clara said, more sharply than she had meant to because suddenly this seemed very important.

"By Bernie Sykes. He works part-time as my gardener. I tell him a few too many of my woes while he prunes the hedges."

"He suggested the charabanc trip?" Clara pressed.

"Not just suggested it, he arranged it," Dr Day-Bowers explained. "When Bernie isn't working in my garden, he is acting as a conductor for the Brighton Charabanc Company."

Chapter Thirty-two

Clara now had more information than she knew what to do with. Mrs Hunt had not been behind the letters, it was the idea of Bernie Sykes, charabanc conductor. A fluke of fate had placed Mrs Hunt in the path of her killer. Had that person decided to murder her when their invitation for the trip arrived, or afterwards when they had found themselves in her company? A good question.

When the following morning arrived she had every intention of tracking down Bernie Sykes and hearing more about his part in this whole affair. But didn't get the chance, for when she came downstairs that morning Mr Stover nabbed her.

"Inspector Gateley wants to see you are once," he informed her with a very serious expression. "There is a police constable waiting outside to escort you to him by car."

Clara glanced outside where the rain was once more slating down.

"He is standing outside in that?" she queried.

"I was not going to have a policeman waiting around in my foyer. There has been enough of that sort of drama around here lately!" Mr Stover slammed shut the guest book he had been perusing when Clara arrived and stalked off to his office.

Clara decided she better find out what Inspector Gateley wanted after all this time. She walked outside and spotted the poor police constable trying to shelter under the porch of the hotel.

"Miss Fitzgerald?" he asked optimistically. He was young and very new at being a policeman. He tended to get all the jobs no one else wanted.

"Yes," Clara replied. "I hear I am wanted at the police station?"

"If you wouldn't mind coming in the car, miss."

The car was a rather old Ford Model T, probably imported during or just after the war. It had a sizeable dent in one door and the pull over roof looked a little cracked in places.

"She was a donation from the wife of a former inspector," the constable explained as he opened the dented door for Clara. "All the constables get to learn to drive in her."

The constable seated himself in the driver's side, behind the huge wheel and grinned. Clearly standing out in the rain was more than compensated for by having this old car to drive. They trundled off in the rain, and Clara soon discovered that when the wind blew water came straight in the windowless sides.

Clara was rather hoping for a cup of tea and the chance to warm up when she arrived at the police station, but almost the moment she set her foot inside she was whisked along by a very efficient desk sergeant to an office. She was ushered into an armchair by an unlit fireplace, before being left alone. Clara took in her surroundings. She was in the inspector's office; a desk sat in the centre covered with papers in neat piles, on the wall behind was a map of the area and a typed list of patrol routes. Near the window was a set of filing cabinets and, just in front of them, a tall hat-stand, currently barren of hats or coats. Clara wondered what she had been summoned here for? It was all rather dramatic if they just wanted to interview her again.

She didn't have to wait long for her answer. She had only just finished her visual perusal of the room when the door opened and Inspector Gateley appeared looking sour-faced. He was followed a fraction later by former Inspector Wake, who smiled at Clara brightly. Clara rose from her seat to greet them.

"Is something the matter?" she asked as soon as the formalities were done.

"That is what we hope to determine in this little meeting," Inspector Wake said, still smiling. "I thought over our conversation yesterday and it struck me there just might be something to the matter. So I rather took the liberty of investigating further."

"I would like to state right now," Inspector Gateley interrupted his predecessor, looking most disgruntled. "that I do not like civilians interfering in police matters."

Clara knew precisely who he was aiming that barb at, even if technically Wake was now also a civilian. Clara chose to ignore the statement.

"What have you discovered, Inspector Wake?"

"It is rather circumstantial, but I think we may have a clue to why Mrs Hunt was killed. We are now satisfied, are we not, Inspector Gateley, that she was murdered?" Wake glanced at his colleague.

Gateley gave a huff which indicated he agreed, even if he didn't much like it.

"Let's sit and I shall explain," Wake continued.

They all took a chair, Inspector Gately taking his behind the desk and feeling a little better for being able to show his superiority to the other two. He was still the only real policeman in the room, after all.

"I came to the station yesterday to look in the archives," Inspector Wake pressed on, not noticing his colleagues' chagrin. "I had a feeling there was a reason the Wignell case had been rather side-lined when we last talked. Just this little hunch that for some reason the death of the Wignell girl had not had my full attention.

That is a very sad thing, I might add, Miss Fitzgerald, but it comes from having too far few policemen at hand to do the work."

"Cases always seem to come in spates," Gateley interjected. "It's how it goes."

"In this instance," Wake carried on, acknowledging Gateley's interruption with a smile, "it happened that we were dealing with a vanished child case at the time Miss Wignell perished. Our full attention was on finding this little girl named Mary who was only ten and had disappeared the previous Saturday. Cases like that always have us jumping because you never quite know what might have occurred. There are unpleasant people in this world."

"Quite," Clara nodded.

"All our resources and time were devoted to finding little Mary when we had the call to Miss Wignell's apparent suicide. With our minds otherwise occupied, it was easy enough to look for the obvious and take it at face value. The girl had dark moods and had tried to do away with herself before. It seemed logical enough to assume that this time she had succeeded."

"A policeman is only as good as the evidence presented to him," Gateley bleated. He was definitely feeling rather undermined on his current case, and didn't like to hear about other cases of policing errors.

"I was the Inspector back then," Wake said. "Any failing over the case falls on my shoulders. I saw what I wanted to see. I didn't have the time to consider another murder."

"Murder?" Clara sat upright in her chair. "Then, you now think Miss Wignell did not kill herself?"

"I went back through the files. At the time I had skimmed over a lot of the paperwork. The jury at the inquest ruled death by misadventure, half the evidence was not even presented to them. We were just so busy. We found Mary shortly after, by the way, alive and well and living with an aunt who was keeping her presence a secret. Seems that Mary's father was rather a ruffian and the aunt had spirited the child away to protect her. Finding Mary just gave us a whole batch of new headaches and by the time they were sorted, Miss Wignell's case was long forgotten.

"When I went back through the files I started to see things I had missed before, and other things jogged my memory. I had had concerns then, but had pushed them aside. I told you about the paintbrush in her hand, but there was more. Miss Wignell had a bruise on her left cheek. It might have happened as she fell in the water, but it rather suggested someone had struck her. There were slight tears in the cloth of her clothes about her shoulders, as if something had forcibly held her down and in the struggle the seams had ripped. None of which would fit with a suicide.

"I looked at the case closer, especially the witness statements and there I found the discrepancy. Mrs Hunt declared at the inquest she had been asleep throughout the incident, but in her very first statement she said she had awoken to the sound of a splash and hunted in the reeds for Miss Wignell before finding her dead. She said this was how she came to have wet clothes when the police were called. It was possible Mrs Hunt had made an error with one of her statements, it does happen. But it had me curious.

"I went through the rest of the statements collected at the time and among them was one given by a Bill Ayres. It turns out this Mr Ayres had taken a shine to Miss Wignell. They were both holiday-makers at the same hotel. They had spent time together and Miss Wignell had confided a lot in him. She told Bill, the day before she died, that she was certain her tutor, Mrs Hunt, was stealing from her parents. She was going to reveal her as soon as they returned to Brighton. Mr Ayres was convinced that Mrs Hunt had killed the girl to prevent her crimes being revealed."

Inspector Wake paused dramatically, glancing

between Gateley and Clara.

"It all made a wicked kind of sense," he continued. "Miss Wignell learned that her tutor was taking money from her parents without them knowing, perhaps siphoning it out of the housekeeping wages, or asking for money for textbooks she never bought. Miss Wignell was young and naïve. She intended to tell her parents but, perhaps before having the chance, she revealed herself to Mrs Hunt. Perhaps they argued and Miss Wignell declared what she knew, or perhaps she was not discreet enough. In any case, Mrs Hunt decided she would have to deal with the girl and what better way than to say she had drowned herself? The girl was known to be temperamental, as it was. Who would question it?

"While out on their daily walk Mrs Hunt struck. Dazing the girl with a blow to begin with and then dragging her into the water. The girl struggled, in the process her clothes were ripped slightly at the shoulders, but in the end she was overcome. Still clutching her paintbrush she drowned. Mrs Hunt then played the distressed tutor, first calling for help, then making out to the police that she had tried to save the girl. Later on, concerned that someone might wonder why she failed to reach the girl in time, she expanded on the idea and said she had been asleep the whole time.

"None of this can be proved with Mrs Hunt dead, but it does offer the idea that someone was out for revenge. The irony of Mrs Hunt drowning in the exact spot her charge did is hard to overlook."

"Did Mr Ayres share his views at the inquest?" Clara asked, thinking that the Wignells were once more looking like prime suspects in Mrs Hunt's death.

"No. The statement was overlooked. My fault, I'll admit. It was flimsy, anyhow. Nothing more than hearsay. Could have even been the case that the police felt he was a rather over emotional boy who had taken the death hard. There was no proof and you can't go around voicing baseless suspicions."

"Was there any indication that the parents had learned of his concerns?" Clara pressed.

"It doesn't look like it," Inspector Wake shrugged his shoulders. "They were certainly not aggrieved by the outcome of the inquest. Had they suspected murder I think they would have pushed the police harder."

"And Bill Ayres? What became of him?"

"That I cannot tell you," Wake shook his head.

Clara sighed. What had first looked like a promising lead now seemed to crumble. Bill Ayres was the only person to suspect Miss Wignell was murdered, but he could be anywhere now, living his own life. Unless he had somehow shared his suspicions with her parents, she could no more say that they had a motive than before.

"It is something," Inspector Wake said gently, seeing her disappointment. "It would give someone a damn good reason for killing Mrs Hunt."

"If they knew of it," Clara said solemnly. "But you are right, it is something, and, if nothing else, it goes to show that Mrs Hunt was more horrid than ever I imagined. If Ayres' suspicions were correct, then she was a cold-blooded killer and a thief as well."

"I'll keep on looking," Inspector Wake assured her.

Inspector Gateley gave another huff.

Inspector Wake showed Clara out of the police station, the day was brightening up and when he offered to summon the car for her, Clara shook her head.

"The rain has stopped, I will quite happily walk," she told him.

Inspector Wake dipped his hat to her and then headed off in the opposite direction. Clara walked up the road, passing the Post Office on her way. She was just coming to the edge of the village when she heard someone shout behind her. She turned and saw the grocer's boy rushing in her direction.

"Are you Miss Fitzgerald?" he asked, running up to her out-of-breath. "The postmistress said she thought you were."

"I am," Clara told him. "What is the matter?"

"Telegram for you. I was going to run it to the hotel. I get a penny for that," the boy handed her an envelope then galloped off once again to get back to his other tasks.

Clara turned over the envelope in her hand, but it just bore her name and nothing more revealing. She tore it open with her thumb under the flap and pulled out the telegram. She read it and her heart skipped. It was from Inspector Park-Coombs and it offered yet another insight into Mrs Hunt's past. It read;

"Hunt arrested for theft 1890 along with husband. Using alias Hardwich. Husband went to prison."

Clara folded the telegram back up.

"Well, well. Mr Hardwich, we shall have to talk."

Clara hurried back up the road to the hotel.

Chapter Thirty-three

Clara was breathless when she entered the hotel. Mr Stover gave her his usual scowl, but she was by now used to ignoring him. Clara made her way to the first of the various hotel lounges and peered in the door. There was no sign of Mr Hardwich, so she headed for the next, that too was empty of her suspect and, ultimately, she found him in the very last lounge she searched. Mr Hardwich was nursing a tall glass of tonic water and looked rather unwell.

Clara settled herself in a seat opposite him and did not at first disturb him. It was enough to observe him and contemplate who this man was. Was he a murderer? He did not much look like one. Mr Hardwich was in his late sixties, he was a stocky fellow, though it would be going too far to call him fat. He was the sort of person who is rather solid, but not from over-indulgence, rather he was born that way. He had a moustache and receding hair, though what remained was still very dark. His face was round and usually quite agreeable, he seemed a light-hearted soul who took no matter dreadfully seriously.

Mr Hardwich was one of life's chancers, and he fully accepted that sometimes, when taking a chance, luck was not on your side. He took this knowledge sanguinely enough and did not allow it to disturb him unduly. He was a genial soul who had done rather well out of his life of dubious opportunities, which he also put down to luck. He was quite comfortable in his retirement, which was more than could be said for many a poor soul.

Clara surveyed him up and down. Mr Hardwich clutched his head in one hand and seemed to be making a determined effort not to open his eyes, thus he had not noticed Clara's presence.

"Are you unwell Mr Hunt?" Clara asked.

Mr Hardwich opened his big brown eyes, which were rather doleful, like a hound's, and at once realised his mistake. He smiled politely at Clara.

"Caught out," he said softly. "Very good, Miss Fitzgerald. Who told you?"

"It was an assumption," Clara admitted. "Based on the information that once upon a time you and your wife went by the surname of Hardwich."

"Ah! The rogue always catches himself out with his own complacency! I haven't used the name Hardwich in ten years. I thought no one would remember."

"People are not so forgetful."

"So I see," Mr Hardwich, now revealed as really Mr Hunt, took a delicate sip of his tonic water. "You must excuse me, I have the most shocking megrim."

"I apologise for disturbing you when you are under the weather, but it was important."

"You want to know about my relationship with my estranged wife?" Mr Hunt attempted to nod his head and regretted it. "I suppose that is logical enough. You are still looking for her murderer and I look most promising."

"That is unfortunately true," Clara agreed. "Not only were you estranged from your wife, but you came here under an assumed name and lied about knowing her. Perhaps you would care to explain?"

"Where to begin?" Mr Hunt smiled sadly.

"Why not start by explaining how you came to be here?"

"If only it were so simple to consider that a beginning... Oh, well, let us try," Mr Hunt took a breath and settled back in his chair so he could look at Clara easier. "Now, I suppose it would be three or four months ago. A letter came through my door. It purported to be from my wife, though the hand was rather unfamiliar to me. The letter writer appeared to have foreseen this and excused the writing by stating they were very unwell. That is, my former wife, Mrs Hunt as she was, was very unwell.

"I was a little shaken by the news. Not least because I had put my wife long out of my mind, or at least I thought I had. That letter dredged up a lot of unhappy emotions."

"Such affairs, estrangements, can lead to a lot of resentment," Clara noted.

Mr Hunt almost laughed.

"If only it was so simple, Miss Fitzgerald!" he said. "I had never wanted to be estranged from Mrs Hunt, I love her today as much as I loved her from the very first time we met."

Mr Hunt became quiet, staring into some internal space where hurt still lingered.

"I am not deluded to the fact she could be a deeply unpleasant woman," he mused. "I have even heard her called wicked. She had her own demons. They ate away at her. I knew her before they had so completely consumed her. I remember who she was then."

"Who was she, Mr Hunt?" Clara asked. "For I have only seen the aspects of a woman who was hard-hearted, perhaps even cruel."

"She could be both of those things," Mr Hunt made no effort to deny Clara's statement. "My wife was a complicated woman. Inside she ached deeply. She was born into what is best described as a slum and her father abandoned the family early on. Her mother could not sustain the family and they all ended up in the workhouse. As was the practice the children were separated from their mother, Mildred and her sister found themselves alone. Their mother died when they were seven and five, so then it was just those two little girls against the world. They became inseparable and they swore that nothing would ever come between them.

"But, of course, life moves on. The girls were eventually found positions as domestic servants in different parts of the county and had to communicate by letter. Mildred began to feel dreadfully alone and began to concoct an idea of how she could reunite with her sister. She saved what little money she had. It was around then that she had been asked to teach at the local church Sunday school. She was actually well-lettered as the workhouse made sure its charges were educated. Mildred took the role and eventually found she had a knack for it. This ultimately led to her persuading her employer to allow her to study to become a teacher. I think the arrangement was agreeable enough to both, as she was not much good as a domestic."

Mr Hunt smiled to himself.

"Mildred did exactly as she said she would and became a teacher. She was an intelligent woman and read widely, improving herself continuously. Ultimately, after she had moved between a few posts, she ridded herself of her past in the workhouse and came up with the story that her father had been a middle-class shopkeeper, who went bankrupt, forcing his children to gain employment."

"From what you tell me, Mrs Hunt made a success of her life? Why should she become so embittered?" Clara interrupted.

"Financially Mildred could survive, and yes, she had improved her lot, but in other ways she felt bereft and deeply hurt," Mr Hunt explained. "She had raised herself up for the sake of her sister, so they might be together again. Then a blow came when her sister wrote to her and told her about a young man she intended to marry. Mildred viewed this as a betrayal. If her sister married then she would have a new life, one which would have little time for a sister. Mildred liked to possess people entirely. Once you were hers then you could be no one else's. Her sister had broken that arrangement and Mildred was struck to her core. She never forgave her."

"That is a harsh reaction to the marriage of a sister," Clara noticed Mr Hunt wince as a fragment of sunlight glinted in the window onto his face. She rose and pulled the curtain.

Mr Hunt gave her a grateful smile before he carried on.

"I don't say Mildred was right, I merely explain how she was. She felt abandoned for the third time. First there had been their father leaving the family so they had to go to the workhouse. Second there had been their mother dying. And now her sister had destroyed her plans for them to live their days out together. These hurts warped her slowly, made her hard so she could not be betrayed again. But, also, Mildred learned to be selfish. She had strived for her sister, worked hard, only to be cast aside. From now on Mildred would concern herself only with her wellbeing.

"We met when she was in her twenties and working at a girls school. She told me the story of the bankrupt father and I believed her. I had an image in my head of her mother and father sitting in dignified poverty, relying on their doting daughter. It was years before I learned the truth.

"I loved Mildred almost at once. I was hopelessly smitten by her. Back then I worked in a greengrocer's, but I had ambitions to improve myself. I was impressed by Mildred, perhaps even a little daunted by her. We did not marry for several years, not until I had worked my way up to owning my own shop, and that was hard, I must say. When we did marry I expected to see her erstwhile parents at the ceremony. When I asked about them, she broke down and explained her true circumstances. I was hurt she had lied, but I understood. She could do no wrong, my Mildred.

"It was 1884. We lived well enough for a time, but Mildred was not content to be a housewife and insisted on returning to teaching. I didn't realise she cared so much about her work. Perhaps she did not, perhaps it was just a way to get out of the house. Since most establishments will not accept married teachers, Mildred reverted to her maiden name and I became one of her best kept secrets."

Mr Hunt sighed. It was a heavy, morose sigh from a man who had been betrayed many times over, but who did not allow the fact to trouble him.

"So we carried on for many a year. Until disaster struck, quite literally. My shop was consumed by fire and the insurance had lapsed. I was bankrupt overnight. We endeavoured to survive on Mildred's income while I tried to find a way to improve my losses, without success. It looked as though we might lose the house, at which point Mildred suggested we try something rather radical. She was working then for a grand family, teaching their three daughters. Mildred said the family always went away for the summer and the house was left quite empty. But she knew where they locked up the valuables. Mildred was convinced we could rob the place and make it appear as if burglars had snuck in.

"I went along with the idea as I always did. Of course, it went badly wrong. A neighbour spotted us. We ran away but when we tried to pawn what we had stolen, we were caught. To my astonishment Mildred created a story about how it was all my idea to raid the house and she had merely tagged along out of fear! I went to prison and my wife walked free. She chose to have nothing further to do with me."

"You must have been angry," Clara said sympathetically.

"I can't deny that I was," Mr Hunt replied. "But it passed. I still loved her. She wanted no more to do with me, or so I thought, until that letter arrived. Thirty years I had waited for just such a thing, and then there it was, stating my wife was dying."

"Did you believe it?"

Mr Hunt was silent a while, processing that thought. Finally he spoke;

"No, I suppose it rather struck me as being out of character. But I was curious, nonetheless. The letter stated that Mildred was going on this charabanc trip and that, if I was to join her, she would aim to make amends. I was fool enough to believe that part."

"But when you got on board the charabanc it was not so?"

"When I got aboard Mildred looked straight through me!" Mr Hunt snorted. "I knew then I had been right when I assumed the letter had been written by someone else. It was either a dreadful joke or some sort of strange way of reuniting me with my wife. In any case, it did not work. I did not speak with Mildred Hunt the entire time we were together on the charabanc, I am not even sure she recognised me."

"Why did you lie about your name?" Clara asked.

"Because I felt foolish and didn't want anyone to know what I was about. And…" Mr Hunt watched the bubbles pop at the edge of his glass of tonic water. "And I thought it might jog Mildred's memory. Remind her of the price I paid for her freedom. But it did none of those things."

"That brings us to the most difficult question," Clara paused briefly. "Did you kill your wife?"

Mr Hunt snorted.

"Why should I? I don't get involved with such things as revenge, they are far too messy. No, I saw my wife alive and so it was. I was genuinely upset at her death," Mr Hunt became solemn. "I meant to speak with her, to tell her I forgave her. I wanted us to be at peace."

"Do you have an alibi?" Clara pressed, thinking Mr Hunt talked a good talk, but had yet to offer her anything tangible.

"An alibi?" Mr Hunt looked sour for a moment, then a thought struck him. "Actually, I do. I was walking by myself along the lake when my peace was interrupted by those two women, Mrs Palmer and Mrs Siskin. I couldn't get rid of them. I was with them most of the afternoon. Ask them."

Clara intended to, but it was a good alibi. Not one but two witnesses could claim to have seen Mr Hunt at the time his wife was being murdered.

"I can see why you would consider me to have motive for this crime, but I really did not harm Mildred. Had she given me the chance, I would have taken her back in an instant."

Clara thought that Mr Hunt had been lucky his estranged wife had not offered that chance. But, he was right, for the moment she had nothing truly against him.

"I hope your headache is improved soon," Clara rose from her chair. "And thank you for talking so freely with me."

"Not at all," Mr Hunt smiled.

Clara left the lounge and headed for her room. Mr Hunt appeared to be a dead end, but that was not the end of the story. Clara just had to find the right way to wheedle out the truth from this mystery.

Chapter Thirty-four

"The reality is I have a number of suspects and none I can actually place at the scene of the crime," Clara informed Tommy and Annie that evening as they sat in Clara's room after dinner.

"May I suggest a rest from all this investigating?" Annie said. "You are supposed to be on holiday and, it seems to me, you are facing a dead end."

"You are right," Clara concurred. "Here I have all the pieces of the puzzle and yet none fit. I have all these people with a grudge against Mrs Hunt on the same charabanc as her, placed there because of a plan concocted by her lover and his gardener, neither of whom, as far as I can see have a motive for wishing her dead. Both were attempting to do her a good turn, to bring her peace after a turbulent life. They located former clients and friends of hers, even finding her nephew and estranged husband, and they brought them altogether in the hope that Mrs Hunt would have the wherewithal to do the rest. Clearly she did not, and clearly she felt threatened by the presence of so many she had done harm to."

"And yet, so far, only one we know of actually tried to hurt her. Her nephew," Tommy pointed out.

"And his attempt failed. But it does at least tell us

something. Excluding the chamber pot incident we can see a pattern. Our killer favours poison. Their first attempt involved poisoned sweets, their second poisoned tea. So, the question remains, who had access to such poisons and the means to give them to Mrs Hunt?"

"And there we come to a dead end," Annie repeated. "Look, tomorrow is our final excursion day. Let us enjoy it. Take a break from these matters Clara and maybe then the solution will appear."

"We can only hope," Clara nodded. "For I fear, once this holiday is over, our killer will have every opportunity to vanish and return to their usual life. Leaving us all none the wiser as to who killed Mrs Hunt."

"If I was to be reckless enough to say 'do we really care', you will probably think me callous," Tommy said thoughtfully. "But the woman spread a lot of nastiness in her time and I can't help thinking she is best off out of the picture."

"She was still murdered," Clara reminded him. "We can't ignore that."

That concluded the discussion and they all retreated to their respective beds. The next morning they rose early to be ready for the last charabanc trip of the holiday. They had been promised a visit to a nearby miniature village that had been built by a local man and then opened to the public. There was also a rumour of a pub lunch and a specially arranged tour of a local stately home. Had Clara not had so many dark thoughts on her mind, she might have been more interested.

They made their way onto the charabanc. There was a noticeable absence of certain key suspects in the Hunt mystery. Mr Hunt was not presence, nor Edwin Hope or Madeleine Reeve. The Wignells, however, were present and seemed determined to make the most of what remained of their holiday. Clara sat beside Tommy and tried to distract her mind from the problem of Mrs Hunt's death. She tried to take an interest in the scenery they passed, or the conversations of other passengers, but to no avail. Time and time again her mind reverted to the problematic murder.

They were just passing through a little village, and crossing a pretty brook when there was a sharp hissing sound and the charabanc lurched to the side. For a brief, troubling moment it seemed the driver had lost control of his vehicle and the charabanc wobbled back and forth across the road. Then he tapped on the brakes and they came to a halt.

Driver and conductor both left the charabanc to see what the trouble was. The driver returned almost at once looking most crestfallen.

"We have punctured a tyre," he informed his passengers. "I'm afraid we will have to stop here a while. I'll try to find a garage that can replace it. In the meantime, this is a very pretty village and perhaps you would all like to take in the views while I get this old girl back on the road?"

With the odd disgruntled mutter about vehicular troubles, the passengers disembarked. Clara stood at the side of the charabanc and stared forlornly at the very flat tyre. She gave it a little nudge with her good foot.

"How long will it take to fix?" she asked the conductor who was busy going around apologising to everyone about the inconvenience.

"I can't say, miss. Depends if we can find a replacement. Don't think it can be repaired. It is proper burst."

Clara gave a sigh. She had been looking forward to the tour of the stately home. The conductor took pity on her.

"Here, why don't I make us all a nice cup of tea?" he declared.

Clara perked up at once. She glanced at the conductor. "How?"

Bernie Sykes, the conductor grinned.

"These here engines run red hot," he said knowledgably. "I worked out a while back that I could rig up a little stand over the hottest part and boil a travel kettle there. I do it all the time."

Bernie vanished briefly and reappeared with a copper kettle and a little trivet that he had personally designed to fit on top of the engine. He unlatched the bonnet hood of the charabanc and folded it up and back, revealing the vehicle's inner workings. Then he propped his trivet and kettle on the engine. He took a canister of water from beneath the driver's seat and filled the kettle carefully, whistling to himself the whole time. Then he left the water to boil and retrieved a teapot from the luggage compartment, two mugs and a large tin biscuit box.

"You are very organised," Clara observed as the teapot was balanced with the mugs on the running board.

"We do a lot of winter trips," Bernie Sykes explained. "And we get no pay to stop at a teashop ourselves. So we make do and keep ourselves warm this way."

The copper kettle began to sing and Bernie Sykes was briefly distracted. Clara moved towards the biscuit tin which had been stood on the running board.

"Does this contain the tea?" she asked, crouching by the box.

"Yes, miss, oh, but I'll do that. You'll get your dress dirty on the running board!" there was a slight hint of panic in Bernie Sykes' tone, he was already replacing the copper kettle on the trivet as fast as he could.

But Clara was not listening. She already had her fingers under the ridge of the tin lid and was forcing it open. She was greeted by a little packet of powdered milk, a bundle of loose tea leaves, two teaspoons, a small glass jar containing sugar cubes and one packet of half used sleeping powders.

Clara picked up the packet and noted that it had a label upon it with the name 'Mrs Doris Wignell' written in ink. Clara glanced up at Bernie Sykes who was staring at her with his mouth open and a look of horror on his face.

"You have some explaining to do Mr Bill Ayres," Clara said.

Bill Ayres turned and bolted. Clara had expected as

much, she glanced at the few fellow passengers still standing by her. None had been paying much attention to her antics until then.

"Catch that man!" she instructed them. Each failed to move.

"Oh for crying out loud!" Clara cast aside her walking stick and started to chase Bill Ayres. Fortunately for the latter, Clara was constrained to a fast hobble by her sore foot.

Tommy and Annie had been sauntering up the road when all the teapot commotion was going on, and the first they knew of Bill Ayres' attempt to flee was when he dashed past them.

"Stop him! He's the killer!" Clara yelled.

Tommy looked on at the rapidly disappearing figure, knowing he was not fit to run and yet desperately wanting to be of help. It was Annie who intervened and saved the day.

"Go fetch the police!" she instructed Tommy and then she bolted after Bill Ayres.

Annie had once done exceedingly well at a school sports event. It had been a sort of genteel assault course for young girls. She was known among her fellow pupils as a remarkable sprinter when the urge took her. Annie had not run in years, but she was still fast and, more importantly, she was doggedly determined.

Bill Ayres was running up a lane. Clara was still calling out for someone to stop him. Two farm labourers were chatting over a wall as Ayres raced past them. They looked up in surprise, but failed to move. A moment later Annie whipped past them and they heard Clara, now fallen behind, shouting that a killer was getting away. They both turned and began to follow Ayres.

Bill Ayres was starting to pant now. He was not a natural runner and he spent most of his days manning a charabanc or pruning rose bushes. The sprint had taken it out of him. Even so, he was stunned when someone suddenly grabbed his arm and swung him around. He stumbled over his own feet, still trying to run as he was spun to face an irate Annie. He tripped himself up and fell to the ground. Annie half-fell on top of him and knocked the air out of him. Bill Ayres was coughing and groaning as the two farm labourers ran up and grabbed his arms.

It was still several moments before Clara hobbled up. By which time Annie had caught her breath and Bill Ayres was almost recovered from his sprint.

"This man…" Clara said, having to gasp for air. "Murdered a woman… I have proof…"

"Rest against the wall, Clara," Annie took her friend's arm and propped her against the nearby wall.

"You are Bill Ayres?" Clara asked firmly.

Ayres pulled a face.

"You poisoned Mrs Hunt's tea and then drowned her in Lake Windermere. You also sent her poisoned sweets in a previous attempt. I presume you laced the marzipan with rat poison, which is so readily available. When that failed you had to become inventive, knowing you could not attempt the same trick twice. So you stole Mrs Wignell's sleeping powders and, when you were alone with Mrs Hunt, you offered her a mug of freshly brewed tea. She was not to know it was heavily laced with the powders."

"I thought they would kill her outright, such a big dose," Ayres pulled a face. "But she kept on breathing, even when she was unconscious. I couldn't fail again."

"So you dragged her into the lake and let the water do the rest. It almost fooled everyone into thinking Mrs Hunt had befallen an accident, but, unfortunately for you, she had previously informed me about the poisoned sweets and the coincidence was too plain."

Ayres sneered. He sagged in the arms of his captors, the fight had gone from him.

"This was all for Miss Wignell?" Clara said more gently.

Ayres' face fell. He looked deeply sad now, almost as if about to cry.

"She killed her, you know," he spoke softly. "No one believed me. But she did."

"I believe you," Clara assured him. "It is most unfortunate that it took this second crime to reveal the truth about Miss Wignell's untimely death. The police now also believe she was killed by her tutor."

"That's good," Bill Ayres nodded. "Even though I shall hang for it, I am glad for that."

"How did it all begin Bill? When did you plot revenge?"

"From the start," Bill said, his eyes drifted up as a policeman became visible hurrying up the lane. "From the moment I knew the police were not going to take me seriously. But I didn't know how to go about it, and then I lost track of Mrs Hunt. I went on with my life. I moved to Brighton, thinking I would find Mrs Hunt again. A part of me thought I could make her confess. I got the job at the charabanc company, but it was only last year that I spotted Mrs Hunt again."

"At Dr Day-Bowers surgery?"

"Yes. I had gone there about a boil on my neck and I saw her. After a few enquiries I learned she and the doctor were on very friendly terms," Ayres gave a bitter laugh. "I offered myself to the doctor as a gardener on very reasonable rates. His garden was awful and he snapped up my offer. From then on I plotted, trying to think of a way to do away with Mrs Hunt so no one would know it was me."

"And you came up with the charabanc idea," Clara filled in the gaps. "What better way to avoid being suspected of murder than to place your victim amid a hoard of her enemies? There would be so many suspects that the police would be pulling it apart for years. And then, as it happened, the police thought her death natural after all."

"It all should have worked," Ayres complained. "I had changed my name, and no one remembered me, not even the Wignells."

By now the policeman had arrived and wanted to know what was going on. Clara briefly explained that Bill Ayres had poisoned one of his charabanc passengers and that Inspector Gateley would understand. The policeman looked puzzled, but agreed to conduct Bill back to the station and inform the Inspector. The two farm labourers, who had been listening to all this keenly, refused to let their captive go and helped the policeman escort him to the small village station.

Clara returned to the charabanc. The driver was just arriving back with the local mechanic, who he had been fortunate to find. He saw his conductor being escorted into the police station and looked confused. But it was Mr Wignell who first asked the obvious question;

"What is going on?"

Clara laid a hand on his arm.

"Mr Wignell, I have a lot to talk about with you and your wife. Perhaps we should go aboard the charabanc for privacy?"

Mr Wignell was baffled, but he agreed to the suggestion. Over the next half hour Clara explained to him and his wife the truth about their daughter's death. It did not make things any easier for them to know she had been murdered, but at least they knew she had not taken her own life. By the time Clara had finished, Inspector Gateley had appeared and new explanations were required. Clara sighed again as she followed the Inspector into the police station to make her statement. She was certain now she was going to miss out on the much anticipated tour of the stately home.

Chapter Thirty-five

Clara was in a lot of pain by the time she finally hobbled back to the hotel. Running, albeit it a shuffling run, had not helped her foot at all. Annie had to help her up to her room and insisted she rest on the bed while she ran to get Dr Masters. When Dr Masters arrived he gave her a disapproving look.

"What have you done now?" he enquired.

"Chased down a murderer," Clara informed him plainly. "Mrs Hunt's killer is now in custody."

"Hmph," said Dr Masters. "So it is all over now?"

"For my part, at least," Clara nodded. "Would you mind looking at my foot while I answer your questions?"

With difficulty Clara had removed her shoe and now proceeded to peel off her stocking. Her foot looked red and swollen. Dr Masters took one looked and sighed in disappointment.

"Really, Clara?"

"Really," Clara said impatiently. "It had to be done."

Dr Masters examined the foot and pronounced that it was just inflamed and should return to normal with rest and a cold compress. The examination concluded he sat in the armchair opposite Clara.

"I think I owe you an apology."

Clara glanced up.

"For criticising my behaviour?" she asked.

Dr Masters grinned.

"No. That deserved criticising. What I meant was that I was rather brusque with you at our last meeting. I took offence at being viewed a potential suspect."

"Many people do," Clara groaned. "But how else am I supposed to solve a case?"

"Well, precisely. But I took offence and then I was rather rude," Dr Masters looked abashed. "Especially over the details of my patient here at the hotel. I was rather annoyed you had seen through my ploy and I became rather surly."

"Then there is no elderly hypochondriac old lady?"

"No. She was an excuse to protect the identity of my real patient."

"The young girl?" Clara had guessed as much. "Why did you feel the need to be so secretive?"

"Because, she is shy and embarrassed by her condition, and she is my sister," Dr Masters shrugged, as if that explained it all. "I would not have been so elusive had it not been for the fact that by sheer coincidence Mrs Hunt had arrived here. I honestly had no knowledge of her charabanc tour, but when I saw her I became determined she would not know of my sister's condition. I did not want her learning about her illness, nor about her in general."

"I didn't know you had a sister?"

"She is a half-sister, really. Another indiscretion on my father's part. Another reason I did not want Mrs Hunt to know anything. I love my sister dearly and would not have her brought into that woman's sphere."

"And what is wrong with her?" Clara asked.

"Simply stated, she doesn't eat. But it is more complicated than it sounds," Dr Masters gave a wan smile. "I hoped this trip would be restorative."

"And has it been?"

"Maybe. Too soon to tell," Dr Masters' smile faded.

"We return to London tomorrow."

"Then, as we shall soon say goodbye, I extend an invitation to you and your sister. Please feel free to come and visit myself and my brother in Brighton. Perhaps the sea air will agree with your sister?"

Dr Masters seemed pleased with the suggestion.

"Yes, perhaps it will," he said, then he pointed at her foot. "I insist you rest. Doctor's orders."

"And I shall obey," Clara rolled her eyes. "But only because it hurts too much to walk!"

~~~*~~~

They boarded the charabanc to return home the following Sunday. There were two noticeable absences – Mrs Hunt and Captain Blake. A pall was cast over the return trip at the memory of what had occurred. For some this holiday had been full of heartache.

Bill Ayres was to come before the magistrates shortly and would probably be committed to trial, he had, after all, murdered a woman in cold blood. It was not hard to feel sympathy for him, and Clara knew that the Wignells had offered to pay his expenses out of their own pocket, even to go so far as to offer to hire a good lawyer to represent him. But, whichever angle you looked at it, he had killed a person and that made him a criminal.

Clara did not precisely feel sympathy for Mrs Hunt, that was somewhat challenging, but she did believe in the system of justice and she served it as best she could. Even so, she hoped the courts would be lenient on Bill Ayres.

The countryside rolled by as they began their lengthy return trip. Tommy dozed. Annie fussed about with a packed lunch she had insisted the hotel prepare for them. Little Bramble was thoroughly exhausted by the change of scenery and stretched out on the charabanc floor, joining his master in quiet snoring.

Clara reflected that, although the holiday had been

somewhat eventful, she had found it rather restorative. Just the change of scenery had been refreshing. And she had not been bored at all, as she had feared. It was ironic, naturally, that Clara required a murder to enjoy her holiday, but she was not going to dwell on that fact. She was just satisfied that the affair had been wrapped up tidily.

Clara leaned back in her seat and risked wriggling her toes. They were sore, but not as bad as before. She thought she might join Tommy and Bramble in catching forty winks. After all, when she reached Brighton she would be expected to report to Inspector Park-Coombs all that occurred. Best to rest now while she had the chance. Clara took another long look out of the window before she closed her eyes. The Lake District had certainly been interesting. Now it was time to get back to business proper.

Clara shut her eyes and joined the gentle snores of her brother and his dog, as the charabanc wound its way home, minus two passengers and a conductor.

Printed in Great Britain
by Amazon